To Ka!
Happy

Suki Lang's
Cozy too

FINDING
NINE

a novel by
SUKI LANG

where everything happens for a reason...

First Printing 2016

ISBNs
Softcover: 978-0-9950786-0-4
eBook: 978-0-9950786-1-1

Suziconfuzi Publications
Surrey BC

www.suziconfuzi.com

Credit: Ellen Bass, "The Thing Is" from Mules of Love. Copyright © 2002 by Ellen Bass. Reprinted with the permission of The Permissions Company, Inc., on behalf of BOA Editions Ltd., www.boaeditions.org

Dedicated

To Roy
For Jason
with a mother's love

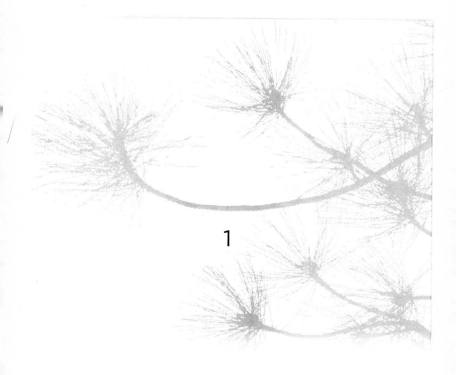

1

Dearest John.

It's the middle of the afternoon and I'm sitting outside in the sunshine with Cozy by my side. You and I both felt a bit upset after today's trip to the cancer agency. Arriving home soundlessly, two depleted souls with nothing left to speak of; by unspoken agreement we both toddled off to our separate corners, our separate spaces, our own little worlds, thinking our own thoughts. Yours are probably a whole muddle of unidentifiable and confusing feelings and emotions that I don't even have the energy to help fix right now. As I write this to you I'm crushed that I'll be no help to you at all for what's ahead. The grief I know you already have. The grief I know will come like a rock slide on the day you read this and the many days after that. Do you feel like I'm letting you down John? I do.

Today, I'm letting you down by hiding myself away but the big letdown will come when I'm gone completely. Sitting quietly here in the sunshine, I will you to come join me so we can talk. And if you did come outside to sit down, if you said, mum let's talk, I just don't know what I would say; even if I could squeeze some words out for you.

What I can do today and every day until I leave, is say I love you. You've heard me say those three words many times a day for all your life; most of the time you say, I love you too mum. And then I follow up with, I love you more. And I do. I love you more.

When you take a chance there will be others who love you, but in a romantic sense; someone special who you will love back. There might be heart breaks, and if there are, always remember you are loved by me, no matter where I am or what you may have done to contribute to the heart break. As you build your life through education and work and making new friends and maybe having children of your own; creating a life you love, I'll be watching you and still I will love you more. A mother's love is strongest....just saying <3!

Right now as you read this I am gone; as you hold this letter in your hands, I am gone. My illness has been hard for you. My death will be harder. You are wishing I was still here and maybe wishing we would be feeling optimistic together. Maybe you're remembering the thrill when we imagined a new treatment or cure or a new prognosis on the horizon. Or you might feel relief now that I am gone and without pain. My pain and your pain; and that's OK, it's natural. My mum died when I was younger than you. I barely knew her; all I have of her now is my name. It's only as I'm nearing my own end that I see how the connection between mother and child stretches on through space and time. As I come to the end of my life, I imagine how my mother may have felt about leaving me, during the last seconds of her own.

Tomorrow or the next day, but within this week, Andrea will help you with arrangements to take me back home. All the arrangements for a safe trip have been planned for you, by me. The party we had on your birthday, my birthing day, was the real celebration of my life. By then I knew it would be the last time we celebrated our wonderful time together, our unit of two.

Andrea has been asked to give you this letter and there will be other letters she'll have for you as well. When you see the messages inside, it'll remind you of all the treasure hunts we used to plan together and execute! Each letter is marked with a number and you are to open them in numerical order. Don't cheat! Your ultimate mission is to arrange a remembrance for me; I don't want a funeral or a memorial service. I want a party. In Ireland there is a custom to hold a remembrance for the dead one month after the loved one has passed away. They call it a Month's Mind. I'd like you to have one for me at the ranch I grew up on. By then you will have been there three weeks!

Right now, right this minute, go upstairs to Andrea and Heather's place because after this summer it will be your place too. Andrea has promised to give you the two front rooms; you may do with them as you please. My art studio can be your art studio, the guest room where you've already spent so many comfy nights, can be your new bedroom. Or do whatever you wish with those two rooms but they are yours now. Andrea will say the same thing.

By summer's end, when you return here, the suite will be rented to another student and her child. Don't be sad. Imagine me - being glad and joyful to know another little mini family is finding a home and aid within four sheltering, loving walls. You and I grew up here and so too will the next tenants with Andrea's kind assistance.

About Cozy—she is to remain here for the summer, don't worry she'll be in good hands.

And although I know she will bring you solace at this crossroad, the journey you are about to take, will be one best taken on your own. With no distractions, no one to take care of; a fresh start. A new adventure is about to open up for you John.

This past year I imagined you taking a trip all the way back to my childhood home. Do you remember the surprise I told you about? This is it. You'll finally meet the people I've told, admittedly, very few stories about. You'll see the landscape I never showed you, barely even described; these are my roots.

Who we become is so much about the people in our lives all along the path. My parents who died so young, and the woman I grew up to call mum-ma Jean or simply mum... And then there was my granddad, and my uncle JJ, and Trish. You'll hear all about Seth, that's Trish's son who died young too, and other people I've mentioned in passing. All the people hinted at, now they will become real.

Throw away all the notions you have formed about them. Clear your mind and arrive with an open heart. I'll be by your side. From time to time you'll feel the warmth of my hand resting on your right shoulder. Talk to me; ask for guidance and I'll do what I've always believed could be done. I'll reach out to you from a parallel universe to give enough guidance for you to find answers to your own questions. And please, you must make every effort to be an open vessel for the guidance that will come your way - from other people, not just me. Promise!

Two more instructions I have for you. Number one and most important is talk about me. For the rest of your life, mention me in conversation, say my name out of the blue, and bring up memories of our time together whenever you can, don't ever forget me. Some fuddy-duddies will feel uncomfortable speaking about the dead. Get used to that; keep me alive in your memory by speaking of me. If you don't, over time you'll forget me, just as if I never lived at all.

Instruction number two; after you and Andrea go to get my ashes from the funeral home, I want you to carry them with you all the way back to my home. Keep them in sight until you arrive at the ranch and then when the time is right place them inside box number 9. It's all part of the mystery for you, part of this treasure hunt.

You haven't had long enough time with me to know all there is to know about me John. When you find number 9 you'll be saying, ah ha, found you. Just like when we've played hide and seek. By the time you find number 9 you will hear my voice saying, I am here. Yes indeed, you have found me.

And as for when and where to read the other letters... you'll just know. You are ever curious and resourceful; questions will come up. When you've gone as far as you can, your next question will be answered in a letter. And yes, I have already given thought to and made an effort to anticipate when, where, what, why and how and have numbered the letters as such. I may be wrong of course and if I am, still follow the next path mapped out for you in my letter anyway; I will give you one hint now.

At the end of next week or before, you will be all set to go and all the five W questions I know you'll have for a safe arrival at your destination, will be answered - in the next letter. I love you John. While I'm getting to know the parallel universe I will say this to you all the time we are apart, you are loved. And until we see each other again, I still love you more.

Love Mum xoxoxoxox

Finishing the letter John rose up slowly. With reluctance and a stiffness of heartache and heaviness of limb, John went into the kitchen to find Cozy, their little dog. She was laying down-heartedly, halfway between her empty food dish and the door to her outside life. She looked as lifeless, as he felt. As sick as his mum had been she always made sure there would be proper care of her little pal Cozy. Dishes full of food and water, her coat hand stripped and cleaned. Eyes wiped each morning with a damp cloth, her coat combed until sleek and shiny.

Yesterday, as weak as she was, her eyes had opened slightly casting a glance toward the kitchen. In that look, John knew it was Cozy she was asking about. Leaving her bedside loudly enough so she would hear and know what he was doing, John filled the empty dog dishes, while speaking to Cozy loud enough so his mum would hear him caring for her dog. But when he went back, she had already stopped breathing. His mother was gone after her last directive had been fulfilled.

John had no interest in reading any more letters today or ever. He had no desire to go on a treasure hunt or play hide and seek or any of those stupid games his mum still loved. Sorely tempted, he wanted to rip the letter to shreds, turn all the pieces into one tiny tight ball and throw it bouncing off as far away as he could. Hurrying into his room, he took a box from beside his bed and crushed the letter as hard as he could inside.

He and his mum had covered this particular box in a brightly coloured paper collage when he was about seven. Since then the coloured paper had been covered over, again and again, with pictures of dinosaurs, skate boards, dragons, vampires, zombies, whatever the interest of the day. Last week he had used gel medium to ad garden twine his mum had once used and some of his mum's hair thrown in and a dried flower from a bouquet she had gotten, included for good luck.

The box contained all his important possessions, a Swiss Army knife given to him by a homeless man when he was three, a lighter that no longer worked, but seemed like a good luck treasure none the less. Water proof matches he had never ever used, an assortment of rocks and shells, a silent dog whistle and a myriad of other treasures he would keep forever, but may not ever use. As he was about to stretch out on his bed, he remembered his mum's request to go upstairs. Changing locations was fine with him. He loved the upstairs, felt totally at home, peaceful, relaxed and a tad more mature upstairs. Heading for the door he called out to Cozy and off they went; the boy and his dog.

Waiting for him in the kitchen, Andrea heard the unmistakable sound of Cozy's nails on wood as the wee dog came bounding up the stairs, followed by the quieter sound of John's shuffling footsteps. Reaching out, she grabbed the basement door handle before John could reach the top of the stairs.

Their eyes met and into her open arms he flew, tears falling unreservedly. Gently rocking his body from side to side, she guided him to the couch in the corner of the room. Easing herself in behind the couch, Andrea began the most familiar of cures, a back rub.

She had been rubbing his back since the day she met him as a baby. Head in hands John continued to weep, hot volcanic tears flooding his cheeks into the neck of his shirt. But when he heard Heather amble into the room and shout, "OK John, it's OK. Mum, make John some tea," the same old calmness settled over him. Giving his cheeks a quick swipe with the hem of his shirt; he looked up at Heather with her arm in a sling, her glasses askew and Cozy in tight, by her side. The dog Cozy passed loving gazes between the two people. In a shaky voice John said, "Hey Heather, did you hear about mum? Here sit on the couch; do you want to play marble solitaire with me? I'm pretty sure mum would want us to do something we both like. But she probably wants me to win this time."

Bending low, Andrea whispered in John's ear, "You, my boy, are a very good and kind person. Your mother's son that is for sure." And then, "OK you two get the game going and

I'll make some tea and toast and we can talk about all our plans ahead."

Hearing Andrea mention the plans ahead, John knew it was up to him to carry out whatever game his mum had in mind. John knew in his heart he would do it for his mum and he would do it for himself. The curiosity that was so intrinsically his, the curiosity his mum had mentioned in her letter now engaged him. He wanted to know more. And began to hatch a plan of his own; a plan that would see him entering a world of great maturity and growth. He felt all the things his mum knew he would, horrified she was gone but also in truth he felt, at least for today, a great relief she and he were both removed from the pain of her illness. And with permission from her, to play some of their favourite games, he was ready to engage in all that lay ahead.

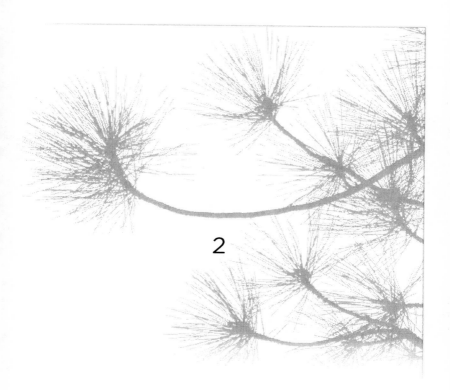

2

True to his mother's word, Andrea took care of guiding John through the many duties that a death brings. During the first days following her passing, Andrea graciously took care of most of the phone calls. John heard her say over and over, "No no, in lieu of flowers she would want you to make a donation to the food bank ..... Oh yes of course there's a plan to have something; it will be out of town in exactly one month. I'll call you or email if you like with the details..."

They went to the funeral home where John was encouraged by Andrea to take an interest in the arrangements and to prepare himself for the cremation. They could have done it all over the phone but Andrea insisted they go together and make a day of it. The day was wet with rain and all John wanted was to get away from the cemetery and go home.

But on the way there they stopped off at a store he had never been to before. It was a camping, rain gear, fishing and hiking gear liquidation centre of outdoor goods. The prices set at a fraction of the cost they would see elsewhere. He'd never seen this kind of selection in any of the stores he and his mum frequented. "John. Your mum asked me to do many things and one of them was to bring you here.

"She found out about this place in the newspaper about a month or so ago and I clipped the ad out at her insistence. It's a pop up store." As she hustled forward John called out, "Hey, what do you mean, a pop up store?" As she picked through some heavy shirts she turned, "It's a store that pops up for a short time.....a week, a month. You see them a lot at Christmas in malls. They pop up for just the season. Your mum had a couple of her art shows in pop up galleries, you remember? They lasted for a couple of weeks. Hey, do you remember the one she had in Victoria? That was a pop up gallery. If a store front is vacant for a short time it just makes a perfect location for something short term to happen." Turning, Andrea looked into John's eyes with her own damp ones, squeezed his shoulder then said, "Let's have a look; you'll need some things for your trip."

The two made their way through the store agreeing to meet up a bit later near some makeshift change rooms. Not knowing what he would need the boy was at a loss. Picking up a back pack to pack his things in and then setting it down again when he thought of his mum's own back pack he could use. After grabbing a couple of water bottles, a new tube of sunscreen, his mind went blank. He had all he needed for a trip at home anyway.

In what seemed like a few minutes he saw Andrea making her way to the change rooms with a cart full of stuff. The first thing he noticed in her cart was a sleeping bag, surprised he said, "What do I need a sleeping bag for? Won't they have beds?" Andrea chuckled, pointing at the cart, she said that some of the stuff was for her and the sleeping bag was for Heather to use at camp this year. Eyeing his potential purchases Andrea guided him over to the footwear section and together they found some sturdy all purpose boots and a pair of sandals. Next they hit the clothing section and Andrea again guided John as he chose between long and short sleeve shirts and a couple of pairs of jeans, some shorts and a pair of sunglasses.

Shopping finally finished they came away with some really good hiking boots, what Andrea called a suitable all purpose light summer jacket, a new hoodie, a little first aid kit, a couple of pairs of jeans, and a couple of new t-shirts. At the last minute Andrea talked John into getting a new swim suit too. Just in case.

John felt a bit guilty. His new freedom from being with his sick mother who was either constantly in treatment, or ill from treatment, or trying to catch up on her art … When compared with the a trip ahead, he couldn't help feeling disloyal to the loss of his mum and the grief he knew would come. Knowing how she felt about reaching for happiness at all costs, he still felt a bit shamed by this feeling of excitement right in the shadow of her death. Over the next few days John had a silent and sometimes not so silent running dialogue with his mum.

When he walked around the house, or sat in the yard, or took the dog around the block, he talked with her. While he was organizing things for his trip, he talked to her. Just as she said she would be, he felt her by his side.

Every step he took, he knew she was there. He didn't feel alone at all. Just the crushing knowledge he would never see her again intruded on his otherwise smooth first week. His tears came unabashedly and without warning and just as quickly they were gone. He couldn't bear to look at her photo, and at the same time wished he had a video of her doing all the things she loved and an audio of her laughter. She had a way of finding so much to laugh about, and laugh at.

John loved how his mother said life was too short to sweat the small stuff. She was full of gratitude for all she had allowed herself to have. John never really understood this sentiment when they had so little. This week though, he too felt gratitude. He was glad her life, the life she created all around her, brought her such contentment. Last week when she talked about life, and the haves and the have nots, she mentioned her uncle and something he had said; true contentment is when you are satisfied with what you have.

Stories of the uncle were rare but always included inspirational expressions or what she called an adage. There was often a moral to learn and especially vocabulary to understand. What the meaning of a particular word or concept was for example. Her uncle JJ she said, would offer up the goods anytime a question came up; describing JJ as quite the guy, the day before she died. Well soon John would see for himself.

He wondered what kind of guy would let his niece just walk away without ever knowing where she was. Why his mum wanted him to go meet the man was so beyond him at this minute. Before he knew it the calm and happy feelings he had been having turned to anger. Anger at his uncle for letting his mother go away, just when she probably needed him most, and angry with his mother for not reaching out for help. And anger that he never had a chance to meet his uncle until now. But most of all he felt angry at her for springing this family on him to have to meet all on his own. Toward the end of the week John was getting antsy to know what the next step was going to be and for the where and how question to be answered.

Still heavy with the loss of his mum, even his legs felt as if they were weighted down with large bags of wet sand. He found himself offering up an, I don't care attitude, while his inside felt torn up; literally torn to shreds. He wasn't eating or sleeping. Just thinking, remembering, blaming, crying, walking and screaming into his pillow. The silent scream, wasn't there an old movie called something like that?

It felt like time to refocus; find out about treasure. It felt time to find 9, and time to hit the road too. When he went in search of Andrea and the next letter containing his mum's next instruction, he found her slumped over on the desk. With her head pressed into folded arms; and the gray roots of her curly hair showing through she seemed so vulnerable to John. He thought she slept, as he'd seen her do in this same spot many times before. But as he turned to sneak away he heard the muffled sound of tears. Turning back and watching as shoulders shook he knew she was crying. He reached out to place a firm hand on her back. All at once his intrinsic strength returned and he remembered his mum's comment that another's weakness often makes us stronger in order that we may lend support to the one in greatest need. He had seen Andrea and his mum lend each other strength during times of weakness, trading back and forth. Today he would look after Andrea, shore her up and prepare her for his departure.

Ever so gently John whispered her name, "Andrea. Andrea I'm making tea for you and maybe some lunch too, I'll be right back." And off he went to put a lunch together for them both. Heather was at the day program she attended for people with disabilities. Today it would be just the two of them; him and Andrea alone together for the first time in his life. They'd have a chance to be open and honest and mature. He felt a maturity sneaking up on him already. His usual adolescent angst seemed to have dissipated suddenly since his mum had gone.

The person full of sullen moments had been replaced with someone he hardly knew. Every hour of each day; with each new experience he felt a shift toward becoming a new stranger. He felt almost like a man. Jaded; his mum used that word, she said it meant dull, apathetic, or made cynical by a particular experience, maybe that is what he felt. Maybe he had become jaded by what had happened in his young life. He did feel like a man though; a very, very old man.

When Andrea came into the kitchen, as if knowing it was the right time too, she had a bundle of letters. Holding them out she said, "Seven letters for you; all numbered 2 through 8. Read them when you need to and read them in order. Don't cheat! Those are my exact instructions from your mum. I have letters of my own, with instructions of my own." She continued to hold the letters out for John to take; hesitating a bit too long, Andrea gave the letters one last shake before placing them in John's usual spot at the table. "Remember, one at a time, in numerical order....hey it looks like I'm getting lunch! I should let you catch me bawling my eyes out more often, I'm starving," patting her stomach she gave a chuckle and said, "not that I don't have a whole life time of extras to live on." Pulling out her chair with exaggerated chivalry, John motioned for her to sit. He continued to bustle, determinedly and with purpose around the kitchen making tea, cutting bread and serving lunch. When he sat, the first thing he said was, "We need to talk." Andrea hearing those four words knew he would be able to make the journey on his own.

A transformation had taken place. A transformation his mum had predicted. With a wash of relief they began a dialogue that would be the first of many before he left. John was ready to step out of his adolescent persona to do a job that in Andrea's opinion should have been left for her and Heather to help him with. This trip his mum was sending him on was a rite of passage; a little early in his life but a rite of passage all the same. He was laying his mother to rest.

> *Dear John,*
>
> *I'll bet this has been a busy week with all kinds of challenges. And I'll bet by now you'll be standing more firmly on the ground than ever before in your life. On the back of this letter you'll find the phone numbers you'll need on your trip; and some additional instructions if things begin to fall apart. For now though, Andrea is taking you to the Greyhound bus, buying you a one way ticket to a surprise destination and then she and Heather will wave you off. When you get to your destination, call the number of Sharon's Shuttle service (it's on the back of this letter). Tell them your name and say you want to get to the lake road by where the old Bar TD feed lot used to be.*

Be sure to pack my old camera, now yours, because the broken down buildings of the feed lot if still there, are pretty cool and no doubt even more broken down after all this time… you'll want to get a few shots off. The shuttle service will already have been notified to expect your call. It's run by the dad of an old friend and though he was always a man of few words, he'll be real glad to lay his eyes on you. The prodigal child returned, so to speak. I know what you're thinking right now. But you know what? I probably miss you too wherever I am and I love you more John. Have a safe and happy journey and remember to keep an eye on my ashes…. I'll be with you every step of the way. Oh… and keep your eyes open for the man who will be late to meet you, on his horse, offering you a hand drawn map too. Oh and one more thing John. Everyone calls me Shelley from home. Only the people in Vancouver call me Margaret…

Love,
Mum xoxoxox

Two days later John was on his way, six unread letters tucked into a front pocket of his mum's backpack. Details of letter number two still fresh in his mind he was ready for the treasure hunt to begin. His first clue would be in finding the man, the horse and the map. Based on the highway signage John knew the direction he was headed. Before leaving that morning, he had scooped one of Andrea's old maps of British Columbia,

18

out of the corner of a bookshelf. With his finger, he followed along passing through the lower mainland of BC. Because they never owned a car he hadn't actually been out of the West side of Vancouver very often, except to go to Vancouver Island. He had only been to the Fraser Valley a handful of times. From the bus window he saw the signage directing traffic to exit at communities along the way where they picked up additional passengers in each stop. After their last stop in a town called Hope the bus driver took route number 5. But route 5, wasn't on the old map John held in his hand.

Leaning across the aisle he asked a fellow passenger two times, where they were now. Finally he was told the Coquihalla Highway. "Where does it go?" He asked. The guy might have been hard of hearing because he just shrugged, without further answer. So John went back to reading the signs and enjoying the scenery. What seemed like a life time later the bus arrived at a small town where the bus pulled over. The sound of the bus driver's voice announced their arrival, telling the passengers there would be a twenty minute break and they could go inside to use the restrooms or get some refreshments.

When John stayed seated, the driver made his way back to where John sat and said, "End of the road for you, this is your stop. The lady that dropped you off in Vancouver wanted me to point out the pay phones for ya... inside. You can't miss them. I'll unload your belonging from under the bus. Come on." Placing his hand gently on John's shoulder he said one more thing.

"Sorry for your loss kid." When John got into the bus station he pulled out letter number 2 again. Flipping it over to find the shuttle bus phone number his mother had written there he walked over to the line of phones. This was the first time he had ever used a pay phone in his life. He watched another passenger to see how they did it and then stepping up to the phone to make his call, saw there were actually how to make a call instructions written right on the front of each phone. It couldn't be easier. Unless he had been allowed to bring his cell phone that is.

Pressing in the numbers and waiting for it to ring on the other end, John noticed a man watching him from the doorway. Distracted by the ringing of his call going through, he turned back to the phone in time to hear a voice answering. "Sharon's Shuttle?" Clearing his throat he said, "Hi, my mum gave me this number to call, and she said I should tell you my name is John..." Before he was finished talking though, he felt a light tap on his shoulder. It was the man who had been watching him from the door. Holding up a little placard that said, Sharon's Shuttle, the man motioned him to follow along outside where a sky blue van waited. After loading his gear on board they silently drove away from the bus depot and out of town, on what John imagined was a secondary road.

All along both sides of the street at first, houses with attached garages dotted the roadside; they thinned out after a short distance being replaced with houses and barns, and then just driveways. John supposed they led off in the distance to more houses and barns. Fencing was sporadic and sometimes when there were fences there were cattle behind them. But mostly John saw bare land with fields used for some sort of crop, or just miles of waving grass, as he passed by.

When they were on a section of road that was completely empty, not a soul, house, not a car, or even a bird in sight, the driver pulled the van over. The ride had been uneventful and very quiet, which made John wonder if the man spoke at all. So far he hadn't said a word. Without turning his head John's way, the man said something in such a soft quiet voice, John almost missed it. "We're here son, sorry about your mum. She was a real good girl."

Without another word, he stepped out of the van, lifted John's travel gear onto the dusty gravel verge of the road and swung John's door open, motioning John to get out. Then the very silent man climbed back in his dusty blue shuttle and just drove off. John never noticed the driver's slight regretful backward glance in the rear view mirror. Nor his lifted hand out the side window of the van. Through a cloud of dust created by the departing van though, John wondered if dropping kids off in the middle of nowhere was a common occurrence in a shuttle bus driver's, bus driving life. Adults were much more careful with kids in the city that's for sure, especially his mum.

Slinging his pack onto his back, grasping the single handle of the old suitcase with one hand, wrapping the heavy twine holding a cardboard box together in his other hand he began to walk in the same direction the bus had gone. In a short time, through the dust created when the shuttle bus pulled off the gravel onto the road, he caught his first sight of the man he'd come to stay with until after the Month's Mind in three weeks. As her letter predicted it wouldn't be a car or truck to come along but a horse and rider; and said horse and rider would be late.

Of course he would be late, that's his way, his mum had said. Not always late but never paying attention to time she said. His mum had hardly ever made mention of her family, but the week before she died she must have been homesick. She talked about home, a lot.

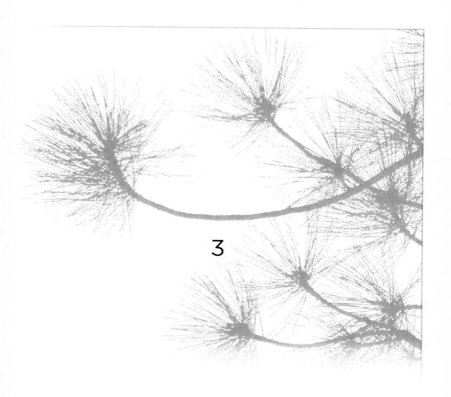

3

When rider and horse were in front of the boy, the man known
as JJ, reached out his hand and said, "You must be John; I'm JJ,
your mother's uncle." John stood still, his shoulders hunched
up almost to his ears, his hands shoved deep in his pockets.
Silently he kicked up a storm of dust of his own with the toe
of his new boot then looked into JJ's eyes. They stared at each
other for a moment then John said, "I know who you are."
After a short pause, of JJ returning John's stare, as smooth as
silk and without too much ceremony JJ languidly lifted his out
stretched hand to reach in his own shirt pocket pulling out a
piece of paper. Pointing and with a nod of his head, he told
John which way was north, at the same time passing down a
hand drawn map.

Deeply amused John wondered if his mum had communicated the map idea to her uncle JJ, but somehow suspected she had not. And this, like so many other things she just knew would happen. She sensed how people would behave and what they were most likely to do. How they'd respond to certain situations. Still holding out the map, John looked up again at the man on the horse and concealing his humour he said something so untrue, "I don't know how to use a map." When JJ laughed and said it was time he did John said nothing. He just listened to what JJ had to say.

JJ seemed to think, since John had been riding in a hot bus all day the exercise would do him good giving him a chance to familiarize himself with the landscape. As JJ turned his horse as if to giddy up, John said, "Well could you at least give a bit of help?" Looking down at the boy as if sizing him up; making a decision JJ said, "Tell you what, hand me up your suitcase, I'll wear your back pack, you can handle the box. Let's see that map … OK the only thing that might be a bit confusing is this part here that says turn right at the Ponderosa pine. I bet you don't even know what a Ponderosa is?"

Pointing across the road, behind what must be the falling down feed lot buildings and up a slope JJ said, "See those trees up there, they're Ponderosa pine. The one you want is the mother of all Ponderosa, she's huge. Turn right when you see her standing all alone on the side of the road, then follow a rough path through the grass. From there keep your eye on the map and you can't go wrong. I'll see you for dinner OK; you're bound to be hungry by then." Reaching his hand into a saddle bag and holding out an offering, "Here, take this apple and some water for the road." And with that off he rode leaving a stunned John with a map, his box, a small snack, a stainless steel thermos of water to hang from his belt loop and that's it.

Well now he had found the first two clues from the letter; the man on a horse and a map. Turning to look across the road, the feed lot was revealed in all its rotting, falling apart splendour to the young artist's eye. Lifting his mother's camera from around his neck and checking the settings John began taking pictures. She knew him so well, his mum. Without the camera he'd be longing to have hers at his disposal. She finally, and very formally, had given John the coveted camera on his last birthday; even though he had been taking pictures ever since, he would always think of the camera as his mum's. Bringing the older model SLR camera up to take a look through the view finder John knew he had never seen buildings like these; in pictures yes, but not in real life.

The environmental elements hadn't so much rotted the wood as sucked all the moisture out of the timbers leaving them grey and ghostly and looking ready to fold in on themselves. Finished with the pictures for now he organized his box of ashes, the camera and water and headed off in the direction he had seen JJ go.

John had kept JJ in his sight for some time before getting side tracked long enough to take pictures. He had watched man and horse amble along at a real leisurely pace but eventually JJ and his horse crossed over the road heading to the left, the opposite direction JJ had told John to go. When John arrived at the point he thought his great uncle had gone, he went that way too. An obviously well used path or animal track took him up and over a short rise above a small lake surrounded by scrub bush. He thought the greyish looking plant, must be the tumble weed his mum spoke of, she called it sage brush. Reaching out John grabbed a piece of the bush rubbing it between thumb and fingers; giving his fingers a sniff confirming the pungent smell of sage. The shore was covered in gravel mixed with flat stones, one small grassy area hugged a small piece of the shoreline; in John's eye the lake was perfect for swimming. Moving down the dried out grassy slope to the lake, he caught sight of what appeared to be a small cave or niche in the hillside. He headed that way to investigate. Poking his head inside he soon determined it didn't go back too far and it looked like the kind of place an animal might use as a den in this dry land; or just as likely, some kids had carved it out as a fort.

His mum told him just a few stories about this country, the place of her birth she called it, telling him one tale of how she loved it; another story of how she couldn't wait to get away. She prepared him for JJ too saying he had some strange ways, and he could be a bit tough at times but her advice as usual would have been - You have to go along to get along. It was one of her famous sayings, each time she said it, carefully explaining as if for the very first time - when you're in a new situation the best way to get on, is to just go along with the way the other person wants things. When you have won their trust, by being compliantly easy to get along with, start to do your own thing slowly. Then before they know it you're getting along without any help. Go along to get along. That's what he'd try to do while he was here.

But first, he'd take a swim in the lake. Off came his shoes, socks, pants, his shirt; his underpants would stay on. The map he stuck in his shoe for safe keeping, into the water he plunged. John loved to swim so had no worries of what lay beneath the surface. Turning over on his back for a bit of a float he saw the sky begin to fill with storm clouds. Floating this way, he watched from his back, the contrast between the blue of the sky and darkness of gathering clouds and his first strike of North Okanagan lightning; he counted one, two, three, four, five BANG! A loud crack of thunder rattled him out of his reverie.

Wow the storm was only one mile away by the calculations his mum had taught him long ago. Back to shore he swam just as the rain hit. Grabbing his clothing he headed for shelter in the only place he could see, the small niche. Making his way across the rocky shore, the map made its way on a breeze out of his shoe, sailing smoothly onto the surface of lake. Dumping his things carelessly, he made a grab for the map and as he did he saw with astonishment the map disappear in a purple haze, as ink bled from the paper into the water.

While he waited out the storm John determined he'd not let his ruined map get the better of him. Once the storm had passed he would head back the way he'd come, crossing back over the road carrying on until he found the mother of all Ponderosas JJ had told him to look for. Turning right at the tree he followed the path through the grass, up the hill he walked. He didn't look at the map carefully enough when he had the chance, to know exactly which way to go once he got to the top of the ridge, but luck was on his side. Looking down the slope he saw the roof of a building so he headed that way all the while knowing his mum would be right when she said, everyone around there knows JJ.

JJ could feel John's eyes on his back as he rode his horse away. JJ was a man who had lived alone and spent most of his time alone for 17 years and his only experience with kids had been with Shelley, his niece, and look how that went. No, this time he would not hover and protect; this time he'd give the kid some rope. Though at this point, he didn't know how much rope to give him. Before crossing the road JJ briefly wondered what John would make of him heading off in the opposite direction the map indicated John should go. No matter what though, he would not look back, no matter what he would not shelter and protect. For now he'd watch and see what the kid could do.

When John got closer to the buildings he'd seen from the hill top, a well laid out farm yard and barn, neat gardens, a house painted in what his mum would call trendy colours of dove grey and white trim, was spread out like a picture. A big motor home parked off to the side; a house on wheels, is what mum always called them. From how his mum described the home she grew up in, he was pretty sure this place was not it; but decided to see if he could find anyone around the place to ask directions to JJ's place. Heading for the main house, movement in the garden caught his eye. A woman sitting sideways on a small wooden box on wheels was working away in the heat; calling out, "Hello?" John caught her attention; jumping at the sound of his voice, she raised her head and then her hand in greeting. Lifting her long slim frame with ease and grace, up out of her gardeners pose she stood, brushed herself off, coming through the gate she said, "You're John, aren't you? I'd know you anywhere. My name is Trish, I knew your mum when she was growing up here." John said nothing, just stared because this was the woman he'd been told about, she looked just like the woman beside his mum in the picture he was shown a couple of weeks ago.

"Her mother, your grandmother, and I were best friends. Your uncle too, I mean the three of us were best friends even

though there were a few years separating each of us in age..."
Feeling a bit disquieted by his silence, Trish had stopped
herself mid-sentence as she realized she was rattling on.
Removing her hat with one hand while sweeping long hair off
her neck with the other, Trish said something she knew every
teenage boy could find interest in, "Are you hungry? Thirsty
too I bet. That JJ! He gave you a map didn't he?" As an answer
John just nodded his head, sharing a brilliant and beautiful smile with her, lighting up his whole persona. "Come on
inside let's find you something to eat." Finally John found his
voice and thanked her as he followed behind, from garden
to home.

Once inside the cool of her kitchen, he asked how she
would have known him anywhere. In answer she pointed to
the fridge where pictures of a boy from birth to play school,
on up to recent photos were secured by beautiful jewelled
magnets. Beneath each photo was a folded piece of paper dan-
gling from a coloured ribbon. The whole effect looked like a
work of art to John, when he said so she threw her head back
and laughed the laugh his mum had told him about that one
time, the laugh of her own mother's best friend, and at times
her best friend too.

Leaning in to take a closer look at the front of the fridge
and all it held; John felt a warm heat of his own discomfiture
crawling up the back of his neck. The young boy in the photos
with the light wavy hair and innocent blue eyes was no more.
The photos on the fridge reflected the changes that followed
him through his years turning him into someone barely recog-
nizable from the early pictures. With this chronology before
him he saw light hair turn to dark brown; next it grew curly
like his mums. His skin had lost the luster of childhood and

now as he hovered between adolescent and man had a soft covering of blemishes and a growing number of dark whiskers; every few days he shaved whether he needed to or not.

He wondered at Trish's comment when she first laid eyes on him that she would recognize him anywhere, when he looked so entirely different from even the last photo his mum had sent, especially his height; he must have grown six inches or more in the last six months and had more upper body mass. These were things he wasn't aware of until looking at the photos. Many moments of the days leading up to this trip found him seeking a maternal resemblance in the full length mirror in the front hall at Andrea's place. The thing was, in this kitchen looking at the back of a little boys head as he hid in a laundry basket reminded him of his mum, and the shape of her head. The way her ears stuck out just a little bit, with her hair in a pony tail, not much just enough for John to see the similarity now. His hand rose to touch one of his own ears, an ear just like hers.

Leaning over his shoulder to look at the same picture Trish said, "In the letter your mum sent with that photo she mentioned you two played hide and seek. She said you loved it. Did she tell you it was one of her favourite games when she was a kid too?" John looked surprised when he said, "Not really, no." Trish carried on with the famous family story of the day Shelley hid for eight hours.

"JJ's mum was still alive and your mum was only four years old. Four year olds are all about doing things themselves and independence and having great ideas and so on. Well one day, right after breakfast JJ's mum, Jean, came running over here looking for Shelley. I had just walked back from taking my boy, Seth, to the road to catch the school bus. Have you seen

Shelley? - she said all out of breath... Shelley had her breakfast and Jean had gone to put on a wash or something and when she came back Shelley was gone. JJ was home visiting, but still in bed and so was Ken, that's JJ's dad, your great granddad. Everyone was woken up and the search was on. After about forty five minutes I called a few other people in the area and the police as well, we just didn't know where she could be. Pretty soon we had a pretty big search party walking the fields and men and women on horseback too."

Trish had John's full attention by now so when she stopped for breath, he asked where his mum had gone, where she was. Trish laughed saying, "I'm getting to that. Shelley loved to play hide and seek and could hide for hours. Jean was really getting worried and for the first time ever, I saw her cry. Not out loud, just the tears streaming down her cheeks. At about four o'clock or so my son Seth came home from school and was expected to join in on the hunt so off to your mum's house he ran. He was nine years old and just at the age when he didn't want to play with little girls anymore."

Stopping Trish got a misty look in her eyes and just for a second John thought she might cry. But no, on she went with her story. "When your mother heard the sound of Seth's voice she suddenly appeared. We didn't know it at the time because she wouldn't tell where, but she was hiding behind a curtain in Jean's bedroom - all day long!" John's sudden laughter filled the room. He laughed so hard tears ran down his cheeks.

He was flooded with memories of playing with his mum, how she loved to play hide and seek. Indelibly etched in his mind, were the reminiscence of hours spent finding the best hiding spot, he knew he'd cherish the memories all his life. She would say as softly as the softest whisper, from her hiding spot, - I'm right here, look with your whole self or knock knock, I'm here. Later on she would suggest looking in the place you don't think anyone can possibly be. I'm right here, right before your eyes, or I'm right in front of you. All of me is right here, look. Just look and I'll appear, like magic.

In the beginning, when he was really young, she taught him to follow her voice or to follow a noise she would make; as he got older she taught him to look for her with all his senses. Sight, look for anything out of place, and sound, do you hear breathing or squeaking, smell the air, is something different, and be sure to touch every surface there could be something or someone hidden there. And if you still can't find the person you seek, learn to taste the air... Now that he heard the hiding behind a curtain story from Trish and he looked back, he realized hide and seek was much more than a game for his mum. It was almost a lifestyle; could hide and seek even be a lifestyle he wondered? He told Trish that lots of times his mum would just seem to vanish and when she did, he knew she wanted him to come find her. And he did, he played along too.

After Trish fed him and before he headed for JJ's she picked and supplied him with vegetables from her garden to take along, saying she knew JJ didn't have a garden but no one expected John to be picking anything today anyway. "Come any time if you want a visit or if you need vegetables, just help yourself OK, that's the way we do it." That said, John began a walk along a well worn path in the direction he was sent and as he did he wondered what JJ's expectations would be. He was pretty sure he'd soon find out.

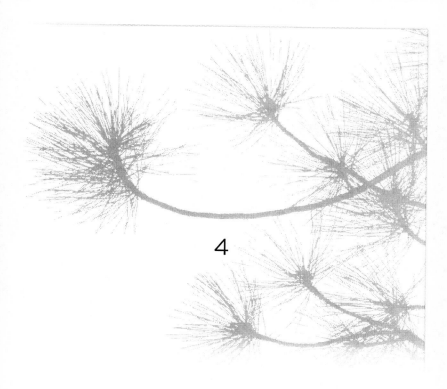

4

Trish first heard Shelley was sick, in a telephone message left by Shelley herself only a few weeks before. When she heard Shelley's voice and the content of her message, she knew deep in her heart the young woman's son would be sent here eventually. Seventeen years ago, Shelley left. It seemed so final at the time and they all came to suspect she'd never come back, and she never did. There were only two telephone calls in 17 years. If it weren't for the letters with news of John and an updated photo once or twice a year, she and JJ would know nothing. Shelley never supplied a return address either. Trish always felt guilty because she knew, with her resources, if she really tried she could have found her. But she never tried hard enough. When someone you thought liked you or even loved you, just walked out of your life never wanting to really talk to you again, it hurts. When they won't even supply a return address on the yearly letter, well that hurts too; the message is clear.

Trish wondered now, as she sat companionably with John in the kitchen what he had been told about what happened or, what he thought of the lack of contact from JJ and her. She'd find out over time but not today. Today she'd tried to let him know she could be counted on for anything. And to somehow convey to him, that he was more welcome here than anywhere else on earth. It had been a long time since she had a young fellow sitting at her table shoveling food into his mouth. He ate as if it was his last meal, and she liked it a lot. Sitting back she fell silent and watched as John had choked down a seemingly endless amount of food; as if he had not eaten in days. And she supposed in his state of grief he may well not have had much of an appetite for some time.

After the meal, a pick through the vegetable patch and a promise to see each other again soon, Trish watched John go along the lane that connected the two homes. The lane had become a bit overgrown from lack of constant use in the past seventeen years, but she and JJ still found reason to use it, if only once a week to check in on each other. The decision Trish made, not to walk John over to JJ's herself was a conscious one. Feeling sure John's journey back to his mother's home was one best done solo. Instinctively she knew it was Shelley's wish to let him have independence during this rite of passage. Leaning against the fence, surrounding her vegetable garden, she watched until his tall frame rounded the bend.

Coming around a sharp curve in the lane, the family farm was suddenly right in front of him. It was just as he'd pictured - no paint, no frills and no cars. Before checking out the barns he went up to the house and knocked. When no one answered he tried the door, knowing from a story his mum told, it would be unlocked. Inside he carefully tucked the precious box he had carried all the way from Vancouver behind a couch, and surveyed the place with his eyes.

Where he stood was just a big open room with two big old leather couches, a sprawling dining table covered in books and newspaper, a kitchen with eating area in front of a broad window that looked out over a quiet landscape. Off to the side was a cubby-hole of a room with a fireplace. This little space, fitted with two overstuffed chairs separated by a big ottoman, was the coziest place to sit. On either side of the fireplace, two glass fronted book cases flanked the wall from the floor, up five or six feet. Rectangular stained glass windows filled the spaces between top of bookcases and ceiling. A staircase leading up to what looked like a balcony was against the kitchen wall. Under the balcony were three doors that begged opening. He'd save those for later. Right now he'd check out the barns before JJ got back.

The barn and outbuildings held no scary surprises, only delights. The first housed chickens at one end with a small hole on the side so they could scoot out to the secure looking chicken yard. The rest of the building housed various feeds, seeds and supplies, old machinery parts and what he thought might be car parts. The second and biggest, a barn he supposed was shelter for horses, though as far as John could see there would be only one horse on this ranch; the one JJ rode today. And the third barn was locked up tight. After circling the whole building looking for a window or a way in, all he found were the two big locked wooden sliding doors at the front, and another door hidden behind bushes that was hard to get to and looked unused. Some roller steel shutters on the other side of the barn were also locked tight. He'd check that building out another day; right now back to the first and smallest barn where he would collect some eggs; a first for him.

All but two of the chickens made their selves scarce when he entered the coop. The two remaining sat on top of what he supposed were nesting boxes. They made a cooing sound while ruffling their feathers. John approached the two hens with caution. He was unsure how to go about lifting the chickens to look for eggs without hurting the birds or getting pecked at. When he tried to lift one of the chickens it started squawking and back peddling its legs in frenzied fury. Setting that chicken down he quickly lifted and pushed the next one out of her box, and there beneath her lay the precious eggs. Folding up the bottom of his t-shirt to form a shopping bag of sorts, he collected six eggs. Two eggs from each hen and two more in a vacated nest; gingerly clutching them to his belly he went out of the chicken house, and back up to the farmhouse and in doors to make dinner. Finding the knives, forks and spoons, bowls and other things he'd need, he set to work making a simple dinner. First he'd get a salad ready, when he thought JJ would be home he'd start some scrambled eggs with some fried potato, onion and cheese he found in the fridge. John was about to sit to look through some magazines on the dining table when he caught sight of JJ riding into the farm yard.

By the time JJ had put his horse in the pasture, his saddle in the tack room and gotten up to the house he could smell dinner cooking. "Well hello John, so you can cook?" As he placed a package on counter he said, "You really used your own initiative didn't you?" When John just smiled, JJ launched into a description of the word. "Initiative means inventiveness, when something needs doing you just do it; without question." JJ paused only a moment before he added, "Not much of surprise that you can find your way around a kitchen, your mum liked to cook by the time she was about ten years old. She'd hustle around here like a seasoned chef! Did she teach you to cook?" John just shook his head in memory of how he'd learned to cook then said, "I taught myself." JJ seemed to be deep in thought when he said he supposed John's mum did too in a way. "She picked up a lot by just watching, then just doing."

While they ate dinner, JJ asked about John's walk home. He guessed John must have managed with the map OK; then he said, "I gotta admit John I was actually a bit surprised you found your way. I thought I'd have to send out a search party." John looked up at his great uncle, not being too sure how to say it, but then just blurted out all that had happened. How he had followed JJ to the left instead of going straight, then finding the lake, the map getting wet, back tracking, finding the tree, then finally finding Trish and asking directions.

He wasn't proud of not taking care of the map but knew he couldn't cover up what he'd done, being sure eventually JJ would find out about the visit with Trish. After JJ heard the whole story and not until John was quite finished he said, "Well aren't you resourceful?" When he saw the surprised look on John's face he went on to say, "Resourceful means, creative, inventive, original, practical, quick witted, knowing when and where to ask for help. You can feel pride in asking for help John, lots of men don't."

With that he got up from the table, gathering the used dishes as he went over to the counter, where he opened his package. Grabbing a couple of clean forks he returned to sit with John, placing with pride, a pie, onto the table. He said, "This is blackberry, made with blackberries picked at the coast last fall. A pal of mine made it fresh today. That's where I was when I headed off in the…" JJ stopped in mid sentence to hold up the index and middle fingers of both hands making quotation marks in the air, "wrong direction. Good thing you went for a swim instead of trying to track me I'd say. Anyway let's dig in." And with that he cut two huge pieces of pie which he assumed they'd eat directly out of the pie tin. Before JJ could dig in though, John hopped up to get some plates; there was no way he'd eat pie out of the same dish with what amounted to a complete stranger!

After dinner John washed up, telling JJ that at home his mum relaxed after dinner on his cooking nights while he cleaned up, then he relaxed on her cooking nights and she cleaned up after dinner. When JJ heard that he laughed, then said, "Well around here, I guess it'll be whoever gets home first cooks and since you're such a good cook, I expect for the next little while you will be getting home first. Don't worry, I can show you where all the food is, you'll know your way around here in no time." As JJ talked it occurred to him after such a long day John would be getting tired so he stood up to show him his mum's room.

When they tried to open the door JJ stopped dead, saying he'd have to find the key he guessed. JJ looked so sad when he told John all Shelley's things were still packed in boxes and remained in the exact spot where she left them. "In a day or two I'll move them so you can sleep there, but for now I've got a nice set up for you to sleep in the barn.

John said, "In the barn?" With complete incredulity in his voice, he could not have been more surprised, in fact this was the first real surprise he'd had all day. "Well yeah, I thought it'd be a good way to break into country life, until your mum's room is clear. Tell you what, do you like to read? Come on in to the inglenook and pick a book." Another surprise, John had no idea what an inglenook was and said so. JJ began to laugh and then John joined in neither knowing what was really so funny. Wiping tears from his eyes, JJ pointed to what John had mentally pegged as the cubby-hole room and they began to laugh all over again. "That's the Inglenook."

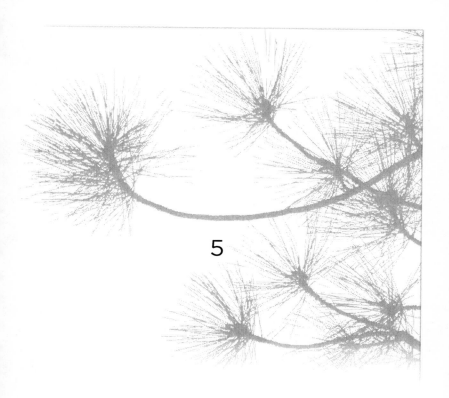

5

JJ and John strolled slowly down to the barn, the evening sky was beginning to dim; the horizon to the west had a rosy hue. Opening the doors JJ turned and said, "Your mother spent many a night sleeping in here; by choice I might add. You'll see why when we get up top. With the barn door open and by the dim light shining through it, John could make out a loft at the far end of the barn. A set of steep stairs against one wall led up to it. Pointing that way John asked, "Is that hay up there, is it a hay loft?" JJ was just about to hit a switch to shed some light on things, "Yeah that's hay. I have it delivered;" he paused then chuckled, "that's not where you're sleeping John. Up here." John turned to look in the direction JJ pointed overhead then saw another set of steep stairs leading up to the top.

Following JJ they climbed up a worn set of stairs; John stared at the hay loft at the other end of the barn with relief. He knew from Heather, that mice lived in the hay. This loft was swept absolutely clean and had two big double shutters that opened up to reveal the night sky; JJ had just opened them showing John as he did how to pull down the bug screen to keep flying things out where they belong. He was in the process of unrolling something and said, "This here's a hammock. Your mother slept in one like it when she lived here, and I slept in it, or one like it too and I believe Trish's son Seth slept up here a time or two as well, and your grandmother slept up here when she was a girl. You might call sleeping up here, a family tradition." With his back to John, JJ began to hang one end of the hammock from a big hook.

His back still turned to John, in a shaky voice he said, "I'm sorry, so sorry about your mother; I didn't even know she was sick. Neither Trish nor I did... She didn't say in the letters to Trish. She left a voice message for Trish, but no phone number we could call her at." Reaching out John grabbed the other end of the hammock, looping it over the other hook. He was at a loss for words so he just said thanks to JJ's back. Pulling a blanket from a tidy little pile of things JJ must have put there earlier in the day, and handing it to John, JJ said, "Well I guess you've had a long day, you need some rest. There's a tap and hose at the bottom of the stairs if you need a drink in the night; closer than making it all the way to the bathroom which is mid barn on the left. Oh and in this cupboard," JJ said as he reached over John's shoulder, "are some other things you might need, a cup, tooth paste...well you'll see. Um I'm beat too so I'm going to head up to the house and hit the sack. See you in the morning." With those last words he reached out briefly ruffling John's hair before giving his shoulder a tight squeeze.

John got himself settled in the top floor of the horse barn with a book and a couple of maps. Before he left the house he had slipped into the Inglenook to scan the books and some surveyor maps of the immediate area that had caught his eye, he wondered how long it would take him to sleep in these unfamiliar surroundings. Reaching his arm up as far as it would go he caught hold of the string that controlled the single electric light bulb hanging over his hammock. Giving it a sharp tug, he pulled himself into darkness. When his eyes adjusted he looked toward the set of double giant doors in the hay loft where he had made his bed. Turning his eyes to rest on the night view out across the landscape lit by the light of the moon; it was the most glorious sight he'd seen all day. With his light turned out and his eyes wide open he took in the night sky. He saw something black and fast flit across his vision. Then another and another; he'd have to ask JJ about that in the morning, as far as he knew only owls flew at night. When he finally lay on his back his thoughts were of star gazing. He was asleep before one star had come into focus.

The next thing he knew, the first light of morning was shining in his eyes. He woke up disorientated, not knowing where he was at first. With a mixture of feelings that couldn't be identified, he knew where he lay but was all at once consumed by misery at being sent here away from everything he knew. But most of all he felt deep devastated worry for himself and how he would manage without his mum.

He remembered a time when his mum was in hospital. She told him when the sun rose each morning the nurses would walk briskly into each room disturbing all occupants. First waking his mum up then making her take some pills, take her temperature, help her to the toilet, open curtains all around the room; in general never allow her to sleep in or wake up naturally, which she always wished she could do and claimed to never have done since he had been born.

Rolling over onto his side, he felt awed by what lay beyond the opened doors of what he would come to know as his hay-less loft; he gazed out the loft doors and thought he must be in paradise. The land as the morning sun spread over it looked so mysteriously captivating and utterly beautiful; the only sound was that of early morning birds and a clicking sound he assumed must be crickets. Soon his second day would begin and he was anxious to get it going. Up he got, thinking he'd go in to rouse JJ.

Once in the house though he saw JJ had been up first, leaving a note fixed to the kitchen table by a long pin. The note said:

I need to tend to business, be back for dinner. JJ

Back for dinner, John mulled this over and guessed JJ wasn't fooling when he said John would be doing the cooking. John cooking; he didn't even know where the supplies were yet. In an uncharacteristic moment of bitterness, John reminded himself he would have to use his own, initiative and be resourceful. Casting bitterness aside he smiled at the memory of JJ's verbosity then looked around for something to eat. He had a quick breakfast, threw together a lunch for later, grabbed a fishing rod off the porch, in the hopes of finding a lake, and hit the road or a path actually. He would stop in the barn to take one of the surveyors' maps along.

John did not know the first thing about fishing, though loved to read stories of adventure and did watch enough television at Andrea's place to know the basics. In his mind his mum would be right there beside him coaching him on - visualizing what he wanted to do. Like last summer at a back yard wedding party, she picked up a hula hoop and began to spin it around her hips as if she'd done it her whole life. Later when she stopped for breath, John over heard her conversation with someone who commented on her expertise; they wondered how they could learn too.

She said, "I visualized myself doing that. One time when I was in hospital I watched that show, America's Got Talent? I saw a Hula Hooper; she was amazing hula hooping lots of hoops at once! Her name was Hoopalicious! So I just imagined Hoopalicious doing it first, then I copied what I saw in my mind's eye." When she caught sight of John listening in, she was sure to tell him exactly what the word visualization and mind's eye meant. She was forever offering definitions for words, just like JJ did; a family trait perhaps.

Another family trait was curiosity and so John planned to spend the day being just that; curious. Before heading off he went into the inglenook and took a compass off its hook. He knew how to use a compass from the orienteering course his mum took him to for a homeschooling project. In the box at home, he had a better compass than this and he forgot to pack it. He'd need to reorient himself to the use of the compass and get his bearings before he left. Grabbing the box from behind the couch John took himself out to the barn before striking out to see the lay of the land.

His back pack, suitcase and box were now all lined up together. What he needed was his own space to put them in. He wasn't about to take over his mums room just yet. And in fact, didn't even want to ever take over her room at all. Taking over her room meant he'd have some level of permanency here. Why would he want that when it wasn't good enough for his own mother to want to stay? Or ever come back to. No she turned her back on this place and the one thing John was certain of was, he wouldn't betray her now by forming an attachment to the land, or the man, nothing would keep him here.

For now though he needed a place to put his own things a place to call his own, for the next three weeks. Climbing up and down the stairs, carrying one item at a time he brought his things to the ground floor. In the front corner of the barn, under his sleeping loft in yesterday's exploration he had passed a closed door. Meaning to check it out later he had become captivated by the loft. Turning the handle of the door now though he found it was locked. Reaching up instinctively, he ran his hand along the door frame and found a key. Smiling to himself he slipped the key into the lock, held his breath and turned it.

Ah ha! It unlocked. Swinging the door open the first thing John noticed was a dust storm of movement the opening of the door created. He supposed the room had been so still for so long that when the door opened, it acted just like a vacuum and sucked all the dust right out. Or a lot of the dust right out.

Inside, the room was a complete surprise. He had imagined a storage room of some kind. Saddles, feed, animal medications… What he saw was a desk, chair and two more big shutters covering what he imagined to be a window, he hoped it was a window. Pulling the shutters open wide did reveal a window all right but there were shutters on the outside, too, so outside he went to get those opened up as well.

Returning to the room he was greeted by a space that was flooded with light from a window obviously not included in the original design. It was as tall as he was and almost twice as wide. The bottom ledge was about a foot off the ground and rose up almost to the ceiling. As he raised his eyes to the top of the window he noticed an attic hatch in the ceiling. A narrow ladder stood just outside the door, so retrieving it, up against the office wall it went. And up he went to take a look. He was surprised to find he was staring right into the loft where he slept the night before. But on second thought this made sense. Returning to ground level, he left the ladder leaning against the wall of the office for future use. Putting his exploration of the land on hold for now, John decided to make the barn home for the next few weeks and began to clean the room up.

He unpacked some of his things and placed them in an old oak file cabinet he'd hauled over from an unused room next to the one he had found. When he opened his suitcase it was packed with pens pencils, sketch books and a number of other necessities for occupying his time. He didn't want things too cluttered and permanent so he set the open suitcase with contents intact on a wooden crate he found laying around. On second thought he lifted the suitcase and carefully laid the box with his mum's ashes in the crate then replaced the open suitcase on top.

Not yet finished, but truly famished from his efforts, John pulled out his lunch, set it on the desk and pulled out the chair to sit. Before sitting he saw both desk and chair needed to be wiped clean of many years of dust and grime. Abruptly leaving the confines of the room, out in to the expanse of the barn he went hunting around until he found bucket, mop and some rags. Hurriedly filling the bucket he squirted in a dollop of liquid soap from a container he found sitting inside the bucket. When he got back, his hunger still strong he left the mop and bucket and headed out doors to find a spot for lunch. There right under the loft doors stood a bench facing the same direction as the view he woke up to this morning.

Seen from a lower elevation the landscape still held a beauty he never imagined, judging from his mum's memory of the place as lonely and desolate. It excited him in an emotional way to sit here in the quiet of the late morning taking in the sounds of birds interrupted only be a deep silence, rustling of grasses and the scenery. Leaning back against the barn, he opened his lunch, pulled out half a sandwich and began to eat.

John never got his chance to sit again that day as one thing led to another and before he knew it he had cleaned out all the horse stalls and swept the entire length of the barns floor. He found another room with the word Tack, on its door and discovered where all the saddles and horse stuff was kept. He cleaned that room a bit too. Just as he replaced the broom, emptied the bucket and cleaned the rags he heard the sound of tires on gravel outside.

Wondering if JJ had a friend coming by or if it was JJ himself, John stepped out into the yard. When he saw an old familiar car pulling to a stop outside the house, John remained in the shadow of the barn. He watched as his mum's friend Todd, removed his long and lean body from the tight confines of the tiny little old hatchback he'd had for as long as John could recall. This sight usually made John laugh out loud but right now he just stood in silent suspicion.

He didn't get why Todd was here. How Todd even knew John was here. Or for that matter, how he knew where here was at all. For just a moment John filled with fury as he imagined Andrea telling Todd where John could be found; this was meant to be his time, his quest.

Andrea wasn't Todd's biggest fan so he doubted she would have a number to reach him at, to tell Todd the news. And he was absolutely positive; Andrea would not have told anyone where to find John. Todd hadn't even been by to see his mum for more than a month, why would he care if she was dead. John was uncharitably thinking these thoughts when he was spotted.

"Hey man, little dude! There you are." Todd came striding toward him with his long skinny arms outstretched ready to pull John in for a hug. Sensing a bit of a cool reception, Todd lifted one poised hand for a fist bump instead. Automatically John raised his own hand and bump they did.

Todd stood in his classic pose with thumbs in belt loops. His other fingers shoved as deep down in the front pockets of his old and faded jeans as they would go; shoulders up as far as they would go, and leaning his torso slightly back as if in a stretch. Todd cast his eyes around the yard settling back on John. "Hey dude, I heard your mum died; and hey - you had to come up here to stay with JJ. Is that true, dude? That's rough little man!" Just as John was about to tell Todd to stop calling him dude and little man, he stopped himself remembering words his mum always lived by. She told him - Don't be the first to talk, let the other guy keep talking until he is all talked out. So John stood still waiting for the right moment.

Placing a hand on John's shoulder, Todd talked on about how he heard from his dad at Sharon's Shuttle service and how he'd been working in Northern Alberta for the past while; he got away as soon as his dad called. He expressed disappointment in Andrea for not letting him know how sick John's mum was at the end and finally said, "Hey bro, just wanted to come out and say how sorry I am. I mean your mum was a great person. Everyone loved her....." When he heard Todd's voice crack John broke down, he didn't mean to. It was hearing kind words from Todd, he couldn't handle it. Todd's eyes were brimming too.

In an uncharacteristically quiet voice Todd said, "You know what John, your mum made me promise not to tell you something big. I'm pretty sure she'd want you to know now though. I grew up around here too. That's how we knew each other. After she left here, I ran into her in Vancouver in a boutique she got a job in. Trish's son, Seth and I were trying to find her and I did find her and told Seth where to find her too. Then I was out of town working and I heard the news about Seth... The next break I got from work, I came back to Vancouver to let her know. He worked with me too. Seth did....he was like, my best friend man."

Todd choked up before he could continue, "That's when she made me promise, many times. She made me promise not to tell anyone where she was and time passed man. I always had to pretend I hardly knew her cause she didn't even want Andrea or you to know about this place or JJ. She said you'd find out some day. She even said she would bring you here herself. And I kept waiting for some day. I never even told JJ or even my family that I knew where you guys were. She made me promise and now man I just feel like shit. I feel disloyal. Because I'm not kidding dude, everyone who knew your mum, just loved her. And JJ missed out on all she was. I loved her; you know I did, both of you. I love both of you." John was speechless now, he couldn't risk speaking for fear he'd cry again.

He had managed to stop the tears but the lump in his throat was too big to handle. He had a load of questions for Todd and told him so but for now he just wanted to be on his own to think about this news. He nodded his head, with a lift of his hand in what was meant as a wave at Todd, he turned and walked away. Todd was wise enough to just let him go, but shouted out, "I'll take off now buddy; I'll go see Trish. And hey man if you need anything call Sharon's Shuttle and ask for me. They know where I am. Or hey, here I'll write down my cell number and email." Todd fished a short stub of a pencil out of his shirt pocket and scribbled out his details on an old receipt. Looking up to see John's retreating back he said, "Bye man. I'll just put my number up here, on the porch table, before I go." His departure was as quick and unexpected as his arrival had been.

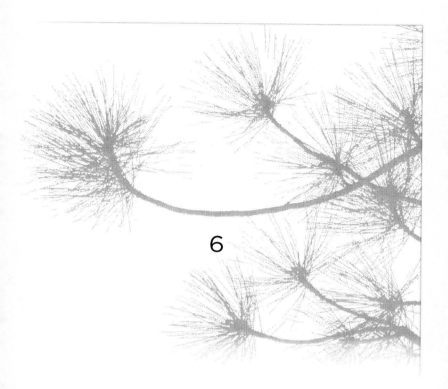

6

Todd's surprise visit had totally altered how the day was going for John. He would have to do some pretty big regrouping, to get his mood back in line. And he had no idea where to begin. One thing was certain though; he would close up the office, he didn't want to bring his sorrow in there. The barn and especially the office would be his place of solace. Going around the side of the barn he pulled the shutters over the big window, in what he now thought of as his own space. Going back inside to lock the office door, he went up to grab a book from the loft and ended up laying down in the hammock for a read. Before he knew it, he had fallen into a deep sleep, full of dreams.

His mother, shaking him awake she said, "John, go do something, don't sleep your life away… come on, time to get a life…" In his dream his mother was well, she had a brightest red back pack slung over one shoulder, and she looked full of life and excitement. Slinging her pack off in one fluid motion, she held it out to him and looked him in the eye. Before handing the pack over they shared a moment of intense and meaningful eye contact. It was during that eye contact, an important message was conveyed. The message was that the backpack contained everything he would ever need. All the memories were inside. Still with a look of intensity, she said, "Look inside, it's all there…" and then she was gone.

Waking from the dream, John was disorientated at first but felt lightness as if, for the moment at least, all his worries had been taken away during his mothers dream visit. That's how he felt every time he woke from a dream of his mother. During her illness she said, if she could, she would find a way to visit him. John treated his dreams like the visits she had promised. To him she was as alive, as if she were standing right in front of him. She had called his name. He heard her voice and knew it was a gift. But it was his gift and his alone.

After reading the letter earlier in the day from Shelley, Trish wasn't surprised to see Todd getting out of his car in her driveway. She knew her house would be the next call after she spotted him driving in front of her on the road out of town. When he made a turn at the driveway to JJ's place every instinct told her, he would be along to her place very soon. Reaching up she set today's letter from Shelley on top of the fridge. Trish surmised it was most likely mailed by Andrea on the day before she and Heather had put John on the bus. Stepping out of the house onto the porch, Trish stood, with arms folded.

As exuberant now, with Trish, as he had been with John, Todd threw open his arms wide in greeting. "Hey Trish; it's been awhile! I guess you heard the news about Margaret...er I meant to say Shelley, bummer eh?" Todd's act wasn't fooling Trish, his eyes were red rimmed as if he had just been crying and she was pretty sure he had.

"Who is this Margaret?" Trish stood not wanting to relax. Her arms folded, she pulled them tighter, waiting for some bullshit answer. Realizing his mistake Todd didn't give one, instead he told her the same thing he told John. "Shelly made me promise, man. I ran into her in Vancouver when Seth and I went looking for her together that time. I saw her and told Seth where she was. I thought he would tell you guys. Look Trish, I feel awful about all this, but now I just need to come clean. Get it off my chest. I have so much to tell you about her. She was awesome." Todd looked so earnest for a change, as he continued, "I don't even know what I was doing so long ago; I was young and the lie just got bigger and bigger. Shelley? She goes by Margaret now. I call her Margaret, everyone calls her Margaret or Maggie or Margot, some form of Margaret. I call her Margs. I mean I called her ....I can't believe she's gone man. I was working in Alberta even way back then, remember, both Seth and I worked up north.

"When Seth never made it back to work on time I just thought he'd stayed with some girl at a music festival he had tickets for. Then I heard the news, and by that time the funeral was over; you never even bothered to try to get hold of me. So Trish, I went straight to Vancouver to tell Shelley and get her back home. But she refused man." Pausing long enough to settle his thumbs in the loops of his pants and the ends of his fingers in to the front pockets, with shoulders raised as high as he could get them, he struck his classic pose. Todd's pose was so familiar to Trish; she had seen it since he went through puberty fast. He grew almost a foot one summer. That's how long ago it had been since Seth brought Todd home for the first time. He brought Todd and another kid home so they could pick up Seth's skate board and Todd ended up staying the whole weekend, and many other weekends throughout the years. Trish was hardly listening to Todd now, but she was aware he was making excuses for the facts she had just now read in a letter. She was suddenly brought back to the surface when she heard Seth's name.

"She didn't want to come; she was shook up, Trish. That girl felt so guilty about Seth. If he hadn't come looking for her, he wouldn't have been on that road at that time. At first she just couldn't face you and then she didn't want to face you; especially you Trish." They were both silent to let this last comment sink in. Then Todd said, "Shelley is gone man. In more ways than one and that poor kid doesn't even know the half of things. It's just one big tangled web."

Simmering for the moment Trish decided to let Todd off the hook, "I already know just about everything. I got a letter from Shelley today; I don't know what JJ will do when he finds out Todd." Suddenly furious once more, Trish launched into a rage. She was in the kind of rage Todd had experienced when he and Seth came home drunk once when they were both fifteen. "Todd what is it you think? Hey Todd? What on earth were you thinking?" Trish could hardly contain herself. She had gone from zero to ten in a flash. She felt as if she was totally losing control of her well honed, and these days, her usual controlled calmness. It just simply evaporated into thin air as she hyperventilated, tears streaming her face, her whole body shook. So shocked to see her like this again, Todd knew better than to come near, to offer comfort or glib remarks.

Trish couldn't imagine what this new twist of events would do to JJ. Trish knew he was already a mess. He hadn't even cracked a grunt or uttered a sound of any kind when he heard the news about Shelley. He just walked off with things to do. JJ is going to be a problem once he finds out Todd knew where Shelley was all along. Unless he really is a changed person as he keeps saying he is.

JJ had been all smiles joking in her kitchen after walking her back from his place on the night Shelley left the voice mail. They had shared an uncharacteristic meal together at his kitchen table, for the first time in maybe a year or two, or even five, neither could recall the last time. Trish invited him back to her place for coffee, because he was all out. And while she puttered with cups and the coffee pot, she noticed her message light flashing.

The next thing she knew instead of staying and talking about the message Shelley had left, to say she was sick, he just looked hopeless before walking off. They hadn't spoken about it that night or since. Because JJ avoided her after that, she doubted now that John was here they'd ever get a chance to talk about the shock of hearing Shelley's voice and the shock of her message. As soon as she hit the play button on her answer machine, they instantly recognized it was Shelley. With an instinctual alertness, leaning in they heard the sound of regret in her voice. JJ went dead silent as if listening for clues, cocking his head to one side. She ended the message with a soft goodbye, JJ stood, asked to hear it one more time then put his jacket back on and muttered a comment Trish couldn't hear and was gone into the night.

Snapping out of her reverie, Trish took a deep breath and ushered Todd inside the house. She asked him how he found out and he said Andrea had called Sharon's Shuttle after she got John on the bus. "After dad dropped John off at the feed lot he thought he better call me." It was as simple as that. "I drove all night to hang with the little dude. But when I got here, it was all wrong man. I did the wrong thing. John looked pissed or betrayed or disappointed or something as soon as I stepped out of the car. And then when I told him I had grown up with Shelley - he was mad. I knew it was news to him but I wanted to come clean. He was so hurt, and I don't blame him."

No one knew that he had known where Shelley was all these years and so far, today, was the first time he had spoken about it to anyone and by the end of the day he'd have shared his secret with almost everyone, except JJ of course. "Hey, do you remember JJ's mum used to have that expression? Your sin will find you out she'd say, and sure enough - bam! If you'd done something one of our parents or relatives wouldn't approve of, soon it would be common knowledge!" Shrugging his shoulders Todd claimed all innocence and he and Trish both shared a knowing laugh.

"It's interesting isn't it that she called herself Margaret. Do you know when that started; why Margaret of all names? Margaret was her mother's name, did you know?" Todd just stared seemingly deep in thought, then said, "She wanted to sound respectable, she said she wanted to bring John up in a way that had a mix of love, creativity and at the same time a bit of conservative mixed in. Calling herself Margaret was largely due to her Mum-ma Jean loving the name so much. She was amazing! Everyone just loved her, Trish...and looked out for her too. She grew up to be so amazing, peaceful and so kind. At first she went through a real tough time. You know how in awe of Seth she always was. His death....well you know better than anyone, eh? Seth was larger than life; everyone loved Seth, right Trish?" Wanting to shift away from Seth and a conversation that might end up being cause for deep pain for Trish, Todd said, "Hey like I told the little dude, I feel like shit about this.

"And I guess part of me liked having my little secret. I was glad I had something over on JJ. He didn't even wonder out loud where she was when someone mentioned her. All he ever said this one time was - I guess she'll come back when she's ready. And apparently he was right. Part of me justified keeping my secret Trish, because I knew JJ wasn't looking for her. He was being JJ, and waiting for her to make the first move. Every time I saw Shelley, she asked if JJ had mentioned her in any way. Both of them stubborn I guess... the one time I suggested she make the first move was the last. She nearly took my head off."

Trish rose from the table to get their coffee, a snack, and to show Todd all the pictures she had of John. She told him the pictures would arrive a couple of times a year with a short letter by way of letting Trish and by extension JJ know she was alive and not to look for her. She started sending them about 16 years ago. The first one came when she somehow heard about Trish's son, Seth; always sent from a different town, all over Canada. Trish wondered now if it was Todd who took care of mailing the letters and she asked.

The subject of Seth was one Todd didn't want to talk about. He was hiding something and always would now that Shelley was gone. He would never tell anyone, he had promised. As far as he knew he was the only person other than Seth who knew where Shelley had been. The fact Seth had spent his last days looking for a lost girl had added to Shelley's grief but it was guilt that had kept her away for so long. If it weren't for her Seth would not have been killed. Trish and Todd shared another pot of coffee and spent another hour or so, of fairly cathartic time together that afternoon. They talked a lot about the old days with Seth and they talked about Shelley too and how hard her early times were as a young mother.

During the conversation, Trish became aware that it was Todd who helped Shelley in so many ways. Without Todd as a life line to home she wondered if Shelley would have just come back to find things out for herself. She didn't mention this to Todd though. She felt certain Todd would have asked himself that question, more than a few times.

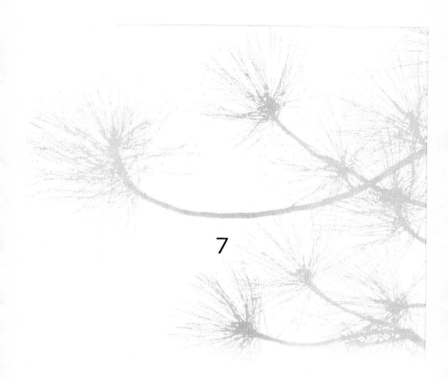

7

After waking from his dream and closing up the barn for the
day, John headed back up to the house. He knew it was time
to read another letter. He just didn't know why so soon. The
letters were surely to keep him from falling apart. To give him
a piece of his mum, so he'd feel her closeness. The house was
still completely empty. He put the kettle on and got down the
tea pot. While he waited for it to boil he reflected on how his
habit of drinking tea, was a direct result of watching Heather's
favourite show, a British soap opera called Coronation Street
on some Sunday mornings at home with Andrea, Heather
and his mum. On Coronation Street the habit, of the shows
characters, of putting a brew of tea on, or slugging a bottle
of whiskey down, in troubled times no doubt inspired the
Sunday morning watchers. At his house the show inspired

them to all drink tea during the show, and Sunday morning tea drinking turned into every day or two or three times a day.

John took his tea cup to the table while he waited for the kettle to boil, turning a chair so it was facing the room he plunked himself down, taking a long slow look at his surroundings. John had been brought up to enjoy quiet time. Using it to think, or just look at his surroundings as he was doing now. The kitchen and the rest of the living areas, if only a few modern appendages had been added, could have been featured in a home and garden magazine or an architectural magazine as far as rustic, open living concept went. John bet the big windows, stretching all across the front brought in lots of winter light. Well thought out, the deciduous trees planted ten or twenty feet from the porch provided shade in the heat, natural light in the dead of winter.

As you entered the house, you passed through a room JJ called an airlock but really it was just a vestibule with an outside door and an inside door. It wasn't big, but was enclosed so the cold air never entered the house in winter. Just inside the door there was an eating area and kitchen to the right, living room to the left and inglenook to the far left and dining area straight ahead. The ceiling was high, two stories high. So far John had not explored in depth the loft and behind the three doors on the main floor. Maybe he would do that after reading his letter.

Turning back to the stove when he heard the kettle sing, he spotted a folded sheet of paper with his name on it. John, it said, I won't be home for dinner; you go ahead and help yourself, JJ. Dejected John felt hot tears burn his eyes. He wasn't used to being so alone, he needed company. Looking around for a telephone he thought he would just give Andrea a call.

No phone. His mum had said she grew up without a phone, TV and all the cars were hidden as if they were criminals or something. Mum said more like crazy eccentrics who viewed the land as untouched by civilization. For the first time John wondered if they even had any cars. He wondered. And he'd find out. Taking tea and his letter into the inglenook he made himself comfortable and began to read his next letter before heading over to see Trish.

> *Dear John,*
>
> *By now you will have done some exploring and I'll bet you didn't get much further than the barn. I know how your mind works and what your hands want to do. I know exactly where your curiosity will take you; I know what doors you will unlock, and I know what is behind those doors. Every step you have taken so far, my feet have travelled there too. The things you will touch, my own hands have touched. We are connected John; zippered together like a nice warm coat.*
>
> *What I am imagining right now, as I sit reclined in bed writing to you is this: JJ setting you up in the barn saying something like, you'll be more comfortable, sleeping in the hay loft. The experience will give you a taste of farm life. By definition though, the land all around you, the land that surrounds you, is not a farm.*
>
> *A farm has farm animals and some crops, or no animals at all and just crops or just a specific variety of animal, such as a chicken or - a pig farm or a dairy farm or just a hobby farm. A ranch usually refers to a large piece of land that*

cattle or other large animals, like horses or lamas, are raised on. I don't know what to tell you about the land I grew up on, or what to call it but it is not a conventional farm at all.

My grandparents Ken and Jean took over a feed lot, when they took over the land. The feed lot comprised the falling down buildings you were dropped off at, and the land all around them. The feed lot was before my time and over and done with, long before I came along. After the feed lot, my grandparents invested and made money in the oil industry and the land became a place to call home. Oh yes, I suppose there might still be chickens and maybe a garden though I bet there is not. You could start one while you are there but who would water it when you go.

Don't let the beauty of the land tie you tight John. That's my advice. Sit on it, watch it and savour the subtle mix of scents in the air. But don't get tied by it. Just allow yourself the luxury of no time constraints or responsibilities for now. Soon enough you'll be bogged down; people, some you know, some you don't know, will begin to stop by to pay their respects, and to be polite they will say, how well I was liked. But the truth is I didn't have many friends when I lived there; I stayed to myself.

If he hasn't turned up already, any day now Todd will come driving down the long driveway. When he does he'll tell you some things that were meant to be kept a secret. Todd won't keep the *secret now. Despite what Andrea thinks of Todd - I know you heard her call him, Todd the Knob. Despite all that he is intrinsically good. I won't reveal his secret to you though; I'll let Todd do that. It was his secret that I asked him to keep for me, and he did keep it; for years and years.*

He helped me John. He helped me to sort out how to put together a future for the two of us; how to move forward in my young life. Coming by like he did so many years ago just out of the blue, was a mystery to Andrea, but not ever to me. I have so much gratitude to him for all he did!

He even found Andrea for us. She doesn't know it but he did and what a find eh? Another prediction for you John is JJ has been very absent since you've been there. That is just JJ. Never wanting to face things or talk things out. You can help him with that. I don't know how you got to be you, but I admire how straight to the point you are. Whenever I hear you say, let's talk, I know there will be something quite insightful on the horizon. The next treasure hunt tip is, keep heading in your well defined direction and soon you'll find YOUR INSPIRATION FOR LIFE, or at least some inspiration.

Love
Mum xoxoxox

The letter induced more tears. He missed her so much and being here reading the letter made him feel her embrace. His feet and his hands touching what she had touched, Wow! All the feeling of not wanting to be here changed in that moment. He wanted to be where she had been, in a place she breathed the air, thought her thoughts, where she grew up. She had been here for almost half her life. She had sent him here for a reason and he would not let her down. Pulling on his jacket he headed off toward Trish's place.

The house was completely dark and her aging RV loomed large as he approached. A light was on in one of the small windows of the motor home. Out of curiosity he headed that way. When he got a bit closer, he stopped just long enough to pick up an empty five gallon bucket he saw laying in the grass. He had every intention of standing on top of that bucket to get a look inside.

What he saw made his eyes water again. He was flooded with emotion. There was Trish reclined on a bed, knees pulled up and surrounded by owls. His mum had made those owls, he felt sure she had. And she was writing in bed, just like his mum always did, with knees up. Suddenly her hand became motionless in mid air, she cocked her head to one side, eyes shifted the same direction and in one fluid motion she was off the bed with the door open, saying, "Who's there?" Climbing from his perch John strolled around the side of the RV and said, "It's only me, sorry, I guess I scared you." What a relief Trish felt. She knew a safer place could never be found than her own home and had never been scared before now. There was something so unsettling about seeing John though. The way he stood, the way he held himself with his assured quiet.

Maybe it was just the fact of Shelley dying that was unsettling on its own. But on top of that, this poor kid was plunked down amongst two adults with a whole life of their own and no clue how to be with people his age. Not now, not way back then either. Trish had never been happy with how things had wound up with Shelley. She couldn't help feeling as if Shelley was reaching out over time with a second chance for them to do the right thing.

About three years after she lost Seth, Trish felt as if there was no strength left to keep her and JJ together. Not just as friends, but as human beings as well. Like little ice bergs they'd floated away on their own sea of grief and each of them now had such a lonely life. Struggling to make things work out in their much smaller worlds, Trish dove into her writing. But what did JJ do? He dove into AA meetings, casual sex and solitude.

On that note, and clinging to the notion she'd been given a second chance to be good and kind and hopefully a mentor too, she grabbed John in for a big tight hug. "Hey, I know it's kind of late but I haven't eaten yet, do you want to share some dinner? I know JJ is usually in town tonight and I bet even with you here he still left you high and dry, right?" John raised his eyebrows and gave a brief nod in answer. "Where shall we eat, inside the house, outside in the yard, or inside Monika, that's my old RV?" Trish said this lovingly as she gave the relatively clean RV a pat.

For answer John turned toward the vegetable garden squinting speculatively through the dimming light, he asked if she had picked yet. When she said she yes, he headed toward the house and over his shoulders he suggested, "How about I make dinner for you tonight. Show me what you have and I'll whip something up? My mum told me she had so many dinners made by you and it sounded as if she would have liked to return the favour and cook for you someday. She was the very best cook, at least I think so. She was so inventive sometimes, with so little... What she did best though was great presentation, and then everything tasted a lot better, because it looked so good.

"Mum was really creative; she could look in the fridge and pick from anything that was there and invent something. We were pretty lucky cause for most of the time we didn't have very much money. But mum had a secret weapon against poverty; she didn't waste food and she never bought processed foods or junk food. I love junk food! Do you have any?"

So far and during the one short conversation the two had the day before, Trish was of the impression that John was on the quiet side. She was pleased and surprised by how forthcoming and chatty John was being now. She imagined single mothers brought up chatty boys. Seth was always chatty. Not so much with men though. He was chatty with women. With men he seemed at a loss of what to say, so talked about sports. This was so untrue of course, just a mother's rambling mind about her son. Everyone liked Seth, all her gal pals all her male friends, his teachers, his friends, their parents. Everyone except JJ who wasn't too crazy about him when Shelley hit puberty, but he was just being protective.

When they got into the house the lights had to be turned on, it was getting pretty dim. In contrast to JJ's house this one had smaller windows letting in a lot less light. Plus the covered porch running the length of this side of the house acted as a shade at this time of year and would make it very dim in winter. When you walked through the back door to this house it was right into a huge kitchen. Spotless counters holding only a couple of bowls, with cleaned produce and a jar of flowers. This kitchen looked like it should be in a magazine. And he said so, telling Trish about going to the library with his mum to get reading material and they would always spend time looking at home improvement and gardening magazines and architectural books. "Mum loved to look at books for ideas on what is popular and lots of - how to books actually.

"When she started making mosaics it was with coloured paper from pages found in recycling, she'd turn them into collages or greeting cards. Then she started painting on her own homemade paper, cutting it up and piecing the shapes together into collages that looked like exotic quilts. One time we went to an art show her friend was having in Victoria, at a gallery called The Ministry of Casual Living. That's when mum knew her work was good enough to show there, or any-where else.

"But what happened was Andrea saw a vacant store front that was having a neighbourhood art show for two weeks. Andrea arranged to take some of mum's art in to have the organizers check them out... it was a surprise for mum. They put a bunch of things mum had done since we had lived at our place...you know like sketches... things in a series, like five or six pieces that were related somehow. She showed a series of the collages, a series of rubbing's from nature, what else, a series of baby paintings of me. All her work is very abstract. A series of rock, drift wood and heavy rope mobile things."

John just kept talking about his mother as Trish watched him go from fridge to counter, eyes constantly moving, searching. Out came a cutting board, knives. He was so self-sufficient it almost made Trish cry as she wondered why and how. She knew this chatter was partly nervous chatter; a need to talk about his mum or a need to talk, after a day of being on his own. And her silence filled a need for her to hear all there was for him to tell about his mum and their life together. She wouldn't tire of hearing. She too had stories and she hoped she would get a chance to share them, before he was gone again. Because once he was gone, they may never see him again.

His attachment to them was just circumstantial at the moment. He came here on a mission for his mum. Once that was complete unless they, each of them, had made a connection nothing would bring him back again. And if JJ went out every night and carried on as if nothing happened, sticking to his routine then what the hell! She and JJ never talked about Shelley, they never talked about Seth either. Didn't talk about her bad marriage, his disastrous relationships; they talked about the land, art, her writing, local politics, various projects and their parents from time to time. She wasn't sure how, but she'd need to talk to him about John, about Shelley and about what the next step would be. Who was she kidding? They needed to talk about what the first step would be.

Snapping out of her musings, she hoped she hadn't missed too much. John was still chatting away. He had moved on to another subject and was asking her a question and she just caught the tail end, "your bedroom," was all that she heard. Then seeming embarrassed and a bit bashful he apologized saying it was none of his business. Without any idea what he would have been asking she jumped right in with, "Well why don't I just show you around, then you can form your own ideas?" This seemed to satisfy John but first he said, "Let's eat," adding very humbly, "it isn't much, but I don't really eat meat much so I just made a salad. Salads are my specialty. I can make salads out of everything." Trish stood up and went to the fridge grabbing some bottled dressing and when she did, John quickly covered the top of the salad bowl with his hands, saying it was already dressed.

Table all set, they sat. Trish silently berated herself for going into a daze and not paying full attention. She hadn't even noticed when he made dressing and there was no evidence he had. The cutting board and counter were all cleaned off. "Let me ask you something John. When you were talking about your mum, my mind wandered back to the old days. The next thing I knew you had finished making this! It is wonderful, absolutely wonderful! You never asked me for a thing, I'm impressed. What I want to know is, what dressing did you use?" John laughed and was clearly delighted that Trish liked the meal. "I used a tomato, crushed and chopped then I added some balsamic and chopped up some orange, added grated cheese, sunflower seeds and sesame seeds too...all found in the kitchen. Then I added a colourful flourish of carrot with the vegetable peeler onto the top for the presentation part.

"Trish, my mum became resourceful...." It took a few seconds to get his breath and still his heart, because at that moment he thought it would break just talking so much about her. "She taught me to be resourceful too. Mum learned how to cook by watching her Mum-ma Jean cook. Well that's what she said, and then in her early days in the city she volunteered at a soup kitchen and learned some hands on things there. John paused for so long Trish thought he had stopped speaking. "One of the things she learned is that everything is not what it seems. If it seems too good to be true, it probably is, and if it seems like the end of the world it probably isn't. She also learned how paramount to success, hopefulness is. To always be looking for the good." John abruptly stopped talking, stood to clear the plates that had been polished clean; taking them to the sink. Trish stood too and came to stand next to him. She opened the dishwasher and began to load,

"When we've finished up here let's go look at the bedroom you are so curious about." And out of the corner of her eye she saw John blush.

Outside again they heard frogs begin their nightly croak. The light was still on inside Monika, and acted as a beacon lighting the way. Stepping into the RV, John felt more at home than anywhere else. On the back of a chair he saw a bag he was sure his mum had made. Making as if to grab for it, he stopped himself from saying this isn't yours, instead he asked where she got it. "Your mum sent it to me two years ago, inside was this?" She held up a little owl made of cloth. John smiled asking where all the other owls came from and Trish laughed when she told him she had become addicted to making owls herself.

"You must realize this isn't my actual bedroom, just one of the places I write. I'm a writer. Each day, when the weather is good I write in here. Usually from about the end of March until Thanksgiving I come out first thing in the morning if it's cool enough that is, to find my muse. The rest of the year I write in my own bed in the house. I don't sleep in this bed John, just write here and not even every day.

"Maybe you being here, Shelley's son, brought me out here to write tonight. I hadn't written propped up like that in a week. When your mum was young I wrote my first book after an afternoon hike with her. She was so inquisitive and after a walk and talk with her about the weather, of all things, I got an idea for a book. It's a children's book about the weather. I called it Weather or Not." Trish smiled at the memory then carried on. "It did get published and has earned me some good revenue. Since then I've written a series of children's books under another name. My pen name is, Suzi Saltaire. If you ever want to hear about how to predict weather by what nature is doing, I'll be happy to tell you what to look for." At that she laughed.

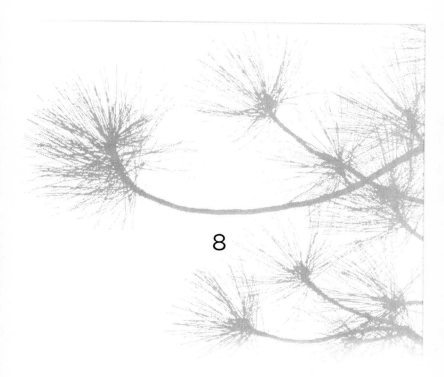

8

Earlier in the day JJ called his horse, Frida, from pasture, saddled her up and taken his usual early ride over the land just to take a look at things in the morning light. He often did this first thing in the morning, the old habit of wanting to check his livestock of which he had none this year. For ten or twelve years he ran a cow-calf operation. Then last year he didn't even make it to one auction before he just changed his mind on buying any new stock; selling all he had to his sponsor. No longer wanting to be that part of the food chain, no one was more surprised than JJ himself, when he sold all his stock and equipment at a bargain price too. Oh he helped the guy out from time to time, but he didn't miss that part of his life. He didn't need the money, the time involved was increasing year by year as he got more stock and most of all, for the first time ever, felt sorry for all the beef on the hoof for sale. Now when he took his morning ride it was strictly for the pleasure early mornings brought, to give his life some routine and to give him a sense, that he was busy.

He didn't know why he tried so hard to keep busy and fill up his time. When he had nothing planned, his time filled up just as fast. Even without a phone people managed to find him and get him involved in their various projects. As he rode he noticed some disturbance of the land up ahead. He knew the land so well that even a blade of grass out of place got noticed.

When he got closer he could see somehow one of the well covers had been tampered with. When he knew there would be no cow calf operation this year he had capped the well just to keep the water clean and stop it from getting contaminated and to protect it from anyone, man or beast from falling in.

The lid had come off, that's what was out of place, but he didn't know how it could have without help. He had placed a large rock on top and the rock had been rolled off. Anyone or anything could have rolled the rock off. But now JJ kicked himself for not taking more care and actually putting a pad lock system on it. He was pretty sure he didn't have anything strong enough lying around; he'd get a lock when he was in town later. And he would have a talk with John about the water and where it came from. Getting from the house to here on foot and back is a bit of a hike so he didn't think it could have been John and when would he have had time. If John was wandering around the place though he'd need to know about the hazard an uncovered well could mean.

Riding back toward the house and from a distance away, he saw a figure with backpack on his back entering the barn. JJ smiled to himself as he imagined the book worm city kid with nothing to do all day but read up in the sleeping loft. Tomorrow he promised himself he would make a plan with the kid.

Stopping just long enough to throw some food together for his ride and write a note to John, JJ headed back out to his horse and the long ride to his sponsors' place where they would ride in the air conditioned comfort of his AA sponsor's truck. He hadn't been to a meeting in a long time until about ten days ago because he didn't need to; until he heard about Shelley that is. He had been going every day. He just went, never got up to share. There wasn't really much to share. His sister's kid died. End of story. Almost nothing to share and then there was John, but he wasn't going to share that.

JJ had already proven he knew nothing about kids and especially teens. One of the reasons he liked the meetings was because everyone was so honest sharing the bare bones of their lives and how screwed up they were, how screwed up their families were because of them. He listened and waited to hear a story to match his own. He needed to know he wasn't alone and most of all he needed to know how to approach the kid. If John were a scared kid needing help, JJ would be in a way better position. But here comes a kid, with self assurance galore and seeming complete confidence in himself and his abilities. A kid who seemed quite fit to do almost anything. JJ felt inept by comparison. So far there had been nothing he could do for John. Except tell him what an inglenook was.

If only John had grown up close by, or if Shelley had let them get to know each other or introduced them in some way. But starting from scratch with only the memory of how Shelley had been as a teenager, made it hard. Shelley was on the belligerent side. Walking on eggshells is what JJ had always done, or at least that's how he saw it. After Shelley's mum died and then some years later her grandmother, it was just his dad, Ken, and him looking out for her. Ken was a real old crusty bastard by that time; he always had been. The only saving grace was Ken and JJ's mother, Jean, were gone so much. Even from the time he was old enough to be on his own looking after his sister, off they would go. They liked to go to Vegas and also had some more land in the foothills of Alberta; they liked it there in the summer. So it was a bit of time in the summer, fall and in the spring too they were always coming and going and when his sister, Margaret, was younger they took her too until she was old enough to stay behind with JJ or the Dixon's.

JJ was twelve when his little sister was born. He remembered the day with such glee. He wanted a brother. And told all his friends at school he was having a brother. The day she was born, he went off to school as usual stopping off at old man Dixon's place to pick up Trish on their way to the school bus. Trish was only six and in grade one. She was pretty excited for JJ about having a sibling. She and JJ were both only children. Trish's mum had left her and her dad, when she was still a baby. She didn't know where her mum went away to for a long time, and neither did her dad.

JJ and Trish were pretty fond of each other, more like brother and sister and they would remain just as close making the new baby sibling number three. Six years separated them, only children in each their own right and at the same time with a support stronger than many familial relationships.

On the morning his sister was born, old man Dixon was coughing up a storm. He'd been sick for a while now and JJ often day dreamed about him dying, so that Trish could come live with them. He didn't die though he lived on and was still living at age 94, remarried and living in the city not too far from where Shelley lived as it turned out. Before getting on the bus Trish had said, "I bet the baby comes today and I know it will be a girl." JJ had already heard her say she wanted a girl but it wasn't going to happen.

As he rode to his sponsors place, he remembered how the day had panned out. They got to school after an hour on the bus. They went to their separate class rooms and about an hour into the lessons the PA system fizzled to life and a crackly voice asked JJ to come to the office. Off he went, face blazing and feeling a mixture of fear, embarrassment and pride. It wasn't the first time he'd been called to the office, and the other times hadn't been good.

This time though he knew it would be OK. As soon as he rounded the corner there was old man Dixon standing right in front of the office with a big grin on his face. He said, "Well JJ the day has arrived, you are finally a big brother," sticking his hand out to shake he said, "Congratulations."

"Is it a boy?" JJ asked still hardly able to speak because he was grinning too. "Well....I don't know about that, they didn't say. All your old man said, was the baby came and they're calling it Shelley." Seeing disappointment on JJ's face, Dixon quickly added, "Maybe short for Sheldon." A beaming JJ ran back to class to the sound of office staff saying, "No running in the halls!" JJ burst into his classroom smiling broadly and announced, "I have a baby brother! And his name is Sheldon but we are calling him Shelley, for short." The class roared with nervous laughter as whispers of, "Shelley" circulated around the classroom. Titters of laughter rang in his ears all day long.

At the end of the school day with just the two of them remaining on the bus, JJ finally told Trish about the baby.

He wasn't sure why he had waited until then except the pleasure of having a brother wore off real quick when he realized every day of that poor kids life he would be made fun of. When he told Trish the news she burst into tears because she wanted JJ to have a sister so bad; together they shared extreme disappointment.

Two very subdued kids got off the school bus that afternoon. Imagining his mum would be in hospital, JJ planned to stop over night with the Dixon's. Opening the door and stepping into the kitchen both kids began to take off boots and coats. "No no," shouted the voice of old man Dixon, "don't remove those boots. You two are to go straight over to your place, JJ. When you two have seen the baby though, I want you to bring Trish back home here. And you better pack a bag and plan to stay a couple of days, too." Boots back on the two kids reluctantly and very slowly took the longest route they could; delaying the inevitable of seeing the baby for the first time.

Pushing open the door they could hear JJ's mum laughing softly and could see his dad sitting in the inglenook cradling a bundle in a pink blanket. The blanket was one Trish had given them for the baby a week ago. JJ's heart sank, he knew his mum was trying to be kind using the blanket, but he also knew if word of this got out his little brother would be doomed.

His mum sitting in the opposite chair to his dad, reached out her arms to JJ and said, "Come have a snuggle with mum first before you see your sister." JJ shouted, "A sister?" And the baby started to cry. Both JJ and Trish hurried over to hover over the wee soul and both were so happy. Trish in her glory because the baby's first blanket was the one she had asked her aunt to make and JJ so relieved it was a girl! Both kids at once said, "Can I hold her?" And Ken looking relieved to give up his seat and get out doors, got up as fast as he could to let both kids squeeze into the chair side by side. Once the little baby was nestled in with the two adoring kids, Ken got the camera out and took a few shots; thinking to himself with real pleasure, the three musketeers. He knew they'd grow up distanced by six years between them, and somehow he knew too the three of them would be completely devoted to each other and as tight as thieves for the rest of their lives.

The baby was not named Shelley after all. Shelley had been Ken's idea or Sheldon actually for a boy. And yes Ken would nick name him Shelley to toughen him up because that's the kind of guy Ken was. A very tough father, he'd stir them all up, then walk away without a care if the dust settled or not. He left most everything to his wife Jean. Ken was a guy short on compliments or kindnesses of any kind and heavy on hard facts and criticism and believed in his form of brutal honesty. In fact the family joke was the biggest compliment he gave anyone was to his own wife when he said of her - Jean has more guts than a slaughter house floor. And she probably did have guts to be married to him. Their life after baby Margaret came along, was much more settled for the first few years then it was back to travelling between their other places on the land.

JJ arrived just as his sponsor was starting up the truck and he had to hurry to get the horse pastured out back of the house. Past experience said if he didn't hustle, he'd miss his ride. That done, when he rounded the house he didn't hear the truck at all and thought he'd missed his ride for sure. But no, there his sponsor stood, back leaned against the truck, eyes staring at the ground. JJ didn't like the look of this, something was up. "Is everything OK, Jim?" JJ asked. The sponsor turned his head, pushed off the truck to stand up straight. He reached out his hand to place on JJ's shoulder and said, "I hear Shelley's son has come, you need to do some talking." JJ felt instant fury at his sponsor for suggesting he needed to share how he was feeling and said so.

"I don't know why everyone thinks I need to talk. What's to talk about, my niece who I'll remind you, took off years and years ago and has never made contact with me since, has died. I didn't know her anymore. I never knew her! If I did, she never would have left. And maybe she'd never have died and she sure as hell wouldn't have had to raise a kid, all on her own! No I don't need to talk about it.

"I'm gonna go through all seven stages of grief they talk about on my own, thank you very much! There is no time to worry about myself. Right now all I want is a way in with the kid. He'll be here three weeks tops, that won't be enough time to get to know each other." The sponsor had not tried to interrupt while JJ ranted; now he just stood still in silence, because he had nothing to add.

They got in the truck then, taking their silence with them and went to the AA meeting. JJ had intended to share his grief at the meeting but after he had cooled down a bit from his tirade on the quiet ride there, all he wanted was for the meeting to end. So he sat with arms folded in close to his body, completely still and silent until it was all over.

After the meeting JJ caught a ride back with someone else, stopped along the way for some shopping she needed to do. He didn't know this lady well but soon after the drive began he realized she was too infirm to drive, that was for sure. So after the shopping he gently took her keys and said he would drive and he would take her for some lunch.

Originally he thought she would drop him off but he ended up driving her home, unloading her groceries, fixing a broken gate, the drawer to the left of her kitchen sink, and putting a new sink in her bathroom. By that time she had a dinner of homemade soup set out and he didn't have the heart to say no.

After dinner though he needed to get his horse and get home to John. Guilt had been crawling up his spine all afternoon. He humbled himself and called his sponsor to come get him, then saddled his horse up and made his way back home. As he came over the ridge he had a clear view of both house and barn and both were shrouded in deep and lonely dark. He felt sick in the pit of his stomach and determined he would put a phone in the house finally. If he had a phone he could have called John to say he would be late.

Except for a small pocket at Trish's place there was no cell phone reception for miles around so no use having one here for John to use. Kicking himself harder, he thought of Trish, she has a phone and that is the one he always used when one was needed. That's how Trish had found out about Shelley first, Andrea had phoned there. Part of him didn't want to involve Trish in this, and the other part knew full well she was just as involved as him and probably was more involved. In fact he would bet John was at her place right now. He couldn't see her place from here but it wasn't a long walk. Pasturing the horse once more, he went inside to clean up before going over to see if John was with Trish. Hoping he was with Trish and hadn't just taken his stuff and left, heading back to Vancouver. That's what JJ would have done in a similar situation.

From the look of the inside of the house no one had been here all day but then he saw the note he had written was gone. Another sick in the pit of his stomach; how could he leave

John all day? He decided to skip clean up and headed right over to Trish's place. When he rounded the stand of poplar he smelt smoke and knew she had a bonfire going. One of Shelley's favourite things to do as a child and Shelley's mums too actually. He wondered if John had ever had bonfires, eaten s'mores, if he ever camped, had ridden a horse. He would find out.

Sure enough there the two were sidled up to the fire, sticks out and marshmallows slowly cooking. A pile of graham crackers and a bowl of chocolate bits were sitting ready for a campfire treat. Trish was drinking from a green bottle of something and so was John. Instantly JJ's hackles went up as he imagined them sharing a case of beer. That was a memory from the past, and it involved JJ thinking Shelley and Trish shared the case of beer. And two nights later Shelley was gone for good. If he had been really paying attention that night he would have known it was only Trish who drank the beer. Shelley was stone cold sober. An angry Trish, much later told JJ that because he was such a drunken idiot Shelley said she would never touch any booze. Ever!

"Hey JJ, pull up a stump! How long have you been back?" Trish stood then and asked JJ if he would like something to drink. His typical reply and a bantering back and forth ensued, "You know I don't drink Trish." JJ said. "Oh no; come on JJ, not even water? Just tell me what you want to drink?" JJ smirked sarcastically as he muttered, "I can see you're well on your way tonight, introducing the boy to booze too, are you Trish?"

At this comment Trish stood stock still, and all joking aside said she and John were having lemon water actually. Would he like some? JJ just nodded. Trish turned to go inside to get him a bottle, when John quickly stood saying he would go. JJ stared after a retreating John saying to Trish, "It looks like the kid doesn't even want to be alone with me." Trish snorted, "Are you kidding me! You are the one who was gone all day! And then you turn up here all holier than thou! JJ, you and I need to talk. Not now, not tonight, but we need to sit down talk and come up with a plan for both of us, for all three of us actually. I'm just as much aunt to John as you are uncle and I'm not going to be too happy if we don't both make an effort to bond tight with him before he goes back."

John went into the house, opened the fridge and quickly got a few of bottles of lemon water they'd put there earlier. His movement made the pictures on the fridge flutter and he knew his mum was there with him. He didn't know what to say to her, so he just sat for a moment at the table and stared at the fridge door. At the artwork magnetized there. He wondered, not for the first time, if Trish had arranged the pictures there when she knew he was coming. Going over to the fridge now he lifted one of the magnets and there in the light from the moon he could see a ridge of dust around where the magnet had been. They had been here a while and this new knowledge made his eyes fill with tears. He felt the warmth of his mum's hand on his right shoulder and all at once he felt strong enough to join the group again.

His mum said JJ was her uncle and when she was growing up Trish was just like an aunt. Trish had been his grandmother's best friend until both his grandparents were killed in a car accident. Trish was also like an older sister to his grandmother when they were growing up. It was hard to imagine his grandmother would have been as young as Trish, but apparently she was six years younger than Trish. He didn't know about his mother's mother, or her grandmother, but this was a piece of the puzzle he wanted to discover. Tomorrow couldn't come fast enough for John and when he went back to the fire he would make his apologies and go sleep in the barn.

He could hear Trish scolding JJ for making him sleep in the barn, saying tonight he should be allowed to sleep in his mum's old room and John was quick to set things straight. "Hey hey Trish, I like the barn. It was a good idea JJ, to set me up there." JJ smiled and said, "Well your mum's room is just how she left it. She packed everything she owned....everything she liked, I suppose. Into boxes and closed the door. I've only been in there once since she's been gone. Everything in there needs to be sorted before the room is habitable." Trish was stunned, "Do you mean you have only been in once since John's mum died or do you mean since she left here, JJ. What do you mean?"

"I mean, I went in to talk to her. Found everything in boxes and haven't been back in since." A sad silence hung over the camp fire and John made ready to stand and leave when he heard his first, coyote howl. "What's that?" He said with alarm. Standing JJ stretched his hand out to John and said it was time to go home and not to be afraid, "I'll protect you." Taking hold of the out stretched hand John allowed his great uncle to help him up. With a quick good night to Trish, a hug, and a promise to see her soon, man and boy left for home. Another nearby chorus of cries from several coyotes put John on slightly shaky legs, as they made their way together back to the house, all to the song of coyotes in the night.

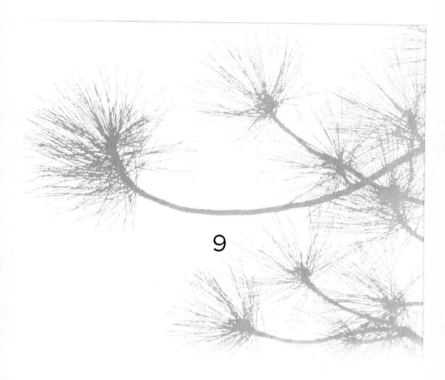

9

When they got back to JJ's the darkened outbuildings looked uninviting after sharing the warmth of all Trish's place had to offer. JJ suddenly felt uncomfortable. On their walk home they had talked. Not a real conversation but the comfortable comments of two guys making their way by the light of the moon. The path was well worn between the two homes after decades of travel back and forth. It was more than an animal track, more than a foot path. Carts, horses at one time a dirt bike and trucks had used this path. It was private and only used by the two households. As they walked JJ wondered what secrets the road would offer up, if it could speak.

JJ had shared his first kiss on this road or at least close to the path, in the stand of poplar. He also knew from rumour that Trish's mum had arranged to meet and run away with a drifter who was just passing through. From here they had used his parent's driveway to get out to the road. He also knew his mum had the beginnings of a miscarriage on this road and that he found Trish crying on this road the day her husband took off...just like her mother had. Margaret made a fort between the two houses in the poplars with a good view of the path. There had been a dog that trotted back and forth between the houses, never quite making up his mind which house he lived at. These were some of the things he had shared with John on the way home. Not all, but some.

Now back within sight of the house both of them sensed tension that hadn't been there moments before. JJ knew it was about John sleeping in the barn. And neither knowing how to part. He didn't know if he should walk John to the barn or just say good night. Instead he invited John in for the rest of the pie.

After John cleaned up and put away the dishes he asked if he could look in to his mother's bedroom. Once more for perhaps the tenth time that day, JJ got a sick queasy feeling in his gut. He felt a deep reluctance to open his treasure back up, after so many years. He wanted John to wait, before he began to start rooting through the room. Finally after a very long pause he said, "When you see the room you'll know why I say let's wait until the morning. You won't see a thing...do you want to wait?" Seeing anxiety on John's face, JJ made the first decision that would turn out to be a good one. "OK, let's go." Reaching for a flashlight just in case, JJ mounted the stairs saying follow me. Once at the top of the stairs JJ could see the big sets of double doors as if they were beckoning him to move forward. The doors were set right in the middle of the loft balcony. Running his hand along the top of the door frame, JJ found the key. Wiping it on his jeans he turned grinning with a nervous chuckle and said, "Good thing I remembered where the key was, but it sure is dusty." And with a laugh to John he said, he wasn't the best house keeper he now realized. When he put the key in the lock it didn't turn. JJ ran back down the stairs telling John to wait there.

When he returned he was giving a can he held in his hand a pretty vigorous shake. "What's that" said John. Giving the can a final shake JJ said, "Oh, it's WD40. The lock is seized up. A squirt of this ought to do the trick." And it did. The key turned and JJ ceremoniously pushed the doors wide open. Bowing low with arm outstretched he ushered John into the darkened room, a shaft of brilliant light from above lit the space. Looking up, John's gaze was captivated by a large skylight; though he couldn't see the moon, light streamed in giving the room a lovely and mysterious glow. But what really captured his imagination and almost made him want to sleep in this room after all, were the thousands of stars that could be seen through the sky light.

In complete awe and turning to look at JJ he said, "You never see stars like this in the city. Even outdoors tonight the stars didn't seem as bright as these. Was my mum happy here JJ? Is this what she wanted me to find, to see? I don't know why I'm here yet." A shudder went through his body and he knew he was crying. A stunned JJ not being sure what to do put his hand on John's arm pulled a hanky out of his pocket, and tried passing the hanky to John. Shaken out of his misery by the knowledge that the dreaded hanky was coming his way, John put both hands up waving the hanky away. "My mum told me about that hanky.....no no not the dreaded hanky!"

And John began to laugh and laugh and pretty soon JJ did too. Even though he wasn't entirely sure why, JJ felt absolute relief and joy in John's laughter. They had shared a laugh yesterday about the inglenook and again today in Shelley's bedroom. This was ending as a good day.

When the laughter died down, John turned to JJ, "Seeing this room tonight was perfect. I'm glad I saw it this way because I know this would have been her favourite time of the day. I can imagine her lying in bed looking up, counting the stars as a way to go to sleep. Why aren't there any other windows in the room?" All JJ said before suggesting they head to their beds was that he was pretty sure there had been a window in this room a long time ago.

Once down the stairs to the living room JJ offered to walk John to the barn and when John said it wasn't necessary, JJ said he would anyway. Along another well worn pathway they went, guided by the light of the moon. When John looked up and saw the outline of small birds zipping across the sky, pointing a long arm upward he asked, "What kind of birds are those?" JJ's one word reply, "Bats," sent chills up the back of John's neck. JJ went on to say he was pretty careful not to let bats get comfortable in this barn. "And that is why there's a screen in the loft window, so no flying bugs or bats get in that way. The feed lot buildings though are full of bats and another unused building at Trish's place too. Bats are a good creature to have on the land." On and on JJ went talking about, and thereby educating John on the world of bats and why they were so beneficial. When they got to the barn they both stepped inside. JJ began praising John for all his hard work cleaning things up. "Your mum loved this barn and she slept in the loft as many times as her Gran, or I, said she could. You must be like her; she kept it pretty clean in her day too, sweeping it out every day. My horse, Frida, likes the pasture this time of year but in the winter she is right over here in this stall."

Pausing long enough to open the half door of the stall so John could look inside, he carried on. "When word of cougars circulate she comes in here those nights too or if I'm around and a storm is on its way. There's also a lean to in the corral with a couple of stalls I use for her in the summer. We don't get many, but if there's a fire almost anywhere, the wild life has to make a move for food. Two years ago I lost a horse to a cougar about three weeks after a fire forty miles away. He didn't kill her on the spot but she never recovered. Did you ever ride a horse John?"

John laughed out loud, "Oh no, never. We lived so far away from an opportunity and never had a car. Mum tried to get Andrea to take us to Heather's riding lessons so I could ride there but Heather wouldn't let her." JJ had heard of Andrea but had no idea who Heather was. "Heather? That's a name I've never heard mentioned and in fact I've rarely heard of Andrea either, until last week in fact." As JJ was talking John got the biggest smile on his face and his eyes became moist. "Heather is Andrea's daughter. When we went to live in Andrea's suite, mum had a deal with Andrea that she would keep an eye on Heather some times in exchange for rent. I grew up with Heather—she's like a sister in a way; except she is way older than me and wiser too." It was obvious to JJ as he listened to John speaking that he had a deep attachment to Heather and so JJ wanted to know more. "How old is Heather?" And the whole story came out.

Andrea had a suite for rent. Some friend of his mum's told her about it a couple of weeks after Shelley had given birth;

John was just a few weeks old. Learning Shelley had been homeless when John was born, brought that sick feeling back to JJ's stomach. Not missing a beat the story continued, with John telling JJ that in exchange for being around when Andrea was at work usually in the evenings, and keeping an eye on Heather they got the suite; a two bedroom ground level suite with their own little yard. They also got two rooms upstairs for nights they slept over. The nights Andrea worked. "She's a nurse." John explained. There were conditions for anyone renting the suite. They had to be a student. "Mum wasn't a student at the time she applied as a tenant but Andrea liked her so much so said yes, and helped mum get into art school. The other condition was to look after her daughter and to become part of Heather's life during the rental period, and a promise to be a life time support forever. We've been there almost all my life; it's my home." said John.

"Mum had a room next to the bedroom upstairs that she used as her studio. And the bedroom was close enough to Heather's bedroom that if she needed anything in the night she could just knock on the door." Feeling a bit confused but still very curious JJ asked again how old Heather was. When John said Heather had just celebrated her 40th birthday JJ was shocked and looked like he was. John just laughed a warm laugh then told JJ that Heather had Down's syndrome, and needed some extra help.

They sat together on the barn bench outside and talked about life with Heather and Andrea for another hour before saying goodnight. When they parted, for JJ it was with a whole new sense of so many things about his niece, about John, and certainly about Andrea and Heather. And Cozy the dog too. Starting to walk back to the house JJ called out, "Be sure to tell

Andrea to bring Cozy to the Month's Mind." Oh yes, she will, thought John as he made his way up the steep stairs to the loft. She'll do that and a whole lot more.

When John woke up to light from the creeping morning dawn the next morning, there was a loud buzzing in his ear. The brightness of the sun light streaming in was making him hot; he had forgotten to close the loft doors again. Sleeping next to him was a cat he had not seen so far. A big orange cat, curled in a tight ball. He looked a bit dirty and rumpled. John knew it was a boy because virtually all tortoise shell cats are female, and all orange cats are male.

Reaching carefully over toward the cat, John gave his side a nudge with the back of his hand. The cat rolled onto his back, all four legs pulled in tight to his body. Front paws pulled over his face. Opening his eyes and seeing John staring back, the cat righted his self in an instant, sat up and started his morning grooming. "Who are you," enquired John; the cat continued quietly grooming. So aloof were cats; his mum preferred dogs but he liked both.

They had a cat; well Heather had a big orange cat for years, he died last year of old age. Andrea said no more cats, too much hair. They all loved Cozy; she was just as good as a cat because she loved to hunt for vermin, which was what she was bred for. Her nose told her when there was a rat or mouse about. Sound and sight and smell, told a cat or seemed to tell a cat, when a mouse was close by. Cozy though, she would spend time following the scent and then move in for the kill. The whole thing was pretty gruesome actually. Lying here just lazing away was kind of nice, but John knew he had to get moving. And when he did the cat moved too, and fast. Off he went completely disappearing.

John headed down the stairs to the barn's main level and thought of the small toilet and sink in a bathroom he'd seen inside the barn yesterday. He hadn't gotten around to cleaning it but he would see if it was functional now. Just as he was using the toilet he heard JJ's voice call out, "Hey, are you awake? Come on up to the house and have some breakfast. Trish is making it." Finishing up in the bathroom John wasn't sure if he should flush. He was a little unsure if there would be a flood or an overflow so he stuck his head around the door and told JJ he was in the can and could he flush. "Oh so you found the bathroom? Shelley, I mean your mum asked me to put it a few years before she left. She said a girl couldn't go on the grass. Next time you go in there, shut the door and have a look at the graffiti on the back. Coming, let's go....? You can bring your tooth brush and stuff up to the house and have a shower after breakfast or better yet I'd like to take you around the place. You can shower after that."

As JJ turned to leave he saw the cat and said, "Hey John did you meet Bennett, our resident cat? He officially belongs to Trish I suppose because she brought him home, but you can tell by the size of him he eats at both our places and maybe somewhere else too. You wanna come too, cat?"

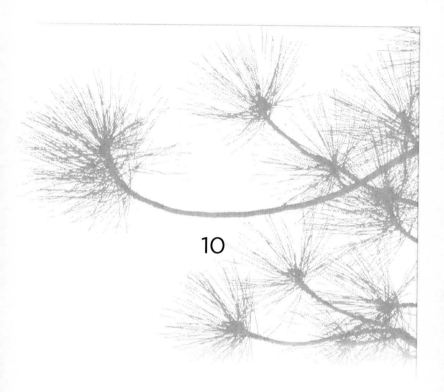

10

All the doors were wide open when they got up to the house. Closing the doors behind them, and before anyone could say a word of greeting JJ said, "Why do you always leave the doors open Trish? You know I don't like it, I don't want flying bugs in here and besides, it's too hot." Not turning around from her job at the stove Trish said, "Oh JJ. We've had this conversation so many times, you never listen. There aren't any low flying bugs in this weather. The air pressure is too high, so the bugs are flying high. In moist weather John, the weight of the moisture weighs flying bugs down, so there are more flying bugs closer to the earth and to the house. When the pressure is low the bugs fly low, when the pressure is high the bugs fly high. Keep the doors closed on days there is a lot of humidity in the air." JJ was shaking his head, "Yeah you've told me that before but I've seen bugs in here on hot days too."

"Well it can still be humid on hot days JJ. I'm talking about the moisture content in the air." Realizing she hadn't even said hello to John, Trish took a chance approaching him for a hug, trying for natural. And sure enough he understood the action. "John you are a good hugger, your mum must have taught you how to hug. She was a good hugger too and do you know who she learned how to hug from? Me!"

"Watch it John, Trish will and always has taken credit for all good things Shelley learned. And if you're not careful, she'll try to identify characteristics you have that have come directly from her. Actually she just did it, you're a good hugger, you got that from your mum and your mum got it from Trish. See!"

John, who was smiling, as all this chatter between the man and woman went on spoke up. "My mum was an excellent hugger. She said to hug, or not to hug was passed down through family. She said, you could teach an adult to hug, but it was better to start people off young. And that's why she hugged me so much and so hard. A couple of years ago when mum said I was going through some sort of independent phase, she insisted I still let her hug me. She told me about you JJ, how you'd be mad at each other but you'd grab her in for a tight hug, without a word." JJ's eyes filled and became moist.

He turned to the table then and said, "I better put some water out for us eh?" When he turned again from the taps there were Trish and John in a warm embrace and suddenly he just lost it, not for the first time since Shelley left home. Both Trish and John were suddenly by his side and they all wept together. Trish had her arms around both of them feeling gratified they had shared this moment. It was tears she believed that

soothed the wretched soul in times of grief. And talk. Grief
was close and familiar. As she cried she was crying for Seth
and for Shelley and for John, for herself and JJ too. John broke
away first, wiping his eyes with the back of his hand. JJ pulled
out his hanky and automatically offered it to them both. Up
came John's hands waving the hanky off once more and said,
"Oh no not the dreaded hanky!" This comment lightened the
atmosphere and they all shared a bit of a laugh. Trish saying,
"Words I heard from Shelley many times."

"Why do you call my mum Shelley? Everyone else calls
her Margaret or Maggie, Mags. I sometimes called her Margo
which she secretly loved, I could tell." JJ and Trish looked at
each other, neither knowing quite how to begin. And both had
heard John speak of his mother as if she was still here. Trish
began, "When your mum was born she was called Shelley. It
was a name, well a nick name her mother grew up with, which
is another long story in itself. Here is the short version....Your
great grandmother was Jean. When Jean had your grandmother, JJ's sister, your great grandfather Ken wanted a boy
and wanted to name him Sheldon, Shelley for short.

"When a girl was born instead, Ken went and told my dad
the baby had come and they were calling the baby Shelley. My
dad assumed it was a boy because he had already been hearing
this name choice for a boy for months. My dad came to the
school, told poor JJ the news. By the time JJ told me about
the baby he was crest fallen to have a brother, one he'd have
to protect from bullies his whole life. And I was so disappointed the baby was a boy instead of a girl. When we finally
discovered the baby was a girl, JJ was thrilled no one would
make fun of him, and I was thrilled I'd have a little.....well in
my mind a little sister. And then Jean said they wouldn't be

naming her Shelley, her name would be Margaret. Does that all make sense so far?" When John nodded and said, "Uh huh," JJ carried on with the story.

"When your grandmother was growing up Trish and I called her Margaret half of the time but we also called her Shelley the other half of the time. It was meant as an affectionate name, we really loved her. Both of us, well the three of us could not have been closer if we had been best friends." JJ's eyes misted up again and his throat got tight thinking about Margaret, his little sister.

Seeing JJ's discomfort Trish took over the story again. "Margaret loved being the youngest and she loved how special the name Shelley was for all of us. She beamed when we called her Shelley and when she got older she started using the name full time; but not for long. When she met your grandfather she reverted to Margaret, and that she remained for the rest of her short life. Well unless it was just the three of us together, then we called her Shelley. When she gave birth to your mother the only one truly surprised that she called her daughter Shelley, was her husband. The rest of us sighed, a sigh of relief that she took charge. Margaret was just a kid herself when your mother was born…

"Your grandfather was a pretty uptight guy and he didn't like the fact we were all so close. He thought of himself as a fifth wheel. Do you know what that is?" There was a pause and just as Trish thought John hadn't heard he said, "Mum told me a little bit about her dad. And her mum, she said they were both killed in a car accident." As long ago as it was, it seemed as fresh as yesterday as soon as John mentioned it.

For both Trish and JJ, her death began a chain of events that seemed unlucky. Trish stood up from the table with such false gaiety, it signified to JJ the subject for today was closed tighter than a drum. He stood too and headed over to the stove and asked when things would be ready. "Hold on, don't touch that! Fill the glasses and sit. I've got it all ready to go. Sit. Sit JJ!" John could see genuine affection between Trish and JJ and briefly wondered if they would end their lives bickering like this.

Once the table was completely laid and they were all seated around it, with John facing the window and Trish and JJ on either side, Trish stopped them from starting to eat. "I'd like us to join hands for a moment." JJ balked until he saw the look of hope on Trish's face. Reaching out across the table he took her hand and felt John's hand reaching his other. As an aside, JJ leaned in to John and told him breakfast didn't usually hold a ritual and Trish mostly left the toasts for the night time. With a look, Trish hushed JJ, "Today is a special day for all of us, we were brought together...we were brought here, to be together, by someone so utterly special to all of us. I am so grateful for this gift." It was looking like it would be a tearful morning after that one, but JJ saved the day by raising his glass and shouting, "SKOAL!"

"What does skoal mean JJ?"

"It's a toast, like Cheers, it originates from the Scandinavian countries Denmark or Sweden, maybe Norway. Trish here uses meals to make toasts and very eloquent toasts they are too; this one no exception. John it is good to have you here." Raising his water glass he said, "To your mother." Said with such warmth that as they raised their water glasses, Trish felt a tenderness of heart for JJ she hadn't felt since her teens.

At this moment Trish felt, no she knew, everything would work out for them. Watching the two eat gave her such pleasure and for a moment she flashed back to her son Seth and his appetite, and all the meals they'd had over here, and with JJ and the rest of the clan at her house. How had things gone so wrong, with two young people gone? Trish realized she had become jaded by Seth's death. She felt desensitized to death. When JJ's dad died last year, she hadn't shed a tear, her dog died and no tears there either. She just felt numb to death and as she rubbed her hands against her legs under the table, she knew she wouldn't get her feelings back that way.

While they ate, the conversation was cheerful. Trish asked about the day's plans and both John and JJ spoke at once. JJ to say he had a pick up to make, and John to say he had something he had to do before he went anywhere. Both comments were mysterious to Trish but she just smiled.

After breakfast was cleared away, dishes done John walked Trish half way back to her place. He didn't want her to see him head into the barn and stay there. As they walked Trish pointed out the stand of poplars that stood at the half way mark. "See those trees? They were originally planted as a wood lot, for fire wood to keep our homes warm and our food hot—when we still had wood stoves for cooking. For some reason it never got used much for fire wood and has just signified the half way point....a spot where the edges of both our properties met. Then the wood lot became so much more to so many. If that little groove of trees could talk! Anyway now it's the mid way point.

"What I love about these trees and about the aspen, and birch and alder trees too… when rain is on the way, their leaves turn over and become a little cup; ready to receive some moisture. Quite beautiful both visually with the silver of the underside showing, and conceptually too don't you think?

Look at them now. There is no sign of rain at all, but come back for a look next time you think it might rain or if you see rain clouds coming our way. You'll be amazed."

Turning to face John, he felt the intensity of her gaze, as if she were trying to memorize his face. Breaking out of her trance she said, "OK - I've got writing to do today John, so I best get to it. I don't know what you and JJ have up your sleeves for today, but have fun taking everything in. Oh and be careful." With that Trish leaned in for another hug, this one a bit shorter, turning away quickly, she headed for home.

Watching her go, John still felt the warmth of her hug, and also the warmth of his mother's hug. It was as if he had actually just been hugged by his mum. The hugs were so similar. Smiling, he headed for the barn. When he got there JJ was inside lifting a rope. JJ jumped when John spoke, "Hi JJ, I thought you were going out?" Turning JJ said, "Jesus, don't sneak up on me like that...I'm too used to being alone and you scared the shit out of me." John stood smiling with his arms folded across his chest; JJ was struck by what a strong family resemblance there was. But a resemblance to whom he couldn't quite put his finger on. Gathering the rope and a harness, off JJ went with a quick good bye and a promise to be back in two or three hours at the most. When he got back, JJ promised, he would pack a lunch and then they would go have a look around.

Once he was gone, John used his key to open the door to the room he had found yesterday; his office. Taking a breath as he stepped into the room, he went directly and opened the shutters, then trekked around the side of the barn to open the ones on the outside. He was just in time to see JJ whistling for his horse. Shaking his head in disbelief that JJ didn't seem to have a car or a truck, John headed back inside to get to know his new office. His office that is what he'd call it from now on. Well, until he went back to Vancouver.

Sitting at the table, he ran his hands over the large cracked leather desk pad that he had briefly dusted off yesterday. He thought of his mum's letter, and knew her hands had been here too, touching what he now touched. He decided to take the desk pad right off and wash the whole desk, give it a proper cleaning. Standing up, in one fluid motion he slipped the pad off the desk and onto the top of the closed suitcase. Taped to the wood of the desk was a large sheet of paper covered with his mum's hand writing. In the centre, at the top of the page was written - Inspirational Messages and Expressions.

So many, his heart started beating faster, the thrill as he recognized his mum's writing was exhilarating. Now he was certain this was her room, her place of inspiration. Before he could even start reading from her list of inspirational quotes, his eyes began to water when he saw the words from her letter. YOUR INSPIRATION FOR LIFE was written above the list of quotes, in the top left hand corner, almost as an afterthought. All these quotes before him were some he had seen or heard all his life.

> *It's impossible, said pride*
> *It's risky, said experience*
> *It's pointless, said reason*
> *Give it a try whispered the heart. Unknown*

> *The secret of getting ahead is getting started.*
> *–Mark Twain*

I never worry about action, but only about inaction –Winston Churchill.

I have been impressed with the urgency of doing. Knowing is not enough; we must apply Being willing is not enough; we must do –Leonardo da Vinci

It was obvious she liked the first one the best, because that first quote, was written softly on the wall in her studio at home. Written in a ghostly grey tone, she said it was like a hush when she showed it to him. She was speaking to a little boy at the time but he remembered her words now. He read the quote again, and recognized how these words if held close could help him through this time. Whispering softly to himself he read the quote aloud again in an effort to commit it to memory. "It's impossible said pride. It's risky said experience. It's pointless said reason. Give it a try whispered the heart."

Removing the old and brittle tape very carefully so it didn't rip the whole sheet, John lifted the paper off the desk as if it were a precious artifact, which for him it was. With the intention of finding somewhere visible to hang it; for now he placed it on top of the desk pad which sat on top of the suitcase. Back out of his office and into the barn John went for the bucket, and this time he cast his eye around the tack room looking for wood cleaner or oil of some sort. Finding what he needed he began the job of cleaning the desk.

> *"It's impossible, said pride*
> *It's risky, said experience*
> *It's pointless, said reason*
> *Give it a try, whispered the heart."*

Reading the quote out loud one more time, reminded John about the next letter to read. His mum had so perfectly predicted he would find this treasure of the quotes, he was anxious to know what other treasures he would find on the hunt. Instead of cleaning he pulled out letter number four and began to read.

Dear John,

I hope the weather is perfect for you, home on the range. Do you remember when I sang that song, Home, home on the range, where the deer and the buffalo play? When I sang that song to you, or when we sang it together in our high exaggerated voices; voices so loud and strong—do you remember? I was always thinking of this place, the place you are now.

Very soon JJ will arrange a tour for you. Maybe he already has. He'll line up a horse for you to ride if he doesn't have a spare. You've seen Heather ride on that video, remember? Just visualize yourself up on the horse. Stay calm and relaxed. Horses have a way of picking up on any anxiety. My guess is before you ride, JJ will have you cleaning hooves, and show you how to saddle up yourself. And he'll have you riding in a riding ring if there still is one. You may do this a day or two, before you actually get out on the range. This of course, in my mind, is a good thing.

When you first get up on the horse, get up on the horses left side. Lift your left hand up and grab hold of the reins and the horn on the saddle at the same time, then put you left foot up, and into the stirrup. Next, in one fluid motion, lift your whole body up, swinging your right leg over the saddle and set your butt in the seat, your right foot in the right stirrup. Got that? Watch out for JJ, he is controlling and protective.

Just relax, and use the reins and your body to guide your horse to let him/her know where to go. You are the captain, and the horse is the sailor. You give the directions, right? If the horse thinks you don't know what you are doing, there will be a mutiny and he'll try to knock you off or take the reins himself. In other words, he will try to pirate the ship. Take an apple for the horse or a carrot or give it some fresh young grass. Be gentle, as you quite naturally are. There may not be time for the barn, which you've already made yourself at home in. You will be out on the range.

When you are riding, steer JJ to the east, or south east; tell him you want to be HOME ON THE RANGE. You'll find a lake. Swim there and I'll watch you, I'll be close by. The lake is a special and a very personal spot for me; it is where I first fell in love....you will feel me there when you look at the hill beyond.

Love,
Mum xoxoxo xoxoxxoxo xoxoxoxo

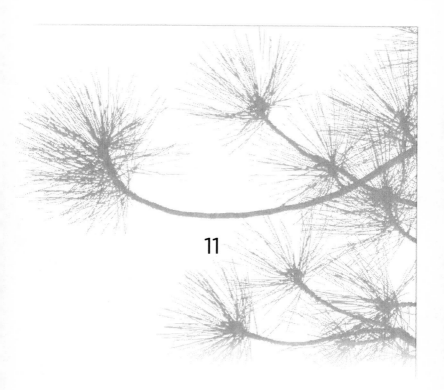

11

John managed to get the top of the desk clean and shining by the time he heard the sound of man and horse outside. John hopped up, closing and locking the door behind him. Just as he did JJ walked in and asked what he'd been up to. As if reading John's mind JJ said, "If you want to get that desk pad really looking good I have some saddle cleaner in the tack room too." Stunned, John stared at JJ. Laughing at the expression on John's face, JJ told him he had seen the shutters open on the side of the barn. "You would have figured it out, but that was Shelley's space where some of her big ideas were born. It's your space now and no worries, Shelley trained me real well on privacy." A grinning JJ carried on down the barn to the tack room with John following at a bit of a distance, unsure what to say.

When he poked his head around the door, JJ wasn't getting the saddle cleaner he had mentioned, he was lifting a saddle down. Turning he handed the heavy mass to John, and reached for a folded horse blanket. Stepping past John without a word between them, they walked in single file out of the barn into the bright white light of the day.

John's eyes so used to the dim barn took a moment to adjust and when they did, he saw his mum's prediction standing tall before him. A horse to ride, with flaring nostrils giving him a good sniff. With a flourish of his hand JJ said, "Meet Ernest, your horse for the day or for weeks or months if you like. We're heading off for a ride pretty soon and it doesn't matter if you've never ridden cause Earnest is old and reliable. He'll just follow me. I know your mum never gave you lessons...." Cutting in here John was quick to say, "She told me what to do though. Except for the saddling part, but you can show me that..." John reached to where the barn met the ground, in the shade of the building and all around the edge grew lovely green grass. He grabbed a bunch and held it out to the horse. Ernest grabbed the grass and it was with great effort, John did not flinch when he felt the hot breath of a horse's mouth on his hand. His instinct was to flinch, but a stronger instinct wanted to show JJ how relaxed and confident he was, so he held firm.

The two saddled up Ernest together, with JJ commenting how some horses expand or puff out their girth so once the saddle is on tight, and the rider is up top, they let out their breath and lose their rider when the saddle slips. "Once you get a horse saddled try to relax it a bit then, tighten the saddle straps before mounting. Ernest is a good old boy though and he'd never try to shake a rider. Am I right Ernest?" Giving the horse a good firm pat on the neck JJ turned to ask, "OK are you ready for the next lesson?"

"What's the next lesson?" JJ smiled and said, "Mounting the horse." With confidence he didn't feel John said, "Oh that, I know how to do that." With one self assured step John followed his mother's instructions from her letter, and suddenly he was sitting on top of a horse for the first time in his life.

Filled with giddy excitement, his heart was beating faster. He had a tightening in his chest which he recognized as sheer joy. Grinning he looked at JJ, "How was that? Now I'm ready for the next lesson. Let's go." Remembering what his mum said in the letter he announced, "I want to be – home on the range." JJ got a surprised look on his face and said, "I know just where I'll take you then." Mounting his horse he said, "We'll go real slowly and honestly Ernest will do all the work. What you can do is hold the reins, and use your body to guide the horse. Use the reins to guide too, but you'll see, when you lean to the left or twist your torso to the left or even look to the left or right your horse will feel your leanings and want to go that way. Try it."

And so it went for the next half hour they rode slowly with little conversation, except for JJ periodically pointing out a few different landmarks which John committed to memory. When they stopped by a giant willow tree John watched carefully as JJ dismounted and he followed suit. JJ just dropped his reins but turned in time to suggest wrapping John's own reins around an old stump. John could tell by JJ's body language that he had something he wanted to say, but when he started talking, John was surprised by what it was.

"Your great, great, grandfather, my grandfather, Ken's father bought this land at the beginning of the 1900's, in 1905.

They never lived here but did run cattle. The house was built by my dad, Ken, in the late 40's. It was my mum's design, she was an artist, and she painted landscapes. That's where… and it's looking like you too… That's where Shelley got her creativity. It comes straight down the line from my mother, Jean. Anyway, when Ken's dad bought this land, the reason he did was because of the willow trees. Where you see willows will be water, was what he always said. There are three good wells on this land that each has been consistently pumping water for over a hundred years. The one by the house pumps the most, but I haven't had the gallons per minute counted in a while. The last count was fifteen gallons, it's a gusher. The other two are used for the cattle; one is just over to the west, we will pass it on the way back. The other is where you and I first met, at the feed lot.

"My grandfather hired a water witch. You probably don't know what that is. In granddad's case it was a man with a piece of a willow branch shaped like a Y. He took hold of the two top ends holding both arms out straight and walked along until his willow dipped toward the earth. This is for real. And I think, the witching, might be a gift because it never worked for me when I tried it as a kid or as an adult. All three of these wells were found by water witching. I'm pretty sure there are a couple more wells too or at least more underground water just waiting to be tapped…but these three are the ones we've used.

"There are a couple of lakes on the property and the cattle could just drink from those too; unless they were in the feed lot, poor creatures. A feed lot is where the animals go before they are sent off to be slaughtered. They go there to get fattened up one last time before they stand on the sale scales… We have one lake and a bunch of land that's higher than all the rest and we fenced it all off from the cattle. That was the lake for swimming and that's where I'll take you now. Hope you like swimming?" And to that John just grinned and headed back to his horse.

After riding for another ten minutes they came to a spot where JJ dismounted again to open up a section in the fence so they could pass through. John still couldn't see a lake and was just wondering when it would appear when he saw some movement up ahead. JJ held up a hand for silence, and they both stopped to watch as a mother moose and her calf came over the ridge. Standing still and not posing a threat, the mother made a fast retreat with calf following close behind.

John was in awe. The sighting of the moose had made his day and here he was without his camera. He'd remember next time to take it along. JJ turned to him from his saddle saying, "Moose can be dangerous, best to just ride with me for a while OK? There are other things out here too, like cougar, that you'll want to avoid; and rattlers. And coyote are usually harmless but ride with care." John was starting to get scared, the hair on the back of his neck stiff with fear. He edged his horse on when he saw JJ had begun to giddy up.

Pretty soon they reached the top of a small hill, below the lake stood clear and inviting. More spectacular though in John's mind was the writing in rocks on the opposite slope. HOME ON THE RANGE. It was written by making words out of rocks and then painting the rocks white. The grass all around the lake in contrast to the sage coloured landscape they had just ridden across, was vibrant green. Almost surreal green it looked so lush. Pointing at the sign of letters JJ grinned saying Trish, Margaret and he had placed them there thirty or forty years or more before. "Seth and Shelley made sure the letters got painted every couple of years. This is where we all learned to swim. Come on we'll pull the float out of the grass and set it on the water."

They gave the horses a drink and tied them in the shade; JJ and John went to work releasing a wooden platform from the long grass, dragging it to the waters edge, and giving it a mighty shove across the shallow shore, until it floated free. John thought the wooden float, looked like a raft out of Tom Sawyer. Turning, to say so to JJ, John saw JJ had already removed his boots, pants and shirt and was walking gingerly over broken rock to the water. John also got ready for a swim, took his clothes off too and jumped right in. After swimming and pushing the raft into the centre of the lake and climbing aboard to dive in, he called to JJ, "Is it deep enough to dive?" In return JJ gave the thumbs up and swam over to do some diving too.

After ten minutes of diving both flopped on their backs to rest before another dive and swim to shore. "Who taught you to swim John?" John lay still remembering the few lessons he'd had then said, "Well I guess mum did. I don't remember. Mum said she started to take me to the public pool when I was a baby. So I guess since I was a baby? I've always swum. I love it. Mum never told me about this lake. She never told me so much about this place but she taught me a song we used to sing. Home, home on the range." As he was saying these words JJ had burst into song already and then they both did. John was feeling tearful at the memory of his mother's voice and he was laughing at the same time; a mix of emotions. He had found the treasure already from his mum's letter. She was right, he was surprised she knew so much about him and as it turned out about JJ too. In the same breath as this thought went through his head, he felt disappointment she had not shared all this with him before she died.

JJ stood, dove in and headed to shore. Standing with arms folded across his chest and waiting for John, with only his gonchies on, JJ looked like an old man as John swam toward him. Getting out and about to pull on his pants JJ stopped him saying, "Have you ever skipped stones? No! OK watch....look for something flat and round, here like this one. And see how I hold it out with my index finger and thumb and then you shoot it like this right? So it is parallel to the water." One, two, three, four skips.

John had been taught to skip rocks by his mum but he made a decision to let JJ teach him. A gift his mum would call this act of generosity. John wanted to give JJ a gift after this day, that JJ had given to him. Riding a horse, showing him the treasure and letting him ride the land his mum had ridden; swimming in the same lake, seeing her handiwork in the white stones.

Picking up a perfect stone JJ placed it in John's hand, wrapping his thumb and index finger around it for him, just so. Stepping back a bit he showed John how to hold his arm reminding him to hold it level to the surface of the water before letting go. John did as he was told and at the last second, shifted position so the stone dropped into the lake without a skip. Trying two more times to skip a stone until finally skipping the rock six times, a grinning John turned to JJ and said, "I did it! Thanks JJ!"

The two continued to skip rocks until their underwear was dry then they got dressed, and planned to head for home by a different route. JJ wanted to show John, one of the most beautiful vista for miles around, in his opinion. And he wanted to share a secret with John. All around the property John spotted stands of various trees. Poplar trees like the ones on the path between the two houses and aspen, and Ponderosa pine too. Their horses were headed toward a stand of lodge pole pine when JJ's horse slowed bringing them side by side so JJ could be heard.

"When Trish was maybe about your age I had a huge crush on her. But she was way younger than me and jailbait to boot. Also she was a bit like a sister so it felt kind of weird. But, at the time, Trish was all I could ever want. I was so crazy about her that I stopped being around when I knew she would be. Whole months went by and I wouldn't see her at all." Their horses were walking side by side when JJ pulled his to a stop.

"One time I came up here and carved our initials in the bark of a tree." said JJ as he got off the horse and secured the reins to a low lying bush. John did the same following to stand with JJ, next to a big pine tree. JJ was pointing at something you could barely make out; the tree had grown around it but there it was. A heart with JJ loves Trish. "I was so lovesick when I carved this, I thought if Trish somehow ever saw it, she would know and I wouldn't have to paint her a picture. Trish saw it one time, just by chance but by that time she already had a grown kid and an AWOL husband.

"The day Trish saw it she was riding up here on her own when she spotted your mum. She would have been about your age, I'd say, and she was carving names in another tree. Come on, right over here.....there see it?" Another inscription, Shelley Loves Seth, had been carved and was now grown over but not enough to disguise the heart and letters within. John turned to JJ, "You mean Trish's son, Seth? Wasn't he way older? What happened to Seth anyway?"

JJ sighed and started to tell the story. "They think Seth was run off the road by a drunk driver. He was on his way back from looking for your mum. He'd taken two weeks off work to go down to Vancouver to look for her. Then he was going to a music festival. The last time he phoned his mum, he said he thought Shelley might be working at a boutique downtown and the next day he would go see if it was her. That was the last time Trish spoke with Seth. We don't know what happened, if he found her or not.

All we know is Seth said if he didn't find her by the next day, he would head up to the Squamish music festival. Then he'd just head back to work in Northern Alberta after that. And we think about seven or eight days later he was driving back to Alberta; it was late at night, when the accident happened. And another week before anyone found his car with him inside. By then Shelley had called looking for Seth... and Trish got mad when Shelley wouldn't say where she was and wouldn't tell her if she had even seen Seth. So Trish told her, Seth, who had been at the Squamish music festival, was spending a few extra days with a girl friend he had. She told her that so she would give up her crush on Seth and just come home." John was silent and JJ took this as a sign to keep on talking.

"Trish loved your mum John, but she didn't think Seth and Shelley were right for each other. And I sure didn't either. Seth had a girl friend in every corner of every town. He was a lover not a fighter. This got said often, when he got teased about the long line of girls. But Seth, Seth never broke a heart, all those gals wanted to be friends afterwards. He was a good guy and it meant a lot to me that he went looking for your mum." John was thoughtful a minute then he asked, "What's jailbait anyway?"

JJ really laughed. He had just told a sad story, one he'd had a hard time telling, and John wanted to know what jailbait was. "Jailbait? It's when a girl is underage. Like under the age of consent, you know to date, and make out with and stuff. Trish's old man would have throttled me if I'd tried anything on with Trish. Then off she snuck with Seth's dad, who was my age, and the rest is history."

"Does Trish talk about Seth much? I mean is it OK if I ask her about him?" JJ gave the question some thought before saying, "Trish and I don't talk about much at all John; beyond pleasantries and superficial stuff we keep it kind of light. But you go ahead and talk to her; I bet she'd like that. I know she loves talking about Seth." JJ was about to turn back to the horses when he could see John had something else on his mind and asked what was up. John just shook his head. "Come on John, what's on your mind?"

"I was just trying to remember one of mum's favourite quotes; it's from Shakespeare, she said it a lot of times when she was sick. Like when we, Andrea and me I mean, would come to the hospital or if she was home after chemo we'd be, like all cheerful and acting fake. Mum would recite this phrase.

"I'm not sure but I think it goes like this... Give sorrow words; the grief that does not speak, knits up the over wrought heart and bids it break ... I think I got it right. And mum said it means that if you are sad, talk about it or else you will fill up with sadness and then burst over and over as your heart keeps breaking. She wrote it down for me to memorize a few times when she was sick. I was thinking about Seth. Trish seems so happy all the time." John looked down at his hands, "I just wondered that's all; if she ... talks about Seth and stuff?" John's eyes suddenly filled again and while he still had his voice he said, "Let's go," and headed over to get his horse, Ernest.

As they rode making their way back home neither spoke. The day JJ had planned had turned sad and this was not his intention. John had a lot to think about on his ride and as his mind churned he looked around him at the beautiful countryside covered by the long shadows marking the beginning of the end of a day. He longed for his camera. Getting near to the barn he slowed his horse and asked JJ where the horses should go that night, the barn or the pasture or did JJ have to return Ernest from wherever he got him. "How about we take them in the barn and I'll show you how to groom them, then we'll give them some feed, water, some hay and set them up in stalls for the night. I think I'll take you and Trish to town for dinner."

"Right on," was all John said but JJ was glad he had come up with a plan so quick and one John seemed to like. After they finished up with the horses he would send John over to ask Trish if she'd like to come for a late dinner. JJ showed John how to clean the hooves, and how to brush his horse. He showed him how he liked to hang the horse blankets on a rail outside the barn, so they could air out and dry out and he showed him the hay and the fork and said, "Pitch some in both stalls, I'm heading up for a shower, then can you go ask Trish if she wants to come with us, before your shower, we both smell I bet. Oh and do you have anything clean to wear?" Said as an afterthought cause it seemed like John had brought so little. Tomorrow he'd show him the washer and the household clothesline or maybe tonight.

Once showered, dried off and cleaned up JJ went to the inglenook in search of family photos. He thought he could bring them along to dinner. They'd go to a slow food place he knew, where reservations weren't a necessity and they were open late. They could eat outdoors off to the side of the hotel and watch from a quiet table next to the trees as the hotels night lights started to come on. He took a look outside and when the coast was clear he made a bee line for the car barn. Swinging open the doors there stood his baby. The first car he had ever owned. Well maintained and barely driven, it was in good shape. He got it from his dad, when he got his BA. A long time ago.

It wasn't new when his dad bought it and had been driven by an older gal, who really just used it to show someone was home at her place. Popping the hood he hooked up the battery and with a prayer turned the key. She came to life and purred like a kitten. His pride and joy; he drove her out of the barn, stopped, grabbed a shammy and gave her a wipe. Went back, closed the barn doors then headed up to Trish's place to give John a ride back for his shower.

When he got there Trish was all alone on the porch reading. All dressed up with her legs tucked under her skirt and book in hand, it was JJ's turn to wish he had a camera; she was a vision. "Hey where's John. Did he leave to go get his shower already?" Uncurling her legs from under her and standing JJ was reminded of the girl he'd had a crush on all those years ago, "Oh I sent him to shower upstairs and got out some of Seth's clothes for him to use. And don't look so shocked JJ. Yes he will be wearing a dead man's clothes. But he was the one who asked if I had any of his things still here and some of his clothes are all I kept; they were all I had to keep... He's a real nice boy isn't he JJ?" JJ scratched the back of his neck and stared at Trish before answering.

"You look really nice Trish. You and I don't see each other dressed up too often anymore do we? I took John up to the lake today. It was good. He's a good swimmer too, a really good swimmer. Like his mum. We rode the view route home and I showed him the trees with all our names carved in them." Trish looked uncomfortable when she heard this and was about to ask what happened, when they heard John come out of the house.

Both JJ and Trish stood stock still as they took the look of John in. Trish had told John to help himself to anything that might fit him amongst what she had kept of Seth's clothing. The sizes ranged from boys, to the men's clothing he wore before he died. What John had on now, when he stepped out onto the porch, made them both smile. He was wearing a white shirt he had found still in the wrapper, a bolo tie, Seth's mustang vest, a pair of Seth's Levi jeans and a pair of boots. The cow boy boots made him look older and they both said at once, "You have your mums smile!" John was grinning, "Do I have time to hit the barn for some saddle polish for the boots before we go....hey WOW! Whose car is that! That's cool!"

Trish answered first saying it was JJ's only real love, and his first true love, she said it laughing all the while. Putting up a finger she slipped back inside and came out holding up a small can of boot polish. "Come up here and I'll do your boots for you." JJ admonished her, "Oh Trish let the kid do his own boots. It's a rite of passage." Shaking her head no, she motioned for John to sit and take the boots off.

Once clean they all piled into the car with John still fawning over the awesomeness of it. Trish and JJ both wanted John to sit up front for the best view but John said no, his mother wouldn't like it; "The woman should always take the front seat." Hearing this JJ knew it was a throw back to his parents and one of their rules of decorum. The lady takes the front seat! No questions asked.

When John got in the back the first thing he noticed were the old photo albums JJ had brought along. As if knowing what was happening behind his back, and as John's hand made ready to lift one of the albums to have a look, from the front seat JJ said, "Wait until we get there."

All along the route there was more land to see. They were surrounded, rolling hills for miles around, bodies of water too. Some very small and laced with white all around the edges, others bigger, surrounded by bright green and lush grass. The grasses in the fields and along the sloping hillsides moved seductively, swaying in the breeze, like watery, rippling waves and John said so. It was mesmerizing and after his long day; his first day in the saddle, John began to feel sleepy.

By the time they got to the hotel John was fast asleep. JJ leaned over the seat gave John's knee a tap. Then he turned to Trish saying, "You sort him out and I'll see about a table OK?" He opened the car door and closed it so quietly and tenderly that if Trish didn't know better, she'd have thought it was so John wouldn't wake up. But the reality was that JJ's car was precious and the doors just got closed quietly. The only long term girl friend JJ ever had, lost her place after one too many door slams. And the fact she wouldn't let it drop, that she would like to drive his car. No one but JJ drove that car.

When Trish turned to look in the back seat John was sitting up rubbing his eyes. They were red and blurry and he looked more like a kid than ever. Trish got out her door, being sure to close it softly and pulled open the back door planning to do the same. But before she could, John took hold of the door making ready to close it and there it went a gently quiet close. Well done, thought Trish.

A hostess was waiting by the door as they came up the stairs. She was about John's age and gave him a winning grin, but he didn't seem to notice. She guided them through several small dining rooms and down some stairs and then out onto a lovely patio. They were the only people there so far and their hostess chatted about how it would fill up soon and could she bring any drinks? Trish ordered three glasses of sparkling water with lime and a pitcher of ice water too. JJ was surprised she hadn't ordered booze and said so.

"JJ I haven't had a drink in two and a half years, you don't notice much do you?" JJ teased her, "Ah, finally went on the wagon eh?" Sadly shaking her head, she said, "Wine started making me feel ill after even a sip so I just stopped. Then a few months later some gal pals were over for a martini night. I made us all martinis and had a sip of mine and had to take a pill and lay down, missing the party entirely. I've been getting migraines ever since when I eat or drink certain things." JJ smiled while raising an imaginary glass, in a toast. John looked from one to the other then asked JJ why he didn't drink. The answer was brisk, "Not now, I'll tell you another time! Hey Trish did either of you get those photo albums out of the car?" John stood then, saying he'd get them, be right back and off he went.

Making his way back inside and the labyrinth that was the hotel, John paused long enough to tuck in the back of his shirt and straighten his vest. Then he sauntered off. He knew he could have just walked around the outside of the hotel but he hoped to catch sight of that girl again. Finally back to the front door he spotted her gathering menus up for the next group of diners. As she turned to lead them to their table she was so taken up with the job at hand, she didn't even notice he was there. Oh well he shrugged, he got the wrong signals he guessed and headed out the door and out to the car. Once there of course he realized he hadn't manually locked the back door so was able to get the albums no problem. Locking up this time around, he didn't bother going through the hotel again he walked around the building instead.

As he approached the table he could see his two companions were deep in silence. Not giving it a second thought he sat down. Silence, deep silence and the comfort of it was something his mum taught him to feel totally at home with. It was chatter for chatters sake that he was uncomfortable with. Just as he was about to broach the subject of the photos, their server arrived saying, "Hi, Trish, JJ. I heard you were out here for dinner. Who's your friend? Oh! Is this Shelley's son?" John stood up then and held his hand out, "Pleased to meet you, did you know my mum? I'm John."

"Oh, good to meet you too John; I am so sorry to hear about your mum. I haven't seen her in years of course, but thought a lot about her. We went to high school together. She was the funniest one liner I ever knew. And boy was she creative....well you would know that. In high school she kept to herself but was super friendly, she just didn't have a crowd of her own but was a piece of everyone's crowd if you know what I mean. We all held her in awe...Oh no I'm rambling here aren't I?

"Have you had a chance to look at your menus yet?" John's reply made both Trish and JJ proud to be out with him. "I'll be out staying with JJ a couple more weeks. We'll be having a Month's Mind for my mum on the 30th if you'd like to come, please do. It will be pot luck so bring something you feel proud of. You know, it never mattered to my mum that she wasn't part of a crowd; she just liked people of all sorts. I'm really glad you remember that about her. It means a lot."

Placing a gentle hand on John's shoulder, she gave it a squeeze then said, "Oh thanks for the invitation. I'm pretty sure I'm scheduled to be working... I'll try to get the night off though for sure. Pot luck eh? OK, sounds like fun and you'll have to tell me about this Month's Mind thing later. But for now how about I take your orders because I know you JJ. You'll want to eat pretty soon." They made their orders and off she went. Turning to Trish and JJ, John said, "We need to talk."

All ears, they listened while John mapped out the plan he had for a Month's Mind. It would be pot luck, and held in the barn. "I'll leave you in charge of the music JJ... No I've changed my mind. Would either of you mind if I asked Todd to take care of the music?" JJ was startled out of his composure asking, "Todd, do you even know him?" Both John and Trish fell silent as John realized his mistake. Recovering smoothly though John said, "Todd came to pay his respects and we talked. He cared about my mum enough to come to find me, and he likes music. I'm going to ask him. I have a feeling mum would be OK with that."

Huffing, JJ asked Trish how she felt about involving Todd, "I'm totally OK with it JJ and you and I can talk about it later, cause the music and who plays it in two weeks, already is a detail neither of us want to tackle. Am I right?" Grudgingly JJ agreed and gratefully John nudged Trish's knee in thanks. Until their meals came the talk about the Month's Mind and who to invite continued. John was in favour of inviting anyone who asked about his mum, JJ said only family and

Trish pulled paper and pen out of her purse to make a list and get organized.

Watching John she realized he was old for his years. He didn't seem to carry the adolescent angst that both Seth and Shelley had done, or she, JJ and his sister either. John was relaxed and comfortable in his own skin. Fine with silence, open and talkative, well versed in the finer things in life such as Shakespeare apparently. Shelley had done a fine job. Trish suspected the fact that his mum was sick for three years had ensured he either grow up in a hurry, or become a problem child. He grew up! And he was really taking the organization of this Month's Mind very seriously.

"Mum would want people to be happy. Maybe we could have dancing later. What do you think? Do you know if she had any favourite songs from her youth? I thought we could have story boards with pictures of mum as a baby, as a teen and as an adult. Maybe have pictures of her family, like her parents and you two and grandparents on one. JJ can you take care of making a story board for ages 0 - graduation? Well you and Trish can OK? And JJ, hope you don't mind too much but tomorrow I'm going to start opening boxes in my mum's room." JJ jumped and was about to say something to the contrary, when he felt the soft toe of Trish's foot nudging him to silence. So he waited while John carried on.

"All the boxes are numbered, so I'm going to open them numerically. I've given it a lot of thought. The boxes are my legacy from her....my only legacy..." There was a slight pause here as John's eyes moistened then he quickly recovered and went on, "If I find anything of use for the Month's Mind, I'll set it outside the door to her room. Otherwise please don't disturb me." Just then their meals arrived. Hot and steaming, just like JJ was beginning to be. JJ and John both looked up and grinned gratefully at the server. Trish wasn't sure if the gratitude was for the food or for interrupting what potentially could have become a heated conversation. Either way it was good seeing two big appetites.

Hers was diminished these past couple of weeks. Knowing of Shelley's death had taken a toll on Trish, bringing back all the feelings of grief in losing Seth all over again. It also brought back the guilt she felt when Shelley never ever called for Seth again. Until a few days ago she had spent years wondering if Shelley even knew what had happened to Seth. The last conversation with Shelley was so rude on her part; rude and cruel. She just wanted Shelley to leave Seth alone. At the time she felt they weren't right for each other and Seth would have broken her heart anyway. He just couldn't stay true to anyone. Even if they had gotten together he would have eventually wandered off with someone else. He was a lover not a fighter. This phrase made her laugh. His dad was a lover not a fighter too, and as soon as the honeymoon was over and their first fight began he was out the door and never heard from again.

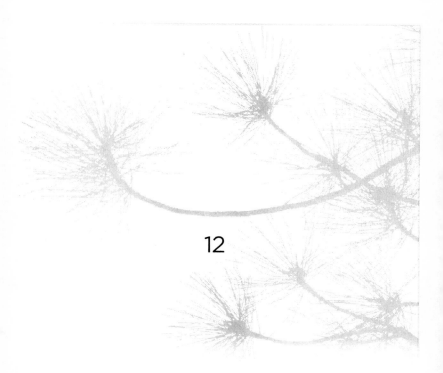

12

The next morning John woke to thunder. He stood up fast, pulled on his jeans, his shirt, a jacket and went down the stairs to use the can, and he ran out the door. From his kitchen window JJ saw John sprint by the house and along the path toward Trish's place. Wondering what was up, but not being moved enough to follow JJ continued drinking his coffee while he read his paper.

When John was half way to Trish's place, the stand of poplars was what he sought. And there they were, as Trish had said they would be; the leaves on the trees had turned themselves over ready to catch the rain. Seeing the leaves like that looking so silvery and vulnerable, John thought of his mum when she was just a girl. He thought of her before she was his mum; just a girl with a crush, maybe waiting and watching from behind these trees. A creative girl with few friends and at the same time lots of people who liked her. A girl who preferred her own company, like him; he liked his own company too. And he liked the company of his mum and their dog.

All the kids he knew through homeschooling lived so far away and were into different things. John started walking back to JJ's and then the sky opened up with a bang. He made a run for it and got there just in time to see a huge lightening crack over the hill behind JJ's. The storm was overhead. The air had a smell that was familiar in a primal sense. When he rounded the corner of the house JJ was standing in the doorway, door held wide, and a big smile on his face as his gaze held the darkening sky. "My favourite kind of day, I'm glad we put the horses in the barn last night. Did you feed them yet?" Wow, thought John he hadn't given the horse's one thought. He did glance at them, but feed them, no.

Together he and JJ headed through the rain to the barn so JJ could show him the ropes. The horses were obviously restless when they entered the barn. The shutters were banging and one of the water buckets had gotten kicked over. The cat ambled out of nowhere and started circling John's legs and meowing. JJ got busy. He didn't hurry. Just did what needed doing with efficiency and then he sat on an old kitchen chair and watched John sweep.

"I was thinking John, why not wait on the bedroom and finish off in the office first. There must be some work you want to finish up in there before you tackle her room. Shelley's desk must be full of stuff you haven't seen yet...and I'm not sure I'm ready to open the doors to you. I mean to your mum's room and her life. I..." Here he stopped with no plausible reason why John should stay out of Shelley's room. He just felt protective of her things, of her memories. JJ had never gone in there after the first time, and there was just something discomforting about John going in now. The bedroom and all it contained was a part of JJ too.

"Look JJ, I'm going to look through my mother's things," John said with more than a hint of defiance, "I'm her son, it's my right. I know it's my right. If it makes you feel better, I'll leave the door open and you can watch me. But I have to warn you there might be tears, eh? And tell you what, I'll just stay in the barn for the morning and come take a look after lunch. Can you wrap your mind around that?" With that John tossed the broom aside and stalked off and up to the house where he would have breakfast and make a lunch to take with him and eat it in the barn before starting on the boxes.

As JJ watched him go, he knew he had just seen John angry, probably as angry as John ever got. And he also felt pretty sure that when he went up to the house all would be forgotten and the subject was not ever going to be up for re-discussion. Looking down at his big hands, JJ sighed and felt a hot splash on his cheek. This wasn't the first time since John's arrival, that he wept for all he had lost. His tears fell for his sister, Margaret and for his niece Shelley. All alone in this barn, on this patch of land for years, isolating himself in the house, friendly but remote with those who knew him; he was also crying for himself.

He could change the direction he was headed if he chose to. At this point though he didn't know how, or when he wanted to, or why he wanted and where he wanted, what he wanted; all the five W's. For just a second he flashed on Shelley and wondered if John knew about her obsession with the five W's.

When he got back up to the house, every darned lamp was on and John was crouched with the cat in the inglenook trying to light a fire. "It's not that cold in here John... Here let me help you." Squatting beside him, JJ took over showing John how to first open the flue, and next how to get a good fire going. "It all starts with structure. Just like anything else you need a solid foundation for any structure. Here look what I did, wood shavings, paper and chips, then twigs and when I get that going I'll add a log. Watch and learn." And John did watch and he was certain when next he tried to build a fire he would visualize JJ squatting close, the stain of tears still on his cheek. John wondered if he had hurt JJ's feeling with his outburst, or if it was just an emotional day for them both. His mum said storms always brought out her sensitive side; first filling her with exhilaration, and leaving her feeling exhausted and needing a long sleep. Maybe that was true for him and JJ too. To JJ he said, "Let's have some tea before I hit the bedroom." The barn was long forgotten.

Before starting on the room he needed to make one stop in the barn to fetch letter number five. It felt like the right time. As he was heading out the door of the house he saw the storm had blown past. Turning he asked JJ if the horses ought to be turned out to pasture today. JJ answered by putting his tea cup and paper down, getting up and just nodding his head and saying, "I'll come with you."

Off they went with John wondering how he would get the letter without JJ catching wind. His letters were private, and for now the only things he had of his mum. Once in the barn JJ headed to the tack room, coming out holding two lead ropes. He threw one to John and put the other around his own horse Frida's neck, opened the stall door and began to lead her away. When John went to do the same, Ernest reared his head up so John couldn't get the rope over at first. He tried a few times before Ernest allowed it. A bit nervously and hanging on tight John led Ernest out of the barn following the path JJ had taken. Kicking his self for not stopping long enough to retrieve the letter he decided he would have to read it later.

The horses pastured, they went up to the house. JJ grabbed his paper, a book and some warm tea and headed upstairs to the loft. Turning on the stairs he looked back at John to say, "I read up here most days. I won't bother you at all. If you need anything I'll be right here." Before he even got settled John called up asking where he would find a vacuum, a bucket and cloth. JJ leaned over the railing pointing under the over-hanging loft to one of the doors, "Right through the middle one there."

When John opened the door he was shocked to find a whole other area of the house, with a hall running straight along with closed doors on either side. He could see at the end of the hall it opened up to another bigger room and he headed that way. Good guess, it was a utility room with furnace, hot water tank, washing machine, sink and there on the floor a small pail with a rag hanging over the edge and another door to the outside and a clothesline. Looking around he saw a small vacuum and a broom and dust pan too. First he took the vacuum with him and the few attachments he could find.

John spent the first hour and a half vacuuming and wiping years of dust and grime off everything. He washed the tops of dressers, vacuumed a giant quilted wall hanging where it hung, wiped the bed frame and night table. Next he took all the bedding off the bed, walked out to the landing with it asking JJ if he would take it downstairs, shake it out then throw it in the washing machine. JJ jumped up as if a fork had been stuck in him, dropping his cup and flying papers all over the place as he did. Gathering up the linen, JJ wondered when he had become so eager to please, in his own house.

Now it was time to tackle the box marked number one. John went back downstairs, got a drink of water and a sharp knife, heading back up the stairs two at a time. The box in question was big. It stood about five feet high by four feet wide but was only about a foot and a half or so deep. Unsure what the box contained and with a rumble of excitement beginning in the pit of his stomach, he slid the box across the floor until it almost hit the wall, he pushed the top side over so it was leaning on the wall for support. John didn't want the contents to spill out when he opened it. And the only way to do that was to slit the tape across the top the middle and across the bottom. Folding back the cardboard John got a big surprise.

A painting or several paintings lined up one in front of another. Carefully John removed the first one. It measured about two feet by three feet. Lifting it up to set atop a dresser so he could see it better; John's heart beat faster as two realizations emerged. The first realization was that the painting was done by his great grandmother Jean and the second was that it was a painting of the area of the mother of all Ponderosa, with the feed lot off in the distance. The next painting was of a close up section of a Ponderosa and he liked this one the best. Taking the two paintings out to the landing he said, "Hey JJ, look what I found." JJ hopped up and almost wept when he saw the paintings. "Hey, those are my mum's. I didn't know where they went, honestly, I didn't know. I thought Shelley would have taken them with her, they were her favourites.

But I guess you can keep them now John, if you want to. They're yours."

"Well, I was thinking they would be good out here. There is no art work in the place. Can I just lean them over against the railing for now; maybe you'll find a place to hang them later. I'm going back inside mum's room."

The next painting that came out was a bit of an abstract but he could make out an attempt of his mother's. Sitting on the bed he just stared at it. The greys and yellows with a soft pinkish coral colour with a hint of a blue blush blended around the two figures. Faceless armless, just shapes. One tall shape seemed to be looking down, with one small shape that seemed to be looking up. The tall shape looked masculine and the smaller shape looked feminine. Leaning in close he saw his mother had signed it Shelley. No date. John sat like that for a long time, looking at the painting and knowing with certainty this was a picture of his mum and JJ.

He didn't take this one out to the landing he needed to know what it meant first. Instinctively he felt JJ would have a breakdown if he saw it. The painting spoke of trust and an intimacy born of that trust. John, head hanging low, legs apart, hands clasped between his thighs was in deep thought when he heard JJ call up to ask about lunch. On stiff heavy legs John stood, walked out of the room, closing the door behind him and went down the flight of stairs feeling the first real affection for JJ. A real affection yes, but also felt a huge loss and a lump the size of a cat in his throat.

JJ had made them peanut butter and thinly sliced onion sandwiches with mayo and a slice of toasted bread heavily buttered on both sides in the middle. After John had taken his first bite, JJ asked, "Do you know what you are eating? It's a barracuda sandwich." A smiling John said his mum made them for him all the time. When JJ heard that, he launched into a story, "When your mum was about your age we heard a story on the radio about a little kid who could not pronounce the name of a particular type of onion. A sandwich made with an extra piece of toasted and heavily buttered bread in the middle. I actually don't recall the name of the onion any longer but knew what was in it. So Shelley and I made one to share and got to see what it would taste like and we both loved it. I've been eating them ever since peanut butter, mayo and onion..." A nostalgic sounding John said, "Me too JJ. Mum made them for me and called them barracudas too, and not because of the onion, but because she said if I could eat onion, and the crust on the toast I'd be as tough as a barracuda AND I'd get hair on my chest!" "Did you?" JJ asked. John threw his head back and laughed, "Well not yet but if I eat a couple more of these at your place, I bet I will before I leave."

"You know John, or maybe you don't know. You can stay here as long as you like, you don't ever have to leave if you decide not to, your choice. Both Trish and I want you to feel at home here and that you can come here any time for just a visit, or to live here. Forever if you want. This is your home. Not my place. This is our place. After your mum left I never once thought of this place as mine. For one thing my dad was still alive so it was technically his. But since he has been gone it technically is mine and Shelley's, and as her son, yours now too. So even though she didn't tell you much about this place, it's also her legacy left to you."

John was looking at the table, he had stopped eating. His mouth was filling up with saliva, his eyes with moisture too. The lump the size of the big orange cat had returned to his throat. He didn't know what to say and didn't even know what he felt. Part of him felt extreme anger toward JJ and Trish and toward his mum. Why hadn't she brought him here? What made her leave? These were all questions at the moment he couldn't even ask. He couldn't even say a word right now. Sensing all the emotions that were swirling around inside of John, JJ got up from the table and placed his hand on John's right shoulder. He placed it there with such care and so lightly John thought it was his mum standing over him for just a moment.

All JJ said was, "Life is complicated." Giving his shoulder a final squeeze before he let go, "I'll leave you alone for a while. I'm going for a ride in about an hour; if you want to come too I'll just be out by the barn doing some work."

John felt as if a ride right now was what he wanted more than anything. He imagined himself up on Ernest's back racing across the land at full speed, heart thumping, his hair flying. But for now, he got up and returned to his mum's room and box number one. The next painting he pulled out was another complete surprise. It was the second largest and was of a young girl sitting at the table downstairs looking outside. In one hand, she held a piece of toast while reaching for a tea cup with the other. Her hair was done in French braids, the painting so skillfully executed, as to be photo realism.

Leaning in for a better look, John was shocked by JJ's initials in the bottom right corner. JJ, wow, he painted this? He paints? This made no sense. Here in this house there was no evidence of a studio or paints or even any art on the walls. Wanting to go right outside and ask JJ about this, he first pulled out the last painting. This one was also a painting of his mother, as a teen. She looked angry, and wore jeans with torn knees, a torn jacket and a mess of really curly hair that was full of hay and bits of paper, paint tubes, brushes, twigs and wool sticking out of it; half impressionist, half realism. Leaning in once more John saw clearly that this one too was done by JJ. Why had his mum packed these up? Was she coming back? Was she planning to have these sent along? He just didn't know. But he sure wanted to. The first thing he needed to know was why paint these two gallery quality pieces, and stop there. Or did he stop there. Closing the door behind him John went in search of JJ.

Just as he said he would be, JJ was out by the barn. When John found him, JJ was taking the blankets from the rail. Seeing John, JJ said, "These got left out in the rain, but they're almost dry now and smell better than if they hadn't gotten wet. Could you take them inside for me, just throw them over a railing for now." Thinking he could get into his office too he took the blankets, did as he was told, then unlocked the office door. Reaching into his suitcase he unearthed letter number five, closing the door John began to read.

> *Dear John,*
>
> *There are only three more letters to go and you haven't been there a week. Today you'll check out my room. You'll want to burn through the boxes. But don't. Knowing JJ, he has left my room just as I left it, after I packed every precious item up. Or he might have put it all out in the barn; my guess though is it is all still in my room untouched. There will be years of dust atop each one, so you'll need to vacuum for this job John. Get busy. JJ will want*

to oversee things. It will be an emotional day for him.

Let him watch from the mezzanine. The area outside the door stretching from one side of the building to the other I called the mezzanine, JJ calls it the loft. There was a couch out there and he'll sit there in the pretence of reading for at least part of the time. Surprise him by vacuuming first. He might get bored and leave you alone.

When you unpack the boxes start with box number one. Box number one should be fun; inside you'll find a JJ surprise. And a great Gran Jean surprise too. A box a day will see you through to the time you need to prepare for my Month's Mind. In box two look for a list.....

Love mum xoxoxoxo

Smiling John threw his head back and laughed out loud. His mum knew them all so well! And she still knew JJ so well. He heard her telling Andrea one time - people don't change really, do they? John hadn't lived long enough to know if they did or didn't. What he suspected though, was everything his mum had taught him would be with him in one way or another all his life. The lessons on manners might slip in certain situations for example, but in time he would recall them, dusting them off to be reused. His mum always said there was no substitution for good manners. Hers were pretty good, though if someone messed with her she never forgot it and took a long time to forgive them. She would hold a grudge. Not a loud, look at me, kind of grudge but a grudge just the same.

He wondered now what Trish and JJ had done to deserve the grudge she held, until recently that is, against them.

To John it was obvious by virtue of the fact she had sent him here, they were forgiven... But what they did to make her want to stay away for so long was a question he would need an answer to. Or maybe it was something she did. Maybe it was something they all did. If she were here she would say, - there is no blame John, just responsibility. Now what part in all this was your responsibility? This said when he was trying to place blame on another. There is no blame. That statement and philosophy had helped him when he was little and was still helping him. "There is no blame, there is no blame, and there is no blame." Said out loud like a mantra as JJ walked past the office. Pausing outside the office door JJ wondered what John was talking about.

Calling through the door JJ said, "Hey John we always had a rule around here, you stay out of my office, and I'll stay out of yours." Swinging the door open John raised his eye brows in a question. "That room right there was your grandmothers, and then your mum's, now it's yours. What you have in there is safety from me, from everyone.

"You can be in there all day long if you like but what you are doing is your business alone. Unless," and now he held an index finger aloft, "unless you want to fill me in that is. Then I'm all ears. Otherwise I know what it's like to be in a zone, my own little world. What I'm trying to say here is - you don't need to close the door to get privacy - especially in summer. You'll boil for one thing."

As JJ was about to carry on with what he was doing John stopped him. "I meant to tell you about the other things I found in the first box. Mum has the boxes numbered and well, you know I'm opening them numerically. In box number one..." holding up his left hand he began folding each finger as he enumerated the paintings. "Two paintings painted by Jean, and a painting mum painted. It's a bit abstract in greys, yellows, kind of a coral colour featuring two figures." JJ held up his hand and said, "That's the first painting Shelley ever did, it was then we all knew she had talent. In case you didn't know, it is a painting of her and me. I loved that painting." JJ's voice caught as he said this last bit. Now John held up his hand, "I'm not finished. Then I pulled out two more paintings. Both of them were of mum. One when she was a kid and the other when she was a teenager, maybe my age... JJ, you painted them."

JJ just looked at John with a look of annoyance, sadness and grief all mixed in one. "Ya I did paint those, is there a problem?" John took a deep breath then said, "No, no problem. Just that I don't understand why, when you said my mum got her talent from Jean... why you didn't say then that you painted too." JJ just sighed, and said, "I didn't tell you because I don't paint. Not anymore! I don't paint, I don't paint at all!" And off he stormed.

The outburst stunned and hurt John, like a punch in the stomach. Taking a moment to review what he had said, he realized it came out like an accusation. And in a way it was a bit of one. He hadn't known JJ painted and felt a bit betrayed that no one told him. Not even, especially, not even his mother. Her technical talent was half what JJ's was if the paintings John had just seen were any indication of JJ's potential. John had to know about JJ the artist, and he had to know today. He left the barn in search of JJ just in time to see him whistling for his horse.

John hustled up to stand beside JJ as Frida trotted over. Not knowing where to start with this man John just said, "We need to talk. If I'm going to get to know you, we need to talk. I'm sorry if you felt I was prying into something you don't want to talk about. But JJ, in two weeks, right after the Month's Mind, I'll be returning to Andrea's and I'll be starting a whole new life." John's voice began to escalate. "Sometimes you seem so angry and if I were you, I'd just say it. Just get it out in the open! I'm pissed too!

"Here I am, for the first time in my life. Don't you think I wonder who you are, what you did to my mother, where she thought she was going, when she thought she would come back. And why - you never went to find her?" John began to overheat with his own anger, standing there under the hot sun.

"How do you think I'm feeling, not knowing? I feel like I've been robbed by my own mother of a life with a family I'll never get to know properly. I'm just a boy, man! Just a kid! Mum put everything on me for the last three years! Everything! Me! I had to be the responsible one. And now she's sent me on a wild goose chase with some crazy idea she would be doing me a favour. I'm just a kid, man!" Tears of anger and hurt streamed over John's red face; his anger was real, it was hot and it was furious. JJ stood still while he heard John's tirade. Roughly he pulled him into a hug. John struggled to pull free and JJ just held on tighter. He should never have walked out of the barn. When would he learn?

"Come with me." Tugging John's arm, JJ headed toward the barn he kept his car and work truck in. The night before when they returned from dinner JJ had dropped John at the door then driven the car around to the barn on his own. When they got to the barn, instead of opening the big double doors, John followed as JJ made his way around the side. They pushed through undergrowth and junk, to a side door virtually hidden from sight. Not missing a beat, JJ pulled a set of keys from his pocket and unlocked the door. Reaching inside he hit the wall and a row of overhead lights came on. Striding across to the other side JJ pulled open a big set of double doors then hit a switch and an outdoor roller blind squealed to life exposing a large set of north facing windows. Throwing his arms wide and swinging his body in circles, around and around, JJ raised his head to the ceiling then looked at John. "This is where it all happened. My painting, I mean. When my sister was born or before she turned one, I started sketching and then painting in water colours. Margaret, your grandmother, was my muse. I was already twelve when she was born. My mother said the baby needed to sleep a lot and that I needed to find something quiet to do, so I wouldn't wake her.

"So for something quiet to do, I'd sketch her while she slept. My dad tripped this barn out for my mum - it was her studio for years. Then on my fourteenth birthday mum said I could use it too. No other gift, just the use of her studio. By then she had stopped painting in here anyway and was painting upstairs in what became your mum's room and can be your room now, if you want it. Here let me show you...."

Walking to an end wall where floor to ceiling cupboards stood. JJ opened one door after another. The canvases stood in rows, lined up one by one, each painting on its edge, one in front of the other. Racks of paintings of all sizes, the racks organized and dated; stacks of sketch pads, paints, brushes, oils, blank canvasses. "But why did you stop." John was pulling the paintings out of their storage places at random. Lining them up against the wall opposite the window, turning he asked again. "Why did you stop?"

JJ shrugged his shoulders and shook his head, "I don't really know. Painters block? Don't worry. I stopped painting before your mum left and maybe that's why she left. I had more time to be nosing around her life, telling her what to do. Trying to control every aspect of who she was becoming, what she did with her time, her friends or lack of friends. I worried about her running with the wrong crowd, when she didn't even have a crowd. My painting stopped in mid air.

"One day I painted, one day I didn't and I've never ever gotten over it. It hurt, and still hurts. My passion is gone, like a puff of smoke." John pulled out a canvas asking, "Who is this?" JJ took a look and realized they hadn't gotten to the photo albums yet or else John would know. "That's my mum, a beauty eh?"

The painting John held out was smaller than the rest and featured a woman from the hips up, standing at the kitchen sink, leaning forward with her hands braced against the edge of the sink. John didn't see a classic beauty, what he saw was a woman in mid life, in a colourful apron, hair pulled into an up do; with a faraway look on her face. It was another painting with a photographic quality. Most of the paintings were por-traits. There was one of Trish that was almost life size. When John pulled that one out, JJ threw his head back and he finally laughed out loud. Then he too began taking paintings out telling a story about each person painted.

Before they knew it the day had gone, both so immersed were they in the job of uncovering this treasure. John of course was mentally thinking of an art show, because these were unreal. And something his mum had always involved him in. JJ suddenly strode over to the wall and hit the switch for the metal roller shutters sending them down with a high pitched scream, not wanting to close again after all this time. Heading over to the door JJ said to John, "Remind me to oil those things....come on, let's go eat."

They headed up to the house, JJ asking about Shelley's paintings and John telling him much of what Shelley did was mixed media. She loved using her own paintings and photography to create collages. She had worked on her art right up to the end. "She started keeping a journal again about two years ago after she knew she was sick. Apparently she kept them as a kid and has been urging me to write in one too." JJ knew her earlier journals were still in her room but on the spot he decided to let John find them for himself.

"The journals mum kept were really nice to look at. I haven't read them yet and thought I'd wait a few years before I do. But she made drawings on the page after she wrote. Then she coloured them with pencil crayons. Every day, every single day....she wrote something. She loved writing and said writing was her new passion. In the last two or three months, the journals became her art."

JJ turned to give John a side long look. "Did you know Trish is a writer? She wrote her first book because of Shelley's curiosity about the world. Everything around her, she wanted to know about it. How things grew, why plants grew, where they grew, why frogs croaked. We had a nick name for her, W 5. Do you know what the five W's of journalism are?"

John was smiling, "I never heard that term, but I grew up with the 5 W's and I'm a bit like mum. It's a deep need to know. Kind of like, right in the pit of my gut I need to know the answers. I have so many questions, JJ, about everything.

The answers will all be revealed, I know they will. But sometimes it's hard to wait. Mum always said to put my questions out to the universe and forget about them. The answer does usually come."

Cautiously, JJ asked, "Are there any questions I can answer for you? Or is this something you need to do on your own?" John stopped walking. "I never knew my dad. I don't even know his name. That was something I was afraid to ask mum. She was sensitive and by the time I was old enough to take an interest, I didn't want to upset her." John suddenly lost eye contact and stood looking at his clenched hands.

JJ was curious about this too and always had been. As far as he knew it was the wrong person or another wrong person and only one reference about him made to Trish, in the first letter she sent home. Not to him of course but to Trish. Before JJ could answer John said, "Not knowing who my father is has always embarrassed me...One, because I don't know and two, because I ought to just be grateful to have such a great mum. It doesn't matter JJ, I didn't think you would know, I was born almost a year after mum left here."

JJ was silent another beat then said, "Trish is the one who would know, if anyone does. Not me. Shelley would never have talked to me about sex after the first time she did... Look after dinner let's sit and see if I can fill in some gaps. I'd like some gaps filled in too. Now that we're getting to know each other, I think it's time to talk about the old days and what she had been up to when she left and since then. I know so little about her."

By now they were at the house. John asked if Trish would be joining them tonight for dinner, and also asked whose turn it was to cook. "Whose turn is it? You really are settling in aren't you?" Run up to Trish's place and ask her round. Maybe she could bring something, we can go potluck. How does that sound?" John and JJ parted company, John heading up the path to see Trish and JJ into the house and a good hot shower.

When John got to her house, he saw Trish getting into the passenger seat of a newer model car. Just before the driver headed off Trish spotted him and waved John over. She introduced the man behind the wheel and asked what John was up to. John wasn't sure why but he lied about coming to ask her to dinner; instead he said he was just wanting to pick some vegetables from her garden. She told him to go ahead and help himself anytime. "What are you up to Trish, where are you going; out to dinner?" Trish blushed and stretched a smile over closed teeth and nodded. She reached through the open window and stroked John's hand before she and her friend drove off. John didn't think much about Trish and the possibility she was on a date. He just headed to the garden and began to pull some salad greens.

When John got back, JJ who was out of the shower was clearly disappointed when he found out Trish wasn't coming. John just said she had gone out, not mentioning she had left with a guy. He didn't mention it because he just didn't think it important to the fact. She wasn't coming to dinner, period. It was nice though just the two of them. John hoped JJ would shed some light on why his mum had left, and for JJ's part, he hoped John would shed some light on a great many questions he had of his own. Why did she send letters to Trish, why did she never mention him in her letters, why did she never give a return address, and why did she write in the first place, if she had no intention of coming home.

They made dinner together that night. John made a salad that truly impressed JJ. JJ wanted to take a picture of it and did. He got John to lean his face in next to the salad, getting him to grin from ear to ear by telling a silly joke. JJ cooked turkey sausages and skewered potatoes and carrots on the barbecue. They ate outdoors, built a small fire after dinner and stayed up late. John talked about being home schooled and JJ recalled how Shelley had been home-schooled for one year due to transportation issues that finally got sorted out. John said his mum had told him about that year, sharing it was the best school year she had ever had.

After the fire was out John asked JJ about Trish's friend whose name John could not recall. He instead described the car and the man. JJ drew a blank but did seem a little put out that Trish had gone out with a man. John said, "I don't think it was a date JJ," didn't help matters. JJ just got defensive saying he didn't care if it was a date and he would have thought Trish was too old for that kind of thing anyway.

John smiled at that, and told JJ, Trish had told him about JJ dating and didn't seem to think he was too old and, "Hey JJ aren't you six years older than Trish," adding as an after-thought, "are you jealous? You are jealous aren't you?" It was said with good humour and fun. JJ just shook his head and laughed. John had a pretty good idea who he was laughing at and it felt pretty good to see JJ laughing at himself too.

It was good to see JJ laughing at all; he was reminded that his mother had wanted this symbiosis of help and guidance, for him. In her first letter she asked him to allow others to guide him and here he was gaining guidance and insights in one go. Today he felt like he had a hand in helping JJ to relax and talk. The growing connection between man and boy was a part of his mother's master plan. Encouraging JJ to talk and relax had resulted in removing JJ from his comfort zone. John had been brought up to look forward to the experience of a lack of comfort zone or challenging the comfort zone. Thinking of his mum and all she did for him in just one little phrase he decided to share it with JJ. "Here's a quote my mum used to say, - Life begins after you leave your comfort zone. I don't know who first said it but right now, right here, I am totally out of my comfort zone. My mum never would have sent me here if she didn't know I could rise to the challenge."

JJ was looking at John from across the fire. He had a thoughtful expression on his face when he said, "Your mum must have been really something John. She did a good job with you. She did a really good job for you. You'll be OK. Now what was that phrase again?"

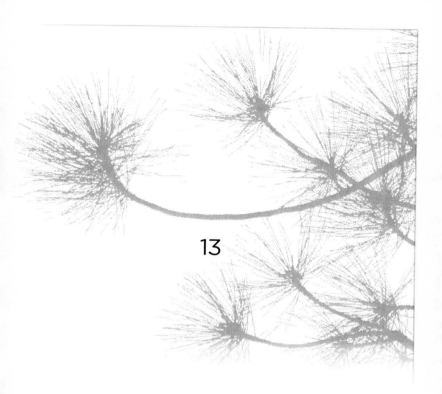

13

The next two days passed in much the same way as the day John had opened box number one. Just John and JJ; two guys sharing time together, they never saw Trish and when John went up to look for her he found a note on her door with his name on it. In it she said she had to be gone overnight to Kelowna, maybe two nights. There was no other explanation and because there was none he thought of his mum when she would say - Just the facts John, just the facts. This comment said by her when he was about to launch into a big long explanation about his whereabouts or his activities. She only wanted the goods. She said she had pulled that line from a TV show long ago. But she couldn't remember which one.

Though they had a TV at his house, it was upstairs at Andrea and Heather's place. They had Netflix and CBC for the news and to watch a Coronation Street marathon some Sundays. A running commentary of the show by Heather; and of course Andrea could be counted on to have cheated and read ahead on-line, so she would know what was coming or what had already happened if a few episodes got missed. Watched from the kitchen table over Spanish omelette with toast and jam and of course tea; and newspapers, school projects and interruptions from Heather as she tried to make out what was said by her favourite Corrie character and love interest, Steve, the barman at the Rovers Return. John suddenly missed Andrea and Heather and Cozy too and was anxious to get to box number three.

The second box got opened and he did indeed find the list his mum mentioned. It was a list of names and also in the box he found journals. He would leave all the journals until he felt ready for them. When he read the first entry he realized it sounded like a diary, maybe a bit personal for him right now. Removing the journals from the box he placed them on a book case alongside other journals already there. When this room was clear of boxes he would make the bed up with fresh sheets and sleep here for a night or two and read some of the journal entries, before heading back home to Vancouver. Even though the bookshelves in the room already held journals, his instinct told him this box held the more personal stuff, the precious stuff.

While he read the note at Trish's place saying she wouldn't be back for maybe two days, he wondered how and when he could make a personal call. He was pretty sure Andrea would accept a collect call from him. He was also sure his mum wanted him to tough it out without a phone call to Andrea no matter the pretence.

Pulling a pencil out of his pocket he flipped Trish's note over to write his own note on the back. He wrote Andrea's number and almost added the list of names found in box number two and added instead - I've started a list of who should be invited to the Month's Mind. I don't know how to contact them, so will need your help when you get back. The names I've written here are friends of mum's from home. Can you call Andrea and give her the list please? I found another list of names in one of the boxes in mum's bedroom; I'll give it to you when you get back.

Thanks, John

On his way back to JJ's, John realized Trish might not lock her door either and went back. But when he tried the handle on her door it was locked. Next he tried the RV and it was locked too. Oh well, another time. John headed home to box number three and before he did he thought about his letters and wondered if it was time for letter number six. No, he decided, he would open up box three then read the letter.

Box number three was about two feet by two feet by three feet high. He tried to lift it but found it was unbalanced inside and really heavy. One side was heavier than the other and something shifted to counter balance things and turn the box into an unwieldy mass. He shoved it over toward the bed where he sat for a moment trying to guess what was inside. He felt sure he'd find a real treasure in this one. Finally slitting the crumbling tape across the top John lifted the two sides of the lid apart and was surprised when he looked inside to find a whole mosaic of cloth. The stitched together brightly coloured fabric so reminded John of his mother. He knew this quilt must be where she got her inspiration for all things collage.

Pulling the quilt out of the box, a strange and pungent smell came out too. The smell was a bit familiar but he didn't know from where. Once out of the box he laid it on the bed and stood back. He would later learn this quilt was called, a crazy quilt. A quilt made from all sorts of fabric of varying shapes and sized material. So colourful with black, red, orange, blue...all the colours vibrant and spectacular.

Textures of all sorts too, soft as velvet, rough as burlap, smooth as silk, joined with strips of an iridescent coloured dark fabric sewed together with heavy wool in what he knew to be a blanket stitch. A piece of art like none he had seen before. A piece of art he wanted the world to see or at least all those who came to the Month's Mind. Lifting the quilt he carried it out to the mezzanine to hang on the railing. He didn't want to hang it outside in the sun for fear it would fade.

Just as he smoothed it out along the railing so it was hanging just so, JJ walked in and looked up. "Oh man! I remember that quilt. My mother called it a crazy quilt because of all the colours and different types of fabric. Your mum worked on it the year of her home schooling. That crazy quilt was a central feature in the inglenook. I wasn't living here by then of course. I had a house in Kelowna, I still have it actually. But don't get there much anymore, maybe just once a month for a night or two...

"I'd come home every week or so John, and there she would be quilting away." JJ had made his way up the stairs and stood next to John. As they stood looking at the quilt and running their hands over it JJ was flooded with memory. He thought the time was right, so he brought up a difficult subject for him.

"That was also the year my mother died. I guess I had moved back before Shelley finished the quilt, there was no way my dad could have handled her. She was a good kid, but my mum took care of everything including Shelley. She had home schooling that year because my mum couldn't drive her to school any more. Mum didn't want her on the bus for some reason and wanted her here. My mum, your great grandmother, was like a mother to Shelley. In fact, she called her mum or Mum-ma Jean.

"Let's go to the inglenook and I'll make us a pot of tea, OK. I just feel like, as your mum said, beginning my life by stepping out of my comfort zone!" Smiling gently JJ patted John's back on his way to the stairs. He took a look at his watch and said, "Its lunch time anyway. Give me ten minutes, finish off what you've got going then join me."

John didn't know what to make of JJ's softened attitude but went back in the room to finish up with the box. He had spotted another bunch of fabric in the bottom of the box shoved in a corner. Still unsure what had been so heavy he leaned in to pull the item up and out of the box. John could barely lift it and soon realized the cloth was used as a wrapping for the object within. Pulling it out and unraveling the surrounding cloth, he found a huge piece of rock. It was a piece of smooth green rock, untouched except for a carved face starring up at him from the top edge. He thought he recognized the face of the woman as that of the one from JJ's painting of his mother. Carrying the rock in his arms, like holding a small baby, John set it on the dresser before dismantling the box to get it out of the room and out to the shed for recycling.

On his way back in the house, he saw JJ setting up a tray on the ottoman separating the two chairs in the inglenook. The big fat orange cat was perched on the hearth, eyeballing what was there. John bounded up the stairs, returning with the rock cradled in his arms, just as JJ came back through with a teapot. Setting the teapot on the tray next to the rest of their lunch, JJ glanced up to see what John had clutched in his arms.

"It was in the box with the quilt. I'm not sure but I think it's of your mother...do you know who carved it?" JJ leaned in for a look. When he did he nodded in the affirmative, it was his mum. But this was something he had not seen before and he had no clue who had carved it and said so. "As far as I know your mum didn't carve; here let's flip it over and look for some initials." Doing so they both saw the bottom was blank and smooth. John said, "Maybe it wasn't finished yet. It is just her face..." Setting the carving on the hearth both stood looking at the face of a woman JJ knew so well, and John had only seen twice in JJ's paintings but never in real life or even a photo. JJ squatted to take a good look saying the technique looked a bit rough, "You're probably right John, looks like a work in progress. Look at her expression though John, she looks like she sees something otherworldly, do you agree? It's really quite beautiful even in its rough state." Turning his attention back to the ottoman and lunch, JJ said, "Let's eat and I'll tell you a little about your family history OK?"

As they both made to sit, the cat as fast and smooth as can be, leaned in with extended claws and delicately but swiftly grabbed hold of the corner of a piece of cheese sticking out of one of the sandwiches. JJ shouted, "Hey!" John laughed with good humour at the entertainment the cat provided whenever he was around.

They ate, and continued to speculate about the carving. Who could have made it, when it was made and so forth? And even if it was actually finished and meant to look rough. "JJ, I know I said all the boxes were my legacy, but would you like to keep this piece? It kind of looks right at home sitting on the hearth." JJ was touched and wasn't sure what to say, so just said, "Yes, thank you, I'd like to. I'll most likely put it beside the door on the floor using it as a door stop if you don't mind. My mum would totally love that. She often said she felt guilty doing paintings instead of functional art."

John put his sandwich down and said, "Speaking of paintings, I'd like you to have the one mum painted of you two." JJ just looked down at his lap and nodded his thanks. He was actually speechless many times around John. At times, John was like an old wise man inside a growing adolescent's body.

And John; John felt as if he had grown both figuratively and literally since he had been here. No longer having his mum to guide, remind and urge him on a daily basis, this was the first time he really got to put into practice his intrinsic common sense, or at least that was what he thought it was. His early maturity in most things, and of course his curiosity, pushed him forward as he tried to mirror what his mum would do or say. John leaned back in his chair after pouring tea for them both. He wanted to hear what JJ had to say about his mum; he was ready for the family history lesson. "So you were saying you lived in Kelowna for awhile?"

Clearing his throat JJ began his story, holding up his hand as he began. "I'll make this as brief as possible and the best way for me to do it, is to just lay everything out and you can ask questions later. There," JJ said pointing to the tray, "I put a pencil and pad for you to write any questions you have, down for later. But please don't interrupt until I'm finished. OK?"

John just nodded, feeling a tiny bit intimidated by this speech and at the same time trying to shrug off the feeling.

JJ carried on, "As I was saying upstairs. My mum Jean, was sick, she had cancer, not the same kind as your mum though. She had ovarian cancer. This is another story! My dad was absolutely no help as far as Shelley was concerned, and in fact he was often out of town, just wanting to carry on with his trips to casinos from here to Vegas and mum was happy to have him go, as long as her girl was here.

"She loved your mum so much, John. She loved your mum like any grandmother does, but also as much as a mother could. My mum said having a grandchild was her chance to be the best she could be. She lost her own daughter, Margaret. Shelley was three. Just a cute little girl, with lots of questions... The guy Margaret married proved to be a real loser, so he would be your granddad and let me tell you, you've inherited nothing of him; nothing at all. Anyway, when Shelley was born all three of them moved into the room upstairs.

In case you don't know, his name was Lorne and he worked in camps in Northern Alberta just like a lot of us around here. My mum thought it would be best if Margaret stayed on here, at home until they had enough money saved. She was just a teenager when your mum was born. Then they could build a house right here on this land. Not the best idea for newly-weds, but that is what she wanted and actually it was also what Margaret had always thought would happen. She had a plot picked out too...I'll show it to you tomorrow if you like." JJ looked up at John and saw the nod of John's head then after a long pause in which JJ just stared into space he continued his story.

"Anyway, Lorne didn't like my old man at all, but the feeling was not really mutual. My dad was neutral, wanting to give Lorne a chance. Really he just wanted everyone to get along, creating no fuss for him. My dad - He just wanted to be allowed the freedom to live his life. Something you don't know John, is my dad was well off. He made some good investments. When my mother's parents died they left her some money, and my dad turned it into a fortune. My friends always have called me a trust fund kid because they thought I never needed to work. But my dad didn't share his money; he thought he was self made and that his kids needed to hustle too. So Lorne had a bit of a problem with my dad and mum expecting him to work hard, and to build a house in a place he didn't even want to live.

"There was a lot of arguing when he would return from Alberta. Between him and Margaret that is. He never spoke to my mum and dad about it, but he spent most of his time sulking when he was here. Almost a whole year went by and he didn't speak to my mum at all, because of something she said ... By that time I'd only be home every few months. I had a good job in Alberta too and had bought my house in Kelowna. I'm pretty good with money! Like the old man. The house I bought in Kelowna has a couple of suites and is close to the college ... so it's a rental. There's a garage out back with a little apartment above and I stay there when I go to Kelowna. The original plan was to pay off the house fast and maybe get married have a kid or two."

Here JJ paused again looking up at John. "You know I feel real bad about not trying harder to find you guys. I know it must have been tough for you. And there is a trust fund for Shelley; my mum had a lawyer set it up after the accident."

John flinched when he heard this and jotted a note. Holding up his hand once more JJ tried to explain, "Your mum knew about the trust fund John. She could have dipped into it at any time. I know she didn't though, except for once and that would have been right around the time you were born. She took fifteen thousand out and that was the last time. I'm going to go back to my story now; we can go back to the money thing later OK."

Without waiting for any acknowledgement that this would be OK, JJ continued in a rush of ignored emotions. "When Shelley was still a baby, Lorne didn't come home on one of his scheduled time offs. He missed the next round too but did come during the third one. He was so upset and begged Margaret forgiveness as he spilled his guts saying, he had been having an affair. That's when my dad hopped into action telling Lorne to just, F OFF and get out of our house. I was home that night and tried to stop dad from interfering, but he just couldn't stop himself.

"Lorne left and I believe that was what he had wanted all along; to be free of Margaret, their little girl Shelley and the whole family. But about two years later he turned up out of the blue, hoping to get back together with Margaret. For Margaret's part she would have forgiven Lorne anything. She was still crazy about him and had invested her life to him. She rarely spoke with my dad after Lorne had left and was just a pretty sad gal. Part of her sadness might have been the baby blues, mum called it.

"So Lorne was back for a few days. He came when dad was off on a gambling junket; both my mum and dad were gone together. So the couple were just like newlyweds, I'd guess. They had the place to themselves... Then mum and dad came home early. Dad apparently blew a gasket when he saw who was here and during his tirade, my mum told Lorne and Margaret to get out of the house for a couple of hours and she would calm the old man. Mum wouldn't let them take Shelley though, she was sleeping. She could sleep through anything, that kid. And it was night and cold, so mum suggested they go to the hotel overnight and she would look after the little one."

Before continuing his story, JJ took an audibly deep shuddering breath. "They did go to the hotel where apparently Lorne got stinking drunk, and even though they got a room, at around three in the morning we think, they set off for home. We don't know why. It might have been to get the baby or it might have been Lorne's anger fuelled by the booze. That was the night they got killed in the accident. Margaret was driving. They went right into the lake by the hotel. Ice on the road maybe, no one was really sure why the car went in. But no one came out of the car, and both of them were found in the morning by the school bus driver. Abruptly JJ leaned forward, smacking both hands down on to his thighs.

"OK. That's it for the day OK? I can't talk about it anymore right now. OK John, is that OK? Let's just go for a ride instead, not on the horses, in the truck." With that, JJ stood and stretched and yawned, while John sat still just staring into space.

Why hadn't his mum told him this? His sense of betrayal was strong, betrayal and disappointment. She treated him like a man, well like a grown up at least when she was sick, why didn't she trust him enough to share some of these truths? She rarely mentioned her mother or father and never mentioned a trust fund. Always seeming too skint to afford much. John wasn't so sure he wanted to hear any more family history for the day so he stood up too and said, "OK let's get out of here!"

As JJ was getting his truck out of lock up, he turned to John and asked if he had seen Trish. "Nope, I went up to the house this morning and there was a note on the door saying she had gone away for a couple of nights." Shrugging his shoulders, he continued, "She didn't date it though, so I don't know when she wrote it, we didn't see her yesterday. I wanted to use her phone, that's why I went there. She locks her house, JJ."

"Oh, I know she does but we have a key. It's behind the kitchen door and it's got a pink key identifier. There are three keys, hot pink, for the house, soft pink for the RV and just plain old dull pink for the barn and shed. Shall we swing by to see if she's back yet? Or do you want to just hang out with me this afternoon?"

For an answer, an unsmiling John asked, "Why don't you have a phone or a computer or anything?" A laughing JJ said he had a computer and kept it in Kelowna and he had a landline in Kelowna too. "You may have guessed by now, but I'm not into technology. My computer is used so rarely. I don't know why I own one. Trish has a phone and a computer at her place though. And she has a cell phone too. And satellite TV. Didn't you know?" JJ said with a smile in his voice. He knew Trish kept all technology out of sight wanting to create the illusion she lived as simply as JJ did. That was why her house was locked and security coded tighter than a fort under fire. She had a whole system storing the books she had written old and new, finished and in progress. All stored on the hard drive. She had a brand new, all in one desk top computer, a tablet, a cell phone and a laptop too. She had a wireless printer, scanner, copier, and a separate hard drive back up, a fax machine and every other bit of technology she could get her hands on. Her TV, he happened to know, was behind a painting in her bedroom and she'd watch Netflix from the comfort of her very own comfy love-seat recliner. Her office was upstairs behind another set of locked doors. That's where all the computer stuff was stored. Poor John, he had been here almost two weeks and he had finally been driven crazy enough by no phone and no internet connection to show he was just an average kid.

"Look John, will you make me a promise?" Reluctantly and for once showing his age John responded with a sultry shrug and a, "Maybe."

"OK John how about we go into town, go to the phone place, and order a land-line?" Casting a long look at JJ out of the corner of a sulking eye, John asked, "What's the promise." With a knowing smile he turned to John saying, "If we get a phone hooked up here, you promise that when you leave you'll phone me at least once a week for the rest of your life? And if you stay, that if you ever need a ride you'll phone me. That's the only thing that would make having a phone here worth it to me." A meek and humble and slightly flattered John responded with a simple, "OK."

Once in town and after asking a few questions and getting directions JJ found a phone store. Getting out of the truck and into the building was a relief from what had turned into a very hot day. Though there was a bit of a line up inside, they were served fairly quickly. Their server was none other than the girl who had been the hostess at the hotel the night JJ had taken John and Trish to dine. "Hi, I thought I might see you again… it's a small town," she said, then went on to explain, "and I have three jobs this summer cause I'm going to university in

Kelowna in the fall and need to save up ." JJ who was in a hurry to get this over with said, "Hey, good for you," rather abruptly, and was immediately chastised by a not too impressed glare from John who said, "We are here to get a phone."

As if JJ wasn't even there she turned her full attention to John and said, "Do you know anything about our cell plans? What's your cell number and I'll look up your current plan for you, I hear you're from Vancouver - very cool. Are you moving here?" JJ was shaking his head no at the same time placing a restraining hand on John's arm in an effort to regain control of the transaction. Even if John didn't know it, JJ realized there was some subtle flirting going on and all he wanted was to get his phone order in and get out of the store and on the road again. As far as he was concerned this girl and John could exchange cell numbers another time or at least wait until his own transaction was over.

"No, not a cell phone, a land line; my place doesn't have cell reception. And before you ask, I am not changing servers; we've never had a phone before. I am a customer though, I have a land line in Kelowna." He then gave her the details, secured a phone number that John picked out based on some magic, but really just picking out something he thought he could remember. After conferring with her supervisor the girl, whose name tag said Lil, told JJ they would either have to charge him a hook up fee directly from the road or get permission from the neighbor to piggy back on their line. "The service line from your neighbour's house will be shorter and won't cost you as much… These are just options of course and personally I don't know all the details because I've never done one of these brand new services before. Is there a number we can reach you at to set up a time and date for installation?"

Then she asked JJ if he knew how to use voice mail and if he wanted call waiting.

"Yes I do and I don't want voice mail or call waiting. I want my phone just to ring busy if it is busy. People can call back.... But I will pick up an old fashioned answering machine just in case I want to hear messages." They left soon after John and Lil said they'd see each other around, with Lil promising to fast track their phone installation, under an unspoken friends and family rule the outlet had.

John reluctantly left his new friend and the air conditioned store and when they got into the truck and were on the road again, JJ told John he had some of their own, friends and family, phone rules. "Use the phone whenever you like. But when it gets installed, let's not turn the ringer on OK? Let's just use it for making calls out at first - not for receiving them. Lil said we'll have call display whether we like it or not, all phones come with it, so we can phone anyone who calls us, back. OK? I've gotten used to not being bothered and I like it, I just like it like that. And don't tell Trish or anyone else the phone number; better yet don't tell them we have a phone." John just laughed and shook his head.

"Where do you want to go, what do you want to see and what do you want to do now?" By this time it was almost two in the afternoon. "How close are we to Kelowna?" John asked, "Or to Kamloops?" JJ thought for a second then took a look at his watch. "I think we can just make it to Kamloops before the stores close. How about we head there, do some shopping for the Month's Mind and then hit a restaurant for dinner. Or we could get something to go and head to the river in Kamloops, and eat on the bank. What say you?"

They never did get to the shopping, but they did get a list written as JJ drove. And they never made it to Kamloops that day either. They got hung up going a back route. Spotting the turn off to a lake JJ liked they stopped there instead, for a late afternoon swim. JJ was really glad John loved the water as much as he did and told him so on their way home.

As they pulled up to the house they saw a piece of paper fluttering on a breeze, from the well used note hanging nail on the front door. JJ kept the motor running, hoping the note was from Trish as John ran up, grabbed it and headed back. Reading out loud he conveyed to JJ, that Trish had sent a dinner invitation. Leaning in the window, John asked if they should drive up the lane. "No while I park the truck why don't you see if we have anything to take along."

Once up at Trish's place, and empty handed, John asked Trish if he could see her computer room. Giving JJ a stern look, and tsk tsking while shaking her head at JJ, Trish said, "Sure," and led the way. Trish had a high tech keypad entry system to prevent intruders. Stepping through the opened doorway, it looked so much like how his mum kept her work space. Everything as neat as a pin and all surfaces so organized in such a way as to give the idea that everything in the world, did have its rightful place. Trish kept her work space looking like a museum display. A big cork board held a map. A handmade, hand coloured map.

Trish said it was an outlining of how her new book was going, and where it was going. The maps were all part of her creative process. Moving in close to have a look, John suddenly turned to look at Trish as he realized, "My mum has a copy of a map sort of like this on her wall. This is yours, you made it right? Do you sell other maps like this Trish?"

Startled at first, then filled with an emotion she couldn't identify, she told him that as she wrote, she mapped everything out to keep track of the events in her story. Lifting her hand she began pointing at the drawings on the map. She said, "Putting a house here, trail there, the town and the ocean… As new events take place in new locations, I draw a curvy road. See right there, it goes from the house to the ocean. And that is where the next event is going to take place."

She told John, after she was finished writing one of the books, her map went along to the publisher too and a pull out version was printed along with the book to either be unfolded from the inside cover, looked at and refolded into the book. Or, they could be torn right out. The realization that Shelley had possibly purchased her book and pulled out a map to hang on her own wall filled her heart so full. A feeling her heart might actually burst right open, overcame her. Going to a cabinet she pulled out a folder of maps.

Spreading them all out, one by one, on a big work table she asked John which of these his mum had. Without hesitation John pointed to one. Folding the rest Trish came to stand over top of the map. "Do you know where this is John? Do you know what place this map was modeled after?" Without waiting for a reply Trish began to point here and there on the map and said, "This is my house, here's the path and there is your house. See there's the barn, and a cat, JJ's car and look, the stand of trees." John felt tears coming to his eyes and clogging his throat. He couldn't talk. And if he could, he would say he loved his mum for having this map. She always referred to it as a special place. A place of magic and said some day they would go there together. He always thought it was just a place out of his little kids' story book. Now he knew why she said it. She was trying to show him home; her home, the place she grew up.

The mystery of his mother and why she held so many secrets would never be understood now that she was gone. Not by John. It was too late. He was lucky. She had a plan and had sent him here, to this place, the place where magic happened; lucky for him she had organized this treasure hunt. Lucky for him these people loved her enough to welcome him home.

Trish and JJ were both, in their own busy ways, lonely people. Even his young eyes could see that. They had both lost someone they loved deeply. Trish had lost her only child, Seth. Remembering his mum's words about how a mother's love was the strongest he wondered, how Trish could be so strong after losing her son. How she could have moved beyond her grief to produce the books that brought so much joy to little kids. He wondered how his mum would have handled his loss, if he had died instead if her. And JJ, losing first Margaret, then his mother, losing the joy of his art and finally, losing Shelley. JJ seemed loneliest of all three of them. Tucking himself away without phone, TV, Internet, he had only a few friends that John had ever seen or heard of; apparently just a long string of romances that never hit the mark. Standing with his back to them both, John could feel a palpable energy, one of neediness, loneliness, and want.

What they wanted, he understood, because he wanted it too, he just couldn't put a name to it. Turning now, he smiled and asked, "When do we eat?" With relief, both Trish and JJ laughed and headed out of the room.

Catching up, John tapped Trish on the shoulder and asked, "Any chance I can use your computer later to check my email?" A smiling Trish jabbed him on the shoulder and said, "Ha ha very funny. What do you think your mum said in the letter I told you about? To quote your mother - this will be a technology free time for you John. And it will be, if I have anything to do with it!" JJ, almost out of ear shot heard this last tag of conversation and felt sad and disappointed and a bit jealous too. He hadn't gotten a letter from Shelley, not ever, not even one. Couldn't believe it! As all three moved around the kitchen with familiarity, the cat appeared at the window.

"Let him in JJ, it's time for his dinner too." Just as the cat came in, the phone rang. John looked up hopefully as Trish went off to answer. Both John and JJ sat to wait for Trish. A few minutes later she came back with a secretive smile on her face and sat down to join them. Then stood up and reached into her back pocket with that secretive smile, pulling out a piece of paper she handed it to JJ. "You have a date JJ that was your girl friend on the phone. I told her you weren't here; that you were busy with your nephew." Blushing brightly, JJ tucked the note into his shirt pocket and denied having a girl friend. Just then John asked about the man Trish went to dinner with. Now it was Trish who flushed all along her neck. Her eyes went to her plate then back up to look from one to the other. "You don't think I was on a date do you? That was my editor, Nick." John happened to be looking at Trish when she said this, so missed JJ's look of relief.

To change the subject and to get on one that needed some discussion, John asked, "Trish did you get my note to call Andrea?" Trish immediately launched into the enumeration of all she had accomplished. "I got just about everyone called from town that I could think of and when you give me the list of names you mentioned, I'll get started on those too.

Andrea's already invited your mum's friends from the coast, she doesn't know everyone will come, but as many as twenty including her and Heather will be here. Oh and she asked about Cozy. Should she come too? I told her I wasn't sure how she is around cats. She also said she's a bit of a flight risk.

"Boy, any dog that's a flight risk around here would soon disappear eh JJ? Do you remember that puppy I got, the yellow lab?" Turning to John, Trish told of getting a puppy for her son Seth when he was a teenager. "I thought a pup would keep him home. I was wrong. And the puppy never stayed home either. The first day we had it, I thought we could all just be outdoors together. You know, that he would just hang around because we were people and he'd want to be with us. By the time he was a year old the only thing we could count on was as soon as our eyes left him, he left us. He never came back without help either. We always had to send out a search party. So one afternoon he just disappeared. Wandered off and we never saw him again. All the other dogs either of us had were good old home bodies and stuck close to home, except him."

John missed Cozy and wasn't too sure how his dog would be up here and if she would behave. But she was his mum's dog, so if anyone should be here she should. As they ate their dinner each seemed deep in thought and then Trish broke the trance by saying she asked Todd about putting together a mixed CD of the music Shelley liked. "And if you two have any ideas tell me now...or in the next day or so." JJ piped up saying Shelley used to listen to the B'52's in the old days, she loved their music and their song, Love Shack was her favourite.

John was thoughtful for moment then said, "She had a song she sang around the house, calling it her theme song but

I don't know why. I think it's called, she's a very kinky girl?" Trish interrupted a bit harshly with, "That song was her theme song? It's actually called Super Freak. I can't imagine how that became her theme song John." John looked stricken with the tone of voice Trish used. "Well, I'm pretty sure mum would want it played if we are picking her favourites. She loved it. She said it reminded her of her own self."

Trish heaved a sigh partly out of guilt, hoping Shelley hadn't painted a picture of herself as a girl a guy wouldn't take home to meet his mother, because of something Trish had said years ago. And partly because truthfully she wanted a tasteful Month's Mind, so she spoke up, "Part of me wants you to honour your mum by doing what she would want John. The other part says honour her by having something tasteful. This is a day to remember her. It's customary to revere people who have died and shine the best light on them."

This wasn't going as well as Trish had hoped. John looked up at her with hurt and angry eyes. "My mum was great Trish... She never tried to hurt anyone and she was always cheerful. People came to her to get ideas even. She was great, she loved life and she was excited by life; she was never dull, I was the dull one. I was always the adult in our relationship. It would be unfair to misrepresent her! She was who she was. She wasn't a song Trish! She was a person who liked a song, one song; she knew all the lyrics to this one song. OK? It's going in Trish."

For the next four seconds John stared defiantly at Trish. And then in an exaggerated voice intended to relieve the tension, Trish stood with great drama, without breaking eye contact with John she placed her hands palm down on the table and then brought them up onto her hips and said, "Well, ya don't have to get mad about it. The song goes in. Shish!" This did the trick and everyone relaxed.

By then dinner was all finished. Trish could see John was emotionally beat and needed a break or a change. She suggested she take care of clean up later tonight and said she would walk them home. "Let's go to the barn first though and make a bit of a plan. You can't do this on your own John, and anyway JJ and I won't let you. We didn't see her but she was in our mind every day and we did love her too. Helping you with this is exactly what she intended; I know it is and you do too, that's why you're here. Or at least one reason you're here."

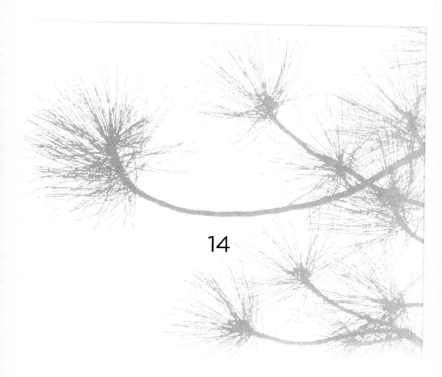

14

When they got to the barn the first thing John did, totally surprising JJ, was to unlock the office door, turn on the light and step aside to invite them in. Removing his suitcase from the top of the cardboard box, he lifted the box onto the desk; his desk. When he turned to speak to them, they were nervous with anticipation.

John smiled a brilliant smile pointing at the box. He took a little bow and said, "Mums ashes. She asked me to bring them here. She wanted to go home, to be home. Home on the range." With this last remark all three laughed a bit nervously. John shared the intimacy of this treasure hunt his mother had sent him on. He told them about all the letters and about box number nine too hoping this would jog a memory. But they both drew a blank wondering what this could mean.

JJ told them, "The only reference I can think of is Shelley thought number nine was her lucky number. She was born on the ninth day of the ninth month at nine in the morning. It doesn't sound quite right but I'm pretty sure she liked number nine for a variety of lucky reasons. Ever since she could count she said number nine was her special number. When she took metal work class in grade eight she got her teacher to help her make a number nine out of sheet metal with a big screw in the end... I remember that. It wasn't her finest piece of work." Trish was thoughtful for a moment and then said, "I remember that nine Shelley made JJ. Didn't it hang up beside the front door for a while, it got all weathered and rusty didn't it?" Glancing at JJ Trish realized he didn't have any idea what she was talking about. So to John she said, "Don't worry John, maybe your mum just wanted to be back here... at home. Maybe there is no number nine at all." Placing the box that contained his mum's ashes back in the crate and settling the suitcase back on top John ushered them out of his office and into the larger space where the Months Mind would be held. John still had confidence he would find number nine even if JJ and Trish had their doubts. He realized in sharing his quest he was also sharing a piece of his mother with two people he felt she would want him to include.

Stepping out into the big wide aisle of the barn, Trish asked John, "What's your plan? Tell me what you're thinking John... your vision or maybe your mum had some ideas she'd like you to share. I'll tell you mine in a minute after we've heard yours. If you have any ideas JJ, you too, share." John walked the aisle of the barn like he had a light inside him. In the short time John had been there, he walked the walk of someone totally at home, like he owned the place. He came alive as he took in all his surroundings. Turning to face them he was very animated. "I'm not sure where everything will go yet but I think it is right if Andrea and Heather come here a day or two early so they feel part of her party – so you all feel comfortable with each other. What mum wants is for people to be happy, comfortable and to talk about her.

"She would want us three, plus Andrea and Heather to be waiting in the barn; ready to greet everyone – you know make them feel welcome. She didn't want a eulogy. She won't want any tears, no tears even during my speech. Oh yeah, even though mum said no eulogy, I say we can make speeches and toasts. You two can make a speech too and Heather and Andrea will for sure and when we're done, we'll invite anyone to come up to an open microphone – that's mum's idea; to have an open mic. I'd like the painting she did of you and her, JJ, to be brought to the barn for the tribute.

"And I definitely want the paintings you did of her JJ displayed in the barn too. If you two could work on a story board for her, you know what that is right?" JJ had no idea but he saw Trish was nodding her head. Without missing a beat John carried on, "Please make sure there are pictures of her childhood, and ask Andrea to get a story board ready to bring with her when she comes, too. The theme will be an art gallery party... I hope Andrea will bring up some of her work; Trish can you ask her? Shall we clear the stalls out or not? What do you think so far? One other thing, I think we need a master of ceremonies, and I'd like it to be you Trish?"

Trish was flattered by the offer and quick to speak. "Thank you John, I'd feel honoured to be MC and I love your ideas John, I can see you have a firm vision. A gallery and including JJ's painting of Shelley would be wonderful, really. I didn't know you two had talked about JJ's painting though. When did that all happen?" Before they could reply Trish carried on excitedly. "Anyway John, I'm glad to go with your vision and if I can take care of the food end of things and where it goes I'm set." Walking around in a tight circle Trish looked up at first one loft at one end of the barn and then the hay loft at the other and at the stalls too not really finding a good spot for the food, then said, "How about we set up the food table at this end under your sleeping loft. From a distance the loft up there with the hammock stretched out looks good. It looks just like it did when both kids were small. Hey, we could have a guest book of sorts where people are encouraged to write a story about your mum? I can send out an email letting everyone know we'll be looking for stories so they can be prepared. I might have a nice journal we could use to put the stories in. And JJ, can you bring my old beer fridge down here so we have somewhere cold to store the food and stuff?"

JJ had been silent so far, he felt so helpless next to these two. He had nothing to offer, or so he thought and he wasn't feeling comfortable about putting his paintings on display either. But he couldn't say that to these two enthusiasts. He just hoped they wouldn't find any more paintings. Finally he spoke up saying, "My mum, Jean, made me a journal once. It's handmade, the paper, everything. The cover is hand tooled leather and she bound the whole thing herself. It's a piece of art so I never wrote in it.

"I've just hung onto it and know mum would love me to use it for this." John took one look at an emotional JJ and said, "Remember what I said! No crying." Then he came toward JJ and gave him a big hug. JJ was totally thrown aback and in awe of John. What a kind and open young fellow he was. Shelley you did a good job, JJ silently said, hoping Shelley would hear it. During their embrace, Trish had wandered the barn and was standing at the bathroom doorway.

She turned asking, "Do you mind if I get this cleaned and painted, maybe a new floor too. It's kind of dingy?" Both JJ and John said at once, "What's wrong with it, its fine like that." Then JJ said, "Don't paint the back of the door though; did you see the graffiti yet, Trish?" Together all three squeezed into the bathroom and closed the door. A bit of a tight fit but they were beginning to feel like a family.

Three sets of eyes scanned the art and writing on the door. The outer edge was painted with a jagged edge of bright gold paint, outlined with hot pink on the inner edge; the two colours vibrancy acting as a frame for what the centre contained. What JJ saw were little figures dancing and messages of all sorts, written in different coloured markers he guessed, judging by the blurry edges and intensity of the colour.

JJ started reading aloud. "Shelley loves Seth. There's a date beside it, making her about fourteen years old." Smiling as he gave Trish's arm a pat he carried on with – "There is no way to happiness, happiness is the way. Good one, we should remember that. This one is by Einstein - If you want to live a happy life, tie it to a goal not to people or objects. Oh she must like Albert Einstein because here is another. - You have to learn the rules of the game, and then you have to play better than anyone else. Oh no here's a heart breaker, it's been crossed out but still - I hate JJ." Trish gasped when she read, "Trish thinks she's a real dish, but she's a real bitch. And it's not crossed out I might add!"

"What I see," said John, "is she mentioned only the people she actually gave a shit about, whoops sorry didn't mean to say that... but look here at the bottom – Mumma Jean you are the best, thanks. It's got a little heart beside it." John stood still for a moment then got an idea, "JJ do you think you might have another door somewhere that would fit this opening? Maybe we can lean this door out in the barn somewhere. Her artwork, including the prose, is really neat. It shows her emerging talent in its rawest form."

JJ was rubbing the back of his head. A gesture John was coming to recognize as inner conflict, and a weighing of his options. When he spoke, what he said gave them all a different choice; one they all agreed on. "How about this, I'm pretty sure the door to the bathroom in the house is this size. It's a bigger bathroom too, so more people can fit inside. This door Shelley made her mark on, just feels too intimate in a way as you said John; it expresses the rawness of her talent. But more than that, it's a personal time capsule. Her bathroom, for her eyes only. How about, I exchange this door for the one in the bathroom in the house.

"I'd like to be the one to look at it every day, or you too John when you're in there; or you Trish, a daily reminder. Do you mind if I do that instead." In answer John gave JJ's back a rub and so did Trish. As they stood in the tight space John was overcome by a desire to make this family his; he felt so close to both these people. He hadn't expected to feel this way but he did. They were family. Then very softly his thought was whispered out loud without self consciousness, "You are my family." He felt a shudder from Trish and knew she had filled with emotions she didn't want to show. Pushing past her shoulder he pulled the door open to let in some air. As he felt the welcome whoosh of the outside air, an idea came to him.

At home his mum had made a curtain of origami creatures; she spent a lot of time making them. They looked like a beaded curtain, and as a curtain it hung between and separating one part of her studio area and her office area. A distant memory surfaced for John. He was really young and still learning the ins and outs of his mum's favourite game of hide and seek. His mum had sat very still behind the origami curtain. She tucked her arms and her head inside her T shirt so she would be camouflaged. This became a lesson to always look beyond the obvious, especially when playing hide and seek.

John could not find her for a very long time. He looked all over the house and every once in a while he could hear tapping from the room she was in. But when he got there the studio was empty. Finally, on the verge of a temper tantrum, he did find her; and she laughed until tears came down her cheeks. Another great hiding spot she used over and over again was to lie cross ways at the headboard of her bed with pillows covering all of her. He fell for it time and again. But thinking of the origami now gave him an idea.

He asked Trish, "Next time you call Andrea would you ask her to pack mums origami from the studio? When you see it you'll be amazed. It's a curtain for a doorway; all made with hanging origami creatures. Mum made them herself when she was expecting me. I'll hang it in the office doorway. It's really brightly coloured, and shimmers in a breeze making a noise that is soft, like ... Well I don't know what it's like, maybe rustling leaves?" Trish was smiling and felt in awe of John. "That sounds lovely John." Clasping her hands together she said, "And you...or should I say we, do we have a plan guys?

"Next week will be here soon so I think I'll head home, what about you two?" JJ turned to John then and said he was going to head up to the house now to turn in for the night. "What about you John, are you coming up to the house tonight, you could sleep on the couch?" John shook his head no saying he was going to stay in his loft tonight. As Trish and JJ left, John heard JJ say, "I'm going to walk Trish half way to her place, so the coyotes don't get her." This comment made Trish laugh in what JJ thought was a very girlish way. Which made JJ laugh too and off they went.

As they walked Trish shared with JJ that there was something about John that reminded her so much of Seth. "Guess it's the age; still kind and caring and wanting to be helpful. Things changed for a few years when Seth turned 17. Do you remember JJ? Shelley wrote I love Seth on that bathroom door when she was about fourteen. He was no longer the kid, John is now. Do you suppose they are together somewhere?"

JJ was quiet. He didn't know what to say, because for him he just didn't know. He knew Trish was thinking about Seth and Shelley when she said, they. He had no belief system at all. Except that if he lived by the golden rule his conscience would always be clear and his sleep would be sound. For the first time since Trish was just a little girl, JJ reached for her hand and held it while strolling slowly along. They walked on this way until they reached the poplars. Trish leaned in to JJ, giving him a long slow hug, whispering thanks in his ear. Returning the hug, JJ brushed a kiss against her hair.

Finally feeling pretty tired after a very long day John too, knew it was time to sleep. Before he headed up the stairs to the loft though, he grabbed letter number six, to read before he hit the hay. The idea of hitting the hay and the expression - hit the hay, had all new meaning for John now that he made his bed in a barn. He wondered if his mum would still know just what was going on, and what new surprise she had in store for him. He couldn't believe he had been here over two weeks already. Such a short time and what seemed like a life time too. John took the letter up to the loft to read and got ready for sleep. Then for what seemed like an unaccountable reason after the good day he'd had, he began to cry.

His tears felt like a dam breaking. He knew his tears were a mixture of feeling guilty; he had a niggling feeling of disloyalty for the happiness he felt being here with people who knew his mum and who seemed to want to get to know him. His mother was gone, never to be seen again. He felt her with him at times. Mostly when he was alone like now; but the more he was alone the less he wanted to be alone.

His mum had left him without telling him her story. And today, that's what left him feeling so bereft. He supposed in her way she was letting him find out things about her from the people who cared enough to cherish the memories. What amazed him most was her long memory and having recalled enough to know what was in each box. To know what JJ would do and what John's curiosity would lead him to do. His mum did have a plan for him, one that had been occupying his time, keeping him busy and distant from the pain of grief. He wondered for a moment how unusual it was to plan a treasure hunt to ease the grieving process.

> *To my Dearest boy John,*
>
> *The boxes must be revealing a few things about me you didn't expect. In fact there will be many surprises revealed about me during your stay. Things you didn't know. Some you will like, some will leave you feeling cheated. One of the best surprises will be the crazy quilt. The*

quilt is where I first began my love of all things, collage. When I was little I liked to cut pictures out of magazines, gluing them with paste made out of flour and water, onto bristle board or just plain old paper or into a scrap book. But the crazy quilt, at least when I was making it, felt like my first real collage; an adult collage.

The fabric used to make the quilt was cast off in a bag of trash found by mum when she was helping a lady in town to de-clutter her house. It was more like, de-hoard, her house. Mum-ma Jean brought it home thinking she would make a quilt out of it for me. Instead, she showed me how to do it. In a way the quilt was made by both of us. Her instructions, some design input from her and some design input from me and all my labour.

The quilt John, is so precious to me. The only thing from home I didn't bring that I have regretted not having. Especially now when I'm so sick and you have been with me all the way. My Mumma Jean was sick too and like you, I had to grow up fast. Did you find the list in box two?

Ask Trish or even Todd, to help you out with inviting every single person on that list to my Month's Mind. I can't recall now, why I made the list in the first place. I wonder if it was fate directing me to do so. One name not on the list is a woman Todd once brought with him to our house. You were just a little guy and played *with her little black eyed, sandy haired girl. The little girl was older than you by a year or two. I don't remember the mums name, just that she and I really connected and you two kids had so much fun together that they all decided to stay overnight. I also knew that she was from my home town. If you get a chance, ask Todd to invite her. The little girl was called Tiger Lily, cute name. Who could forget that name!*

You might be way ahead of me by now John, you may have found the quilt, and if you did you also found the soap stone carving. I want Trish to have that carving. Her son carved it. It wasn't ever finished but he gave it to me just before the woman I called mum died...Trish will treasure the carving even though your instinct will be to give it to JJ. It is meant for Trish. You'll understand the importance for Trish, of running her hands over something Seth had touched too. Give it to her on the day of my Month's Mind. And John if you haven't already, tell Trish and JJ about this treasure hunt, see if they remember number nine.

Love mum xoxoxo

Putting the letter aside, John smiled at the irony. His mum knew he would want JJ to have the carving and now he had to find a way to give it to Trish instead. John would tell Trish what his mum had said; imagining Trish running her own hands lovingly over the stone getting a thrill at the touch. Just like he did every time he opened a box of his mother's things, or rode a trail she had been on or sat at her desk in the barn. Looking out the window she had looked out, or laying in the hammock at night; jumping at sounds in the dark she may have jumped at too. The treasure hunt his mum had devised was showing him not only who she was, but giving him insight into who he was, and what kind of person he wanted to become.

In the morning after breakfast he got to work really cleaning the barn. JJ popped in to ask when they would go for their ride but John was too into cleaning to be disturbed. A short time later JJ returned with a door strapped to a dolly; he went right to work exchanging it with the bathroom door. Calling out for help when he needed it, John hustled to give a hand.

Once the doors were exchanged and with the old graffiti door out in the dim light of the barn JJ decided it needed to have a cleaning but worried about removing anything. Saying he would figure something out he strapped it onto the dolly and headed up to the house. Over his shoulder he asked John, "Can you come up to the house in about half an hour, I'll blow the horn."

When John heard the loud squawk of the horn he was now getting familiar with, he dropped his mop and went up to the house. The first thing John noticed was on the table, JJ had set up what would become part of a story board for his mum. One lone picture of Shelley in her late teens was tacked to the board, it was her grad picture. Heading to the bathroom John found JJ waiting for help to lift the door up onto the hinges saying, "I had to move the hinge bracket by chiseling it out here," moving aside so John could see where he meant, JJ pointed to his handiwork, "see right there? Just a fraction is chiseled out to make it fit but here goes... OK are you ready? I'll lift and you set the pins in right there. Let's go on three - one, two, three." And up it went. When they tried to close it they noticed almost for the first time there was a small window high up in the door and wondered how, and if people would feel exposed. The glass was opaque with old fashioned wavy ridges though, so you'd only see a back lit shadow if you were tall enough to see anything at all. "And most of the time I'm here on my own anyway. Unless you're here, you can stay on if you want, you know that right? This is your house too." This last comment had been said before but now it was said with great comfort, both by the speaker, JJ or Trish and by the listener, John.

In reply John said, "I see you got the story board started, I like that picture of mum. She hasn't...I mean hadn't changed that much." JJ was already shaking his head. "You know John, I never really thought to look at photos until you were here and we still haven't looked together. Last night I opened photo albums one after another and most of the pictures of your mum had been taken out. Do you think she has them, I mean do you think she took them with her? There were blank spaces throughout the books. She might have taken other pictures too, I don't know." John felt his face flush as he heard blame. He had never seen many pictures of his mum and said so in a bit of a belligerent voice.

Noticing John's fuse shortening, JJ held up both hands in a placating motion of peace. "I don't know if it was your mum who removed them John, and I honestly never looked at them at all. Let's ask Trish and see if she took them or if she has any. She'll have pictures of Shelley and Seth together for sure." John felt shame at his reaction and said it made more sense that his mum had taken them but again he had only seen a few of them, if she had. "That's OK John I was just feeling bad that

I couldn't find them, for all I know I took them out myself in a fit of drunken rage years ago."

Surprised by JJ's admission John asked, not for the first time, why she left. "I honestly don't know; she didn't even leave a note! And hey! I was too drunk to take notice right away. Trish says it was my drinking and maybe something Trish said to your mum. But that's her story to tell. All I know is that for a short time before she left, she was… oh I don't know. She was restless and moped around the house and just not her usual self. Sulking around staring into the distance, she was not living in the moment that's for sure.

"She seemed anxious and angry and hurt, pacing like a caged animal. Shelley, your mum, she left for a whole multitude of reasons. It wasn't on the spur of the moment, was it? She packed all her stuff didn't she, even numbering the boxes, for Christ sake?" JJ paused and began rubbing the back of his head again; he looked directly into John's searching eyes and just shook his head and shrugged his shoulders. "I don't know, she never said and by now you'll know, I'm not the most insightful person, so I never came up with an answer.

"What I do know is this. I thought I caught her drinking beer with Trish a week or so before she took off. I got mad at both of them. When we left Trish's place together, Shelley and I brought that mad along with us home here. Things were said by both of us. And a week later she just got up, packed her things and left." There didn't seem like there was anything left to say on the subject, so John said he was going back to finish up in the barn and if JJ had some free time to come help.

Before John could get away though JJ said, "You asked about my drinking, right? Well my drinking started just before my painting stopped. It got worse and more frequent and I was an ass hole most of the time. I hated myself for not painting, but Shelley... she hated my guts for drinking, hated me for being a quitter and the last time we were together we argued... that's putting it mildly John. We really had it out with each other. At the time I didn't really even remember much of what I said to her because I was so drunk. But what I do recall was about me mainly. How self centered is that?

"She said I was a quitter and a failure. I did tell her she wasn't either because she was too darned scared and immature to even try something new. Told her she was letting her feelings for a guy who didn't even know she existed stop her from getting a life. She had graduated from school two years ahead because she was so darned smart for Christ sake! She was just wasting her life waiting around for that Seth to notice her." Realizing he may have gone too far, JJ stopped speaking and couldn't think of anything to add. Again John said, "Let's go to the barn." On their way out the door John thanked JJ for clearing that one up at least. As they both headed out of the house to work in the barn, John thought about what JJ had told him. It really never got him any closer to knowing what made his mum go and then to actually stay away. And he guessed he would never know.

An organized John had made a list of all the jobs needing attention to get the barn ready for the Month's Mind. JJ could see just how seriously John was taking his mums wish to have a Month's Mind. Together, like they'd been doing it all their lives, John and JJ worked side by side as they cleaned up the hay loft then swept out the barn. They thoroughly cleaned out the horse stalls too, first sweeping them out, and then hosing them from ceiling to floor. Stepping back to take a look at how clean the stalls now seemed JJ decided to add a few bales of hay to sit on in each horse stall in case anyone wanted a quiet place to chat, away from the crowd. JJ explaining to John, "We're lucky to find hay bales at all. Most hay is rolled up nowadays. You've seen them in fields, those long white rolls? That's hay. My hay guy though, he never went to that system and I still get my hay from him, he delivers too."

When they heard the sound of tires crunching on gravel, they shared an identical shoulder shrugging look, then went out to see who was there. It was Trish with a young guy in tow. Making introductions Trish said, "This is Matt, he's going to do a refresh on that bathroom. Matt, meet JJ and John." Grabbing the supplies out of the back of her car they all headed inside. Trish had already been to the paint store and flooring store saying she took a guess on the floor size and got a roll end. "Matt will be here for a while doing the painting and floor." Grabbing the paint can from Matt Trish used a tool she had in her pocket to open it up. "How do you like this colour?" It was bright sunshine yellow. They weren't too sure so they asked about the flooring. It was a soft looking bluish grey with dark flecks, like gravel. JJ thought it looked like something you'd find in a school hallway.

They all went to the bathroom now to look at the sink and shower. The shower was white acrylic and the sink and toilet were white too. "These colours will be a bit of a nod to Shelley's painting of you two, JJ. We can put the painting right here," said as she pointed on the wall just outside the bathroom door. "Good idea Trish," uttered an unsure John, "we'll trust you. Won't we JJ?" Rubbing the back of his head again JJ said, "Oh sure." Walking away JJ leaned in whispering to John that he hated yellow on a wall. Smiling, John threw his head back and laughed loud and hard.

186

Matt was very fast, and in a few hours he had finished the job. The yellow looked great even by JJ's standards. They all went up to the house to get all the paintings of Shelley, and by Shelley, and to talk about other arrangements. Trish was questioned as soon as she got there about the missing photos. But she claimed ignorance saying she had enough of her own, many of which were family photos of Seth too. Trish suddenly launched into talking about the funeral she had for Seth.

"We had it within a week after he was found. And it was quite a formal funeral wasn't it JJ? Not in a church but with chairs lined up in rows. Lots of people came but it felt so rushed. I was devastated," her voice caught and she had to stop talking… "I'm still devastated. JJ will tell you…and none of us knew where Shelley was.

"Oh John, sorry to say, for a long time I was so angry with your mum for leaving. I even blamed her for Seth's death; he went to Vancouver to look for her saying that was where she always wanted to live. If he hadn't gone, he wouldn't have been in the wrong place at the wrong time." Hearing these words, John wanted to interrupt and somehow defend his mother, but the touch of JJ's hand on his back stopped him as he realized Trish had to say this.

"I don't know what I would have done without that anger John. The anger held the grief at bay. It kept me from falling apart completely, the anger kept me here. I didn't even know if Shelley had been found. The last time Seth and I spoke he hadn't found her, but thought he knew where she worked. He said he was going to a music festival on the way home. When I asked, he said he hoped he would be taking a girl there too, and I knew then it would be a week or two before I heard from him again. Once he got hooked up with a girl he was all business.

"When the phone call came; not even a house visit John! A phone call came asking about Seth, then telling me he had been in a fatal single car accident. I… well do you remember JJ. I went crazy for a very long time. Then, a very long time later I got the first letter from Shelley with pictures of you. By then JJ had gone to Vancouver to look and put ads in the personals, then just gave up I guess, didn't you, JJ? We heard stories about having seen her. Todd once said he had spoken to her at a dragon boat festival, and she was OK but didn't want to get in touch.

It was about a month after Todd saw her, wasn't it JJ; I started getting letters from her. No return address just letters with news. There was mostly news about you, and photos of you too John, the ones hanging on the fridge. You can read the letters any time you want to… by the time she wrote she said she had heard about Seth. I could hear the devastation in her message, and all at once I forgave her. And I forgave myself too; in a way she saved me by sending all those letters and giving me a chance to watch as you grew up. It gave me a new focus instead of the grief that has been a recurring crushing blow. I waited for the letters to arrive and marveled at what she did by making each one a mini masterpiece, in its own way. All that time and never even knew about Todd's involvement in all this… Well until her latest letter. It came as a complete blow to know the whole time Todd had been letting her know our news." As soon as she said it she realized her mistake.

A look of complete confusion struck JJ's face; followed by anger, immediate and complete anger, heart wrenching hurt and anger. He thought he had let go of these feelings long ago, but not so. His reaction to this news was immediate and took him right back to how he felt when she left, and during their search for her.

Leaving John and Trish in a rush of anger, JJ broke completely. He had endured years of knowing Trish got letters and pictures and he had gotten not one word from Shelley, and now this? Todd knew where she was all the time. John followed him into the bathroom where JJ was hunched over the toilet grabbing handfuls of toilet paper. John's first words surprised even him, "Don't blame Todd. There is no blame JJ. Just responsibility and it was mums responsibility, not Todd's. The fact is Todd came around a lot and I don't think Andrea even knew why he did or who he was, or how mum met him. I know I didn't know, not till I saw Todd the other day.

"When he came to our place, he always helped us in some major way. I remember this one time he brought and installed a dishwasher. And last time he came he brought and set up mums hospital bed in our tiny living room; rearranging everything as she directed him too. Andrea never liked Todd and I was neutral. Sometimes I found him really funny, sometimes I didn't, but I was always glad to see him because when he came, mum got so excited.

"After Todd left the other day I realized every time he came to see mum, they would either go for a walk together or mum would say to me, go read or play, I need to talk to Todd about something for a minute. And there they would be, Todd doing all the talking in a hushed voice. He was different from all her other friends. Now though, now that I know what he was doing, I'm grateful to him. I don't know why mum never came back here JJ. It's so clear to me she loved this place. I don't know the answer at all.

"Mum would say that people and the what, and why, and when, and where, and how, they do things is a complete mystery. Some actions people choose, end up looking like there is just not a reason." JJ started to protest and John just carried on speaking. "Mum wants us all to be happy. Now I know why she sent me here. That's the reason JJ. But please, don't be mad at Todd, be mad a mum." Turning JJ grabbed hold of John and with wracking sobs managed to say, "You're just a kid! How did you get to be so smart?"

The rest of the day was spent by all three of them, going through Trish's photos. John finally seeing and watching the love Trish had for her son, Seth. They managed to find more photos than Trish had thought she had of just Shelley, on her own. Gathering the photos and handing them to JJ, Trish said, "You take care of the storyboard tonight JJ and if need be I'll rearrange it in the morning. Right now if you two guys don't mind I need some quiet time." A surprised John looked at JJ who wasn't surprised at all, and they headed home. Once there JJ asked John if he would like to spend the night. "No, not tonight, I still have some boxes to unpack though, so maybe I'll just go up now and try to do at least one."

Stepping into the bedroom, John softly closed the door. He went over to the bed that was illuminated in a wash of light and lay down on his back to look straight up at all the stars shining down on him, the same stars that shone on his mother. He lay this way deep in thought and unmoving for several minutes. Finally John sat up on the edge of the bed, flipped on the bedside lamp, and grabbed box number 4.

He was falling behind so he leaned over and grabbed box number 5 too. Box number four revealed some old jackets; many looked homemade. One by one he began to pull them out and at the very bottom was an old brown leather jacket with a fringe. Smiling John stood to hold it up in front of his body noticing the closure, was for a man's jacket. Holding the jacket up against his body and stepping over to the mirror he took a look at himself and laughed out loud and said, "Fashion?"

When he slid his arms into each of the sleeve holes and zipped himself in, he took a second look, he liked what he saw. A bit unsure where to put all these jackets, he decided to keep the leather one out and put the rest of them in the closet. Opening the closet doors he realized, he had been so focused on the boxes, he never had looked inside until now. The closet was wide and deep trailing off into the slope of the roof and almost completely empty. Reaching his hand in to the stack of hangers on one of the shelves closest to the door he stopped in mid air. Caught there in the light from the room was an envelope with writing on the front. The envelope looked like it had been there awhile. John's hand automatically reached for it when he noticed it was addressed to JJ. John stood stock still; he turned and went out to the mezzanine calling for JJ to come up.

Pointing to the open closet doors John asked JJ what he saw. "I see nothing, except just some hangers ... an empty closet. Why?" John gave his back a light shove pushing him closer. "Take a look JJ." Lifting the hangers JJ grabbed the letter with speed and tenderness when he saw and recognized Shelley's hand writing. Pressing the envelope to his chest, JJ was engulfed in emotions he had never felt. "What does it say?" An anxious John wanted to know. Then recovering himself, knew JJ would like to be alone to read it. Guiding him to the bed John left the room saying he would give him some privacy.

Hi JJ,

One look in this closet and you'll know I'm gone. Many things have happened lately that have nothing to do with you JJ. Ever since I finished school I've felt as if I'm waiting for something fantastic to happen to me, but am afraid to stick my toe off the property to go find it. If I get a job or go to school I know I will miss seeing Seth when he stops in… The night I had that argument with you just made me think, you are right. I can't sit around here waiting for life to come to me. Waiting for Seth to notice me, or to take me seriously, is a total waste of time. You and Trish are both right. Seth isn't the right one for me, he's too old for me or I'm too young for him… he loves it here with plans to stay here all his life near his mum and I don't love it here period. And as you say he isn't interested in having just one girl friend, he wants many girl friends. So I'm taking your advice and am going to get a job and maybe even go back to school. For the next two weeks I'll be with Fay Gardener at a house she is looking after in Vancouver. You can call me there if you want - find the phone number and address on the back of this page.

If I need it sometime, then I'm taking money out of my trust account to get me going, but won't take another dime until I retire early at 45. Ha ha ha. That's my goal, same as yours right? A self made woman....I'm sorry for all the rotten things I've said to you and about you in the last while... but the truth is I meant every single thing I said to you. I've been feeling angry at myself and at Seth and at Trish and at you too, but not just at you. You know what Mumma Jean always said. It's easiest to hurt the people who love you, because you know they can be counted on to forgive you, over and over again. But you know what? I hate trying to work things out when you're drunk, so I thought I'd slip away while you slept it off. Is that harsh?

If you can stop drinking long enough to actually quit drinking for good and long enough to forgive me, then call me. But JJ, if you don't call me or make a move to get in touch with me, I'll know you don't want this burden back. And I won't ever come back.

Shelley xoxoxo

JJ read and re read the letter over and over trying to under-stand, and briefly trying to remember who Faye even was. Finally JJ lay down on the bed and fell fast asleep; into a sleep full of dreams of Shelley. In his dream JJ was standing at a counter of what looked like a car rental company. Many employees were lined up on the opposite side of the counter. He said out loud to anyone whose attention he could get, "I'm looking for Shelley." A voice out of nowhere said, "Sorry she has gone, she's already gone. She's not coming back, you're too late."

Behind the counter JJ could see a set of large double glass doors. And through the doors he saw lush green flora and fauna, tropical looking. JJ said to the invisible counter attendant whose voice he had heard, "But I just need to give her a message, to just talk to her for a minute, can I go in?" The attendant said, "No, it's not time for you yet." Suddenly the palm fronds behind the glass doors began to sway and shudder and out crashed Shelley. Pushing through the leaves and throwing open the doors she came from around, or right over, or maybe even passed right through the counter, and threw her arms around JJ's neck giving him the biggest hug. And as she did, he knew it was the last one, one of forgiveness and love. Gradually JJ's eyes opened and it was morning. He could smell the welcome scents of cooking breakfast. Bursting out of the bedroom like a man reborn, JJ bounded down stairs to tell John about his dream and about the letter too.

Both John and Trish were making breakfast side by side. Laughter and good cheer made the kitchen feel brighter and more open. JJ felt like Scrooge waking up on Christmas morning. Smiling broadly he told the two to sit so he could have their full attention. Then, a still standing, grinning JJ shared the contents of the letter and most importantly the dream where Shelley had forgiven him with a good bye hug he was convinced he felt and like a soft and tender bruise could still feel and would never forget.

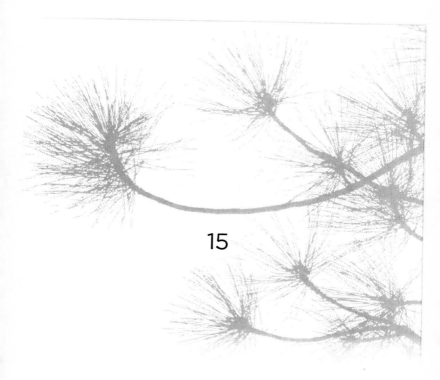

15

John still had boxes to unpack. He wanted to get another letter to read too, and he had never gotten back into the barn to check out his mums desk drawer and the treasures it surely held. So when Trish asked if he wanted to head into Kamloops with her to shop, he suggested JJ go in his place. John noticed Trish and JJ cast a nervous glance at each other. Interpreting the look to mean, worry over him, he urged them to just go saying, "I'll be fine here on my own." Still Trish and JJ looked hesitant, and again he told them he would be fine and to go.

Giving them an added purpose he asked if they would pick up some party streamers for the horse stalls, "So you know... people will know the stalls are to be used for sitting in, on those hay bales." JJ started to say no to streamers, but Trish stopped him by grabbing his arm and saying, "Good idea John that will brighten things up a bit for sure. What colour do you think your mum would like? Or you?" John looked deep in thought and he finally said, "Just get whatever colour you like Trish. My mum had similar taste to you, but she loved white and she loved silver and gold. Hey, can you pick up some of those tiny little white Christmas lights too?" Grinning Trish was instantly caught up in the visual of the barn being tripped out in tiny white lights. "Sure John, great idea!" Turning to JJ she asked, "Want to drive me, in your car? Or do you want to drive me, in my car?"

Watching them from his perch on the porch, John wondered about loneliness and if his mum was ever lonely. He wondered if she ever longed for a partner or boyfriend, someone her own age. Andrea and most of the other people his mum knew were all way older than her, or way younger. She never had a boy friend as far as he knew, just male friends. Looking at JJ and Trish today as they got ready to go out in JJ's car, his instinct told him that perhaps this was the first time in years their loneliness of grief was put aside or forgotten. He wasn't taking credit necessarily, but he too, realized being with them, eased his own loneliness and grief. As if his mum was close by, he heard a quiet voice from years ago say - Well aren't you a wise old guy, in a little guy's body.

JJ surprised Trish, when he said, she could drive his car. Without hesitation Trish went to the driver's side ready to jump in and take the wheel saying to both John and JJ, "I'm the first person to ever drive your car JJ. Aren't I?" And then whipping her hair into a pony tail so a breeze from an open window didn't shift it across her face while she drove, turning to the porch, she gave John a little grin and two thumbs up before sliding into the driver's seat.

Hello Dear John,

Today began as a sad day for me. You came in from your bedroom where I thought you were attending to your studies and you didn't even say hello. You went marching right past full of purpose, without even looking my way. I stared at your retreating back and dreamt up ways to win you over. Willing you to at least turn and look my way. Then you surprised me by bringing Cozy in, plopping her, a freshly sanded wooden tray and all our coloured pencils and wax crayons onto the bed. Cozy curled under the blanket nudging up against my side, while you and I coloured our hearts out.

Colouring with you today was such a thrill for me. I'm pretty sure it will be our last time colouring together. And look at you being so creative! Only you would have thought to colour on the wooden tray itself. You said the heat of tea, meals and sunshine would mush all the colours together, penetrating them right into the wood - thus making the vibrancy of the colours permanent for all time. I hope you somehow sneak that tray to my Month's Mind. Ask Andrea to bring it, and then sit it out in the gentle heat found in the shade by the barn and sure enough the colours will all mush. How is it that you and I got so hooked on functional art? My gift to you, my mother's gift to me, a circle....

In my room at JJ's, the large tapestry you see hanging on the wall was made by your Great

Grandmother, Jean. She started to make it for my mother, Margaret, when she was a baby. It took her years to finish apparently, and then for years it lay rolled up in storage; waiting for a time my mum would leave home to make a home of her own. In those days, fathers would sometimes build a cedar chest for a daughter. Mothers would fill the chest with precious things to make a future home beautiful, as well as functional. The cedar of the box kept bugs away and those boxes were called, hope chests.

My own mother died when I was just a wee little thing. She had not established a home of her own yet, and inside her hope chest the tapestry resided. It stayed there until the week before I left home. It had never even been out of the chest since it first went in, so when I unfurled its beauty, I hung it on the wall. Marvelous isn't it! Way too girly for you though John, so I'd love for you to remove it from the wall, but be sure you do not take it down until after my Month's Mind.

It is a gift to Heather from me. She'll love and treasure the beauty of it. I can just see it perfectly hung on the wall facing her bed. Can you imagine her sitting with her karaoke microphone in hand while she sings, in her sweet quivery voice; singing to the lovely ladies in the tapestry? I can. That's why I want her to have it. Tell her the gal on the far left is me. Do you notice all others are looking in the same direction to the right? But I am looking right out into the room. Wherever you stand, I am watching you. My grandmother never told me what her intention was when she chose to design the tapestry with one young woman appearing alone from the rest. But when I hung it up, I related to her and for years have thought of her standing keeping an eye on my room. Waiting for me to come back…

After you've removed the tapestry you'll have one letter left to read. I know there will only be one more of the letters left as I wrote that one first. I won't be able to write much more so I am sure this will be the last. Have you enjoyed the letters so far John? Keep them, read them over and over again as the years pass, if you like. You'll be reminded of me; you'll be reminded of this special journey you've taken. You'll be reminded of how you went from cared for boy, to cared for young man. They care for you John.

They, you may ask? They - are all the people who have touched your life and whose lives you've touched. They are the living people who care for you; Andrea, Heather, Todd, many others you've met along the way… and especially two new people, Trish and JJ. You've changed their lives by being part of theirs, I am 100% sure of it. You've brought joy and hope back to them. My hope is now they have met and fallen for you they will have set themselves

free enough to fall for each other too. And if
that happens, you'll have played a big part.

Love always,
Mum xoxoxoxoxox

John folded the letter back into the envelope and was wowed, by his mother's careful consideration for everyone, as she made this plan. Not just for him as it turned out, but for JJ and Trish too. Giving closure to her disappearance from their lives so many years ago, causing them both unknown grief. Sending her only child back to be with them now though, was the right thing to do. Every day since he left Vancouver, John had questioned the wisdom of being sent here. Wondered, what good would come of his being here? Recalling the comfortable laughter John heard from JJ and Trish, and his own laughter made him realize a change had already taken place. Listening and watching as JJ and Trish got closer and closer, good friends giving in to something bigger perhaps. John hoped their trip into town today would give them enough time alone to bring them even closer still. And like his mum said, fall for each other.

Trish as it turned out was not allowed to drive on the highway. This was fine with her as she had a feeling, JJ wouldn't want his car going as fast as some of the yahoos on the road would like. She had never even been alone with JJ in his car; well not since she was old enough to have her own car. In the old days, if there was a joint family outing they went in her car, because as JJ said, "Kids are too messy for my nice clean car. Yours on the other hand … well it's as messy as the kids. Let's take yours." When there was an occasion that just adults were heading somewhere, then usually there would be a few more than just JJ and Trish.

JJ seemed comfortable enough with Trish behind the wheel, but personally he always liked to take the scenic route whether in the car or the truck. He felt this particular vehicle though, on a highway, just seemed wrong. The car was old, the highway was new. And he liked to watch the scenery, sometimes stopping for a swim at the same lake he and Seth had stopped at.

Today though JJ didn't think swimming would be on the agenda as Trish chatted about all the things she needed to pick up. "Did you even bring a list Trish?" JJ asked. It was his experience that Trish kept a running list in her head, so he reached in the glove box for a pen and pad of paper. "Tell me what we are getting and I'll write a list." Trish snorted with laughter, "We don't need a list JJ, it's all up here," she said pointing to the side of her head. Frustrated, JJ said, "Just tell me what you want to buy. And tell me slowly so I can write it down…for my own use, OK?"

Still laughing, Trish began to list off all the things they would need and finished up with, "And I'll take you for lunch when we are finished." When JJ began to protest, Trish reached her hand over touching his thigh which sent an electric shock up his entire body. JJ was well aware he felt a mix of nervous excitement to be spending the day with Trish, all on his own. He had waited a life time for this, or at least that is how he felt. As Trish talked she kept patting his thigh or his arm or rubbing his arm. Was he imagining things; did Trish's touch contain more than friendship and camaraderie. He didn't think so. It was just wishful thinking.

While she talked JJ watched her profile, watched her glance his way from time to time and watched the smile in her eye, when she did. Finally Trish asked why he was watching her so intently and why he was so quiet. JJ laughed at that because he felt like she was doing all the talking. He didn't need to do any at all. When he told her that she fell silent and JJ worried he had hurt her feelings until she said, "Do you know JJ this is the very first time we've been in this car together? There was a time it was you, me and Margaret. And a time that was very short lived because I met Seth's dad, that I fancied me and you making out in the back seat. Did you know that JJ?

"So today, I'm not sure why, but I feel a bit nervous. This … chat … is nervous chat. Space filler so we don't have to feel uncomfortable in silence. More specifically, so I don't have to feel the discomfort of silence." When JJ didn't say anything Trish cast a glance his way to see a little smile on his face, making her think he was laughing at her. "Well JJ, now I'm embarrassed to have shared that with you, thanks a lot!"

Trish had a way of diffusing an awkward moment with exaggerated angry sounding humour; both laughed, the diffusion had worked. They drove along in silence and then JJ got an idea he wanted to go swimming after all, to cool off. Pointing, he instructed Trish to take the next left up a dirt lane. When Trish hesitated he told her, he was taking her for a swim. "Are you kidding, I don't have a suit with me?"

"Wear your undies then Trish, just like a bikini." Trish was silent for a few beats then turned a red flushing face his way and said, "I go commando." Confused JJ asked, "What do you mean by commando?"

"Oh JJ, I don't wear underwear, I go commando. You haven't heard that expression, have you?"

"Nope, it's totally new to me. If you don't want to go, commando, then just sit and have a rest while I swim. I bet you've never been here before. In thirty years of finding it, there's never been a soul in sight. Once I saw an old guy in a truck, come to check me out and said to swim any time I liked. So I do. Other than running into him rarely, the only person I've brought here is John. And now after what you just told me, I wanted to take you there too." Casually JJ carried on talking, telling Trish he too, had wanted to get her alone in the back seat of his car; many times, and off and on over and over again throughout the years. "I always had a thing for you Trish... you know that." Again they drove along in silence. Trish felt as if her throat had closed, she couldn't speak, didn't know what to say. Her feelings for JJ had grown in a new direction, since John had turned up. Watching the two of them together, knowing John's presence had begun to bring JJ back to himself, a deep fondness and attraction grew. She felt herself resurfacing too, she felt ready to love again. Since John had arrived a small fissure of hope had appeared in both their hardened shells.

On the surface, Trish knew she appeared to have coped well with the loss of her son. But inside, just below the surface, her heart felt empty and incomplete. Not a day went by that she didn't shed a tear or a river of tears for her loss. She knew how lucky she was, to be able to plunge herself into writing as a way of bringing her son to life, it was such a gift. Much of what she wrote about was inspired by real or imagined events in their life together. Write what you know - her editor had reminded her in the early days after Seth's death. And so that is what she did.

JJ hadn't been so lucky in his life. No painting or other creative outlet to get his motor running again. He always just seemed like he was going through the motions, of pretending to have a life with his many short lived and superficial romances, his house in Kelowna, his horse, favours for other people. All these things gave an appearance of busyness, but Trish knew he was just waiting for something really good to happen. Just like her. They were both playing a waiting game. Not for the first time, Trish wondered about all the people who lived life in a holding pattern. Not moving forward, just standing still waiting for life to begin. For someone else to take their hand, saying - Let's go.

Getting near a wide part in the road, JJ instructed Trish to pull the car in. The road always seemed to be maintained to a level JJ felt his car could drive safely on and told Trish he wondered if long ago, this pull in, was a place to park while the ranch owners family swam or maybe it was just a wide spot in the road. Taking the keys from Trish, JJ got carefully out of the car so as not to damage the paint job, then went to the trunk and took out a blanket and some towels. Looking up at Trish holding her hand up to shield the sun from her eyes, JJ felt stunned, she hadn't ever changed, still the same essence of natural beauty; in his eyes, at least. "Towels and a blanket, I always carry them just in case I get a chance to swim in summer or have a break down in winter and need to stay warm.

"Come on, follow me. It isn't far." Silently they made their way, and JJ was right, the lake was just up and over a bit of a rise in the land. On their silent walk, the music of crickets and birds filled the air. The day felt just perfect to JJ and to Trish.

She could see why JJ would like the peaceful beauty found here, and asked if he ever brought Frida.

"Of course, Frida and I have been here lots of times. I park the truck and trailer back at the beginning of the road. Then we ride in. Actually that's how I found the lake. Not with Frida, but with another horse I was selling her for a friend of mine that I worked with in Alberta. The directions I had were backwards, so I took a wrong turn. Pretty soon I realized I couldn't turn around anywhere. When I got to where we left the car, I parked and came up the rise to see what I could see ahead. Like a driveway, or a place to turn around. Anyway, that's when I saw the lake. Went back to the trailer, got the horse out for a bit of fresh air and fresh grass and had a swim. I never could figure out where the horse buyer was and ended up buying her myself. I gave her to Seth. Do you remember?"

"As you were telling the story, I wondered if that was the same horse you gave Seth. Real kind of you JJ…" That might have been the last kindness from JJ to Seth, he was pretty sure. But when Seth was in his teens he was hard for anyone except Trish, to handle, they rubbed each other the wrong way. JJ hadn't liked his attitude toward Shelley. All she ever wanted was to hang out with him and his friends. All he wanted was to get rid of her as fast as he could, after he was about thirteen. Then when Shelley was about fourteen, JJ didn't want Seth anywhere near Shelley. She had such a huge crush on him and had developed curves in such a way, that JJ thought he caught Seth ogling her. He never told Trish though, but thought he might soon.

Trish was the one who brought it up though. "You and I were so protective of Seth and Shelley. We tried so hard to keep them apart. I wonder what would have happened if we had just stayed out of their business... I have no idea, now, why I was so anxious that Shelley never get close enough to Seth, so they could date, I mean. One of my biggest regrets, especially now."

That said and out of the way, JJ pulled off his shirt. Realizing he no longer had the body of Adonis, he turned to say so to Trish, just in time to see Trish had released her hair from the elastic band; with her back turned to him, and in a flash of vibrant colour her summer dress glided easily over her head. "Do you want me to close my eyes while you get in Trish?" JJ called out.

"Sure, just turn your back and I'll let you know when I'm in... OK, you can look now JJ." Deciding to go commando too JJ stepped out of his under shorts. Covering his privates with his hands, JJ turned in time to see Trish slip into the water; her long hair floating out onto the waters top, completely surrounding her like a wreath. Smiling she watched as JJ walked on tender feet toward the shore. His sun browned face held a sheepish grin. What caught her attention was, his farmers tan, and the bright whiteness of the rest of his body. Holding his hands in front of him as if he were protecting something precious, at the last moment he let go and plunged into the lake surfacing right next to Trish.

Turning to face each other, Trish reached out her arms to place them lightly on JJ's shoulders. His hands slid onto her hips. And there they stood searching one and others face as if for clues. Later Trish would comment to JJ, that the moment they shared was completely awesome. "Awesome is an overused word that has lost its true meaning. Please forgive me for using it." Trish said. A word, she herself had never used but wanted to try it out on this occasion, for lack of another. In the buoyancy of the water, Trish's legs floated up as if on their own to rest around JJ's hips, her arms hanging lose around his neck, his arms around her back and together they swayed, face to face, making a slow circle in the water. Two people, a watcher might say, way past their prime. But for JJ and Trish, each felt utter innocence about the feelings welling up inside. They could have been as young as a couple of teenagers introduced to all the feelings of love, for the first time.

And like young innocents JJ and Trish retired to their blanket and lay chastely holding hands, looking up at the sky above. Naked, each with a farmer's tan they lay content and happy to just have human touch with another. They felt not a bit shy at their exposure, with only a sense of complete freedom to be naked in front of one another, without judgment. Picking out clouds and making up stories about what they saw in the sky they lay like that until JJ's body shifted, so that he was on his side. Reaching out for her, he carefully helped Trish as she turned toward him, and held her there. With evidence of JJ's arousal between them, neither seemed sure of where to go from here, or what to say.

JJ was torn between his animal instinctual desire, and another less familiar instinct that told him to hold back. He sensed they each knew what they wanted. And it was to take things slowly. It was JJ who opened things up for discussion. Drawing her hair away from her eyes, JJ brushed his lips across her forehead and held her tight. "Trish…" He began, then pulling back from her so he could see her face, he said, "I've wanted this for so long - but let's take things slow OK? This - being together and feeling so much, is almost overwhelming for me. I don't want you to hurt me, and I surely don't want to hurt you, Trish."

Trish's body tensed as she began to object, "I don't intend to hurt you JJ. But I know what you mean. We're both so vulnerable and have been for so long. But JJ, I know what I feel. I know what I've been feeling... I can't put into words what it is, except to say, it's a magical surprise - It's awesome." They laughed into each other's eyes then JJ said, "I feel the same way, Trish, I feel like the long awaited gift of you, has fallen into my arms. I just don't want us to get mixed up by our feelings about John, and the bounce he has brought back to our lives. I feel new Trish. I feel ready, and I want, us, to wait."

Pulling her to him again, he said, "This, what we have right now, feels like we are moving toward a celebration, like there ought to be fireworks, you know? That sounds corny coming from me... I want you, and I want to wait for you. I want to wait for a special time for just us, to be together. That's what I'm trying to say. We have so much going on, I don't want something with so much potential to, not, be celebrated on its own."

Trish again pulled away from JJ, but this time it was to take his face in both her hands. And on his lips she placed the lightest kiss, packed full of promise. "I feel the same. Let's wait until after the Month's Mind for our own celebration." Knowing the day was getting away from them, without another word they soundlessly pulled apart, dressed, folded up the blanket and made their way to the car. This time JJ took the wheel, got the car turned around and off they drove into Kamloops to hold hands in public for the first time, and to shop.

On the way back later that day, Trish suggested they stop in at the hotel for dinner. JJ, hesitated because he had already left John alone far too often, and he didn't want to keep making that mistake. "No worries JJ, I called Todd when you were turning the car around and he said he planned to stop by to see John, anyway. He'll let John know we will be later than we thought and said he would take John into town to have dinner with his folks." JJ, who had been driving since they left the lake, went into an instant sulk. He didn't get why Trish would trust Todd at all. But she seemed to. As if reading his mind Trish reached her hand out to stroke his cheek and said, "Now don't spoil our nice day out JJ. Todd isn't so bad. OK?

"What is that prayer you used to spout, the AA prayer or the Serenity prayer? How does that go again?" Grudgingly, JJ recited the part she meant, though the whole prayer was much longer and he couldn't remember it. "God grant me the serenity to accept the things I cannot change, courage to change the things I can - and the wisdom to know the difference." Sinking back into the passenger seat Trish heaved a sigh, just as if her breath had been held tight and indeed it had. As she saw it, things would either go easily one way, which was her way that is, or not at all.

She said, "There. Now apply that to the past. Any one of us can only move on from this spot we are at, from this moment. There are no do overs in life we can't change a darn thing about the past, JJ. I hate the expression but - it is what it is. The first time I heard that prayer was when you said it to me, on the one year anniversary of Seth's death. Do you remember? It didn't help me that day but it sure made me angry. Since then though I've reflected on it many times, and it's helped me. It might help you too. When you think of Todd that is..." Reaching for his hand she brought it up to her lips and a feeling of peaceful contentment filled JJ's heart.

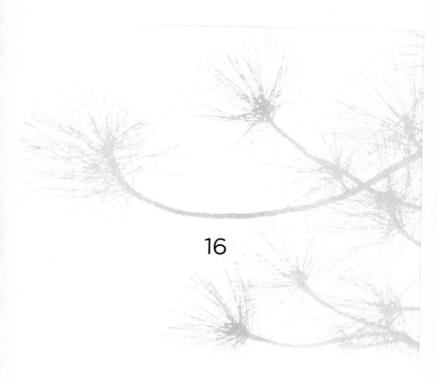

16

Still not being too happy with Todd the next morning, JJ decided to drive into town and have a talk with him. Watching JJ get the car out of the barn, take a chamois to it, then head up the driveway got John very curious. But not in time to find out where JJ was off to. As John made a move to go find out what was going on, JJ drove away. Instead of calling ahead, JJ drove directly to the home of Sharon's Shuttle which was also Todd's family home.

He knew Todd would be still sleeping and his parents would be gone for the day, so he knocked as loud as he could. Pretty soon it became evident no one would answer. When he turned away going back to his car, a kid hanging his head out the window of the house next door asked, "Who are you looking for? Todd?" JJ nodded yes and the kid told him Todd was at the animal shelter working. Baffled JJ headed that way, wondering as he drove, if Todd had gotten into some kind of trouble and was doing community service.

There was only one person at the shelter office this early, and it was a veterinarian JJ knew. "Hi Terrell, what are you doing here so early?" The vet looked up from his paper work, offering a weak smile, "Well JJ! We haven't seen you around for a long time. How's Frida?" Before he could answer, Terrell told JJ he was acting as an emergency vet for the shelter and got a call about two hours ago when one of the volunteers came in. "But JJ, I've got another emergency call I'm heading too. So...Is there something I can help you with before I go, tell me quick?"

"Oh yeah, I'm looking for a guy named Todd, I was told he works here?" The vet really smiled for the first time saying JJ would find Todd down the hall, first door on the left, saying, "Just call out, you'll find him." JJ found Todd alright; he was holding a tiny new born kitten in one hand, and a baby bottle in the other. JJ was already surprised Todd worked here; he thought he had a job in Alberta. Whispering Todd asked JJ what he was doing there, and was everything OK with John.

"Oh ya, everything is OK with John, but not with me Todd!" Todd lifted the bottle and putting a finger up to his mouth motioned for JJ to keep his voice down, saying loud noises would scare the kitten. In whispered annoyed tones, JJ told Todd he'd finally found out what kind of a liar Todd had been all these years. Instantly Todd looked hurt and somewhat comical, as he stood holding a baby bottle for a kitten that must have only been a couple of hours old. This wasn't the picture JJ had of Todd at all. It was just after seven in the morning and the guy JJ thought of as someone who worked in northern Alberta, came home pulling a few all nighters, just didn't fit with the guy with the bottle. Softening somewhat, JJ couldn't muster the anger he felt ever since he found out Todd was keeping the great big secret of Shelley's whereabouts.

In a soft very quiet voice Todd asked JJ to wait outside in the parking lot while he finished up in here, "This sounds like a conversation that might take awhile, and I don't want bad vibes to upset the place." Calming down, JJ offered to help, just to hurry Todd along. As they worked side by side, cleaning out kitty litter boxes and putting fresh food and water in all the cages, Todd told JJ why he was here.

"You know what it's like in those camps right? I work sometimes sixteen hour days, which I like for the money for sure. Then I come home for either four or nine days depending..... When I'd get here JJ, I needed something to do, so I came in here to see if they could use my help with anything for a few days each month. I love animals man...most times more than I like people...

"I've done painting, plumbing, and electrical, swept and washed floors, and walked dogs. And today I've put in time feeding that kitten. I do everything I can for them when I'm here. You should come volunteer too JJ, they could use a guy like you with the horses they get in once in a while." JJ wasn't sure about that, but one thing he felt very sure of was, he had Todd all wrong. And he was pretty sure most people did.

When all the work Todd had on his list for that day was done, the two left the building, got in their separate cars and by agreement stopped at the closest coffee and donuts place and each man, got both to go. They agreed to meet for a private talk out by the hotel, almost right at the spot JJ's sister, Margaret and her husband had gone off the road into the lake.

JJ got there first, parking in a pull out he sat behind the wheel for a few minutes deep in thought. By the time Todd got there JJ was filled with resolve. He didn't want all the events of the past to keep him from having a happy future. John's words resonated in his head...there is no blame. And Trish's reminder yesterday of the serenity prayer helped JJ make a decision that he'd go easy on Todd, as simple as that; there is no blame.

For the next hour or so Todd filled in many gaps, including a very few words about who John's father was. In Todd's opinion, he was a poorly chosen womanizer Shelley had it bad for. In the end it was what turned out to be a one or two or three night stand, at most, "She never mentioned his name once it was obvious he wouldn't be giving her a call...and I know for sure she never saw him again. I don't even know if his names on the birth certificate or not." JJ asked him not to mention any of this to John, about his father that is, not now at least.

Just three days before the Month's Mind and almost everything was in place. Todd had gotten the music ready and felt a lot better, having had a good talking to by a less than happy JJ. It turned out that once they got the conversation out of the way, Todd and JJ got on well and worked well together. During the last day or two they had bonded over more stories about John growing up and revelations about Shelley.

While Todd and JJ were taking a break on the bench outside the barn, Andrea and Heather arrived in a trail of dust the tires kicked up. They were driving a rental, compliments of zillions of air miles Andrea said she had and had never used, but decided to use them for this trip. When the door opened, out bounded a small black and tan dog with short legs and a short furiously wagging tail. "What the heck is that?" A startled JJ asked. He had a vision of a little fluffy lap dog, not this wired with energy hound.

Todd told him, somewhat proudly, she was an Australian terrier named Cozy. Around and around, and around she ran, sniffing the ground and squatting, with leg lifted as if she were marking her territory here and there just like a male dog would do. Every once in a while, it looked like she picked up a familiar scent then the circling would start all over again, and she'd make a crying noise. She saw and happily recognized Todd, barking and squealing at the sight of him. Stopping her antics long enough to pick up another scent she seemed to know, off she raced into the barn where she circled a couple more times then stopped outside the bathroom door. Standing still, her head cocked for a moment, before she started scratching vigorously with all her might at the door.

When the door opened and John stepped out both boy and dog demonstrated pure unadulterated love for one and other. John fell to his knees while Cozy's little short legs propelled her up and down jumping, circling and crying and barking.

The reunion was broken up when a voice from the barn door said, "Hey John, what about me! Aren't you happy to see me too?" Looking up John saw Andrea smiling behind mischievous looking Heather, who was decked out in jeans, a plaid shirt and a cow boy hat. He stood up and bounded over to both women encircling them in such a warm and tight hug that Heather's hat popped right off her head. And before anyone could grab it, the sly little black and tan dog got a hold of it and made a mad dash, holding it aloft, while she ran circles around and around the barn. Laughing at the dog, Heather looked up at John and said, "John grew mum."

Andrea just nodded and smiled wordlessly, a signal John knew meant that she was close to tears. And so was he.

Once everything settled down and introductions were properly made, Andrea told them she and Heather were staying at Trish's place, "...as per your mother's instructions." Turning to JJ she said, "Margaret just wants us to try out the guest room she stayed in so many times when she was a kid." Momentarily confused, with a glimmer of recognition a baffled JJ thought to ask, "Why did Shelley change her name to Margaret?"

Andrea didn't know the full story so stuck with what she had been told. "Shelley told me Margaret was her real mother's name. She said your mum, Jean... Her Mum-ma Jean, right, mostly raised her after that accident. Calling herself Margaret was her gift to your mum. She said Jean never really liked the name Shelley!" Turning to John, Andrea asked if he would be so kind as to get in the car and show them the way to Trish's place. "And JJ, Trish will want you there for dinner tonight. Dress up. And you Todd, are invited to come too if you'd like?"

"Hey Andrea thanks a bunch man! I've got some plans happening. But tell ya what, if I'm free early I'll check by phone before I come out to see ya. I've gotta get going now anyway, so we'll hang with all of you later eh? And hey Heather! Nice to see you girl you're looking good in your country gear! See you soon eh? And see you too, Andrea." Lifting his fist for a bump, said to John, "Later little dude." Giving JJ a wink, he folded his tall frame into the driver's seat of his tiny car and slowly pulled away.

As Heather waved goodbye laughing, she shouted out at a retreating Todd, "Good to see you too my man." Turning to the remaining group she began to share accolades both John and Andrea had heard many times about what a great guy Todd was. JJ had seen Todd around since he was a kid and it was only today, he realized why he'd barely said so much as hello since Shelley had gone.

Todd always gave JJ a wide berth whenever they met. He'd say a quick hello and step on by. Rarely looking him in the eye, and barely if ever, speaking more than a few words; Todd would always be hustling off, or out of the room, if JJ turned up. Well I guess that is what you need to do, when you have a secret thought JJ; some of his questions had been answered today.

JJ told the others to go ahead, and he'd just clean up. He said to John, "You ought to have a shower too. Hey. Andrea and Heather why don't you two come up to the house, while John takes a quick shower. Let me at least give you a cold drink or something before you head off to see Trish. How would that be?"

John got the message and went up to the house to take a shower in the little bathroom off his mum's bedroom. Cozy ran along beside him watching his every step all the way there, but once inside the house, she did not follow him up the stairs. From below, he heard the commotion of Cozy meeting the cat, Bennett. Then dead silence. John went back out to the mezzanine, leaned over the railing to get a look at what was going on. The cat was sitting on a chair totally engaged in grooming himself, while a seemingly disinterested and unconcerned Cozy sat bolt upright with her head turned away from Bennett. No doubt suspecting correctly, it was wise to avoid eye contact if she wanted to stay out of trouble. Watching them from his perch, John had no doubt they'd be friends by the time he was out of the shower. The white shirt and jeans he had worn to dinner were still clean so he wore them again, along with Seth's vest over top and the bolo tie.

Just for fun he got the fringed leather jacket out, he would put that on too. It was a little big but he'd grow into it someday. Today was a bit hot for leather but instinct was telling him to put it on, if only for a little while. When he was in this bedroom he felt a special closeness to his mum, he had never felt in the week after her death. It was as if she were truly with him, by his side just like she said she would be. Almost dressed he sat down on the edge of the bed to think before heading down to join the others.

When he was in the barn today, he finally got to the desk drawers in the office. The drawers were packed with all kinds of things, notes, pens full of dried up ink, coloured pencils, dried out erasers and all the office supplies an office should have. He also found a bundle of letters and notes held together with an elastic band that had lost its stretch, so that when he went to remove it, the rubber just fell away in his hand. Everything was then sealed up tight in a plastic bag. Through the plastic John saw the letter on top was from Seth. Sorting through them once he had torn the plastic off, all the others under it were returned letters his mum, Shelley, had written to Seth.

Should he share the contents with JJ and Trish? He didn't know for sure, but what he did know, was he was closer than ever to knowing why his mum left. It looked like his mum loved someone else, before she loved him. And that someone was Seth, she really loved Seth.

When John began to read a letter Seth wrote to Shelly he could see the love was returned in a brotherly way, but also wondered if his mum read another meaning into it. John couldn't help comparing them to Romeo and Juliet; especially since in the end they were both dead. The things to do after the Month's Mind were stacking up and now this bundle of letters. Folding up the unfinished letter John decides to share all the letters with JJ and Trish, after the Month's Mind. He has a feeling that when his mother left home, it might have had more to do with a broken heart than with JJ and his drinking. Or whatever JJ had hinted, Trish had done.

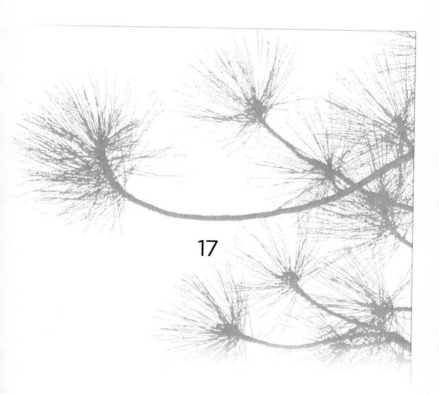

17

When John came down the stairs with the jacket over his arm, Heather was quick to tease, "Oolala, hub bah, hub bah. Look at John. You're a real cow boy now John. Where's your hat, oh and where's your horse?" With that comment John strode over to Heather, placing a hand on one shoulder turned her around so she was facing the window. "See those horses... that dappled grey one? That's mine, mine to ride anyway. Tomorrow JJ will take you out for a ride too; he'll take you ... Home on the range. And I'll let you take my horse." JJ didn't look too sure about that but just smiled all the same. Heather was quick to add, "No worries JJ, I'm a master horse woman."

John laughed out loud and added for JJ's benefit, "Heather has been riding horses for years. She started at a therapeutic riding place and now shares a horse with two other girls at a stable, a few bus rides from home." Heather was quick to pipe in, "I take the bus there by myself."

After the three had left for Trish's place JJ had a quick shower too. On impulse on his way to see Trish and the rest of them, he stopped to pick some roses gone wild, by the side of the house. He took them over to the hose and gave them a wash in case of ear wigs, then wrapped the stems in damp newspaper. He decided to walk over and for the first time in years felt really happy, almost giddy.

It wasn't just the requited love he felt for Trish or the letter to him from Shelley that John had found in the closet. It was John being here. He felt a bond with John and knew no matter what happened John was here, in JJ's life to stay. He felt the promise of new beginnings with Trish too and could feel her relax, every time John was around. Her grief had knotted her so tightly for so long; the lightness of heart she had been showing the outside world he now realized was a facade. But in the weeks that John had been here there was a new lightness to both their steps and a thawing of both their hearts.

JJ always felt an attraction to Trish, she was the first girl he ever had feelings for, though she was too young for him to act on them at the time. And the first girl who, unknown to her broke his heart when still too young she fell for, and got pregnant by, a guy the same age as JJ. The attraction he now felt was coming directly from Trish.

The way she looked at him, touched his arm, leaned into him smiling; laughing at his jokes. And he sensed her trying to care for and protect him. He felt loved for the first time in ages. Loved by Trish but also he felt loved by John, and forgiven by Shelley. The flowers he had picked were a celebration of all three of those people and how much he cared for each of them.

Andrea drove, while John directed her to go a route he had only taken once with JJ. Up and out their own driveway, turning left at the main road, around a bend and past two more driveways before turning left again down Trish's driveway. This was only the third time John had come to Trish's place by a route other than the pathway. The first day on foot, he advanced on Trish's place from further along the road and a bit higher up and the second time was in JJ's car. Now here he was again arriving to her house, in what he felt was a new direction, and with two totally different people.

Death changes everyone he supposed but Andrea seemed more fragile, and Heather seemed more grown up and matured. When they got there John said it would have been quicker to walk along his much loved pathway. Andrea rejoined with, "I know Hun but we have the suitcases too John and the car, what about the car? Trish says JJ doesn't keep cars out in the open at his place." This last comment made John laugh out loud. "The only reason JJ doesn't have a car for all to see Andrea, is he keeps it protected in the barn. Other cars would be OK I'm sure, though I haven't really seen any yet except for Todd's; not from the house or barn at least.

"Anyone who comes over probably parks behind the barn. But you're right; the cars are all out of sight. What's that called - an idiosyncrasy? JJ's unique!" That said as they made their way down a well kept driveway to Trish's house with a promise from John to show them the pathway very soon.

When they got out of the car, John sent the two ladies up to the house to be greeted by a waiting Trish while he got their luggage. Calling from the drive, John made introductions. He watched as all three women were already embracing up on the porch. He imagined by some of the things Trish had said over the last couple of days, that she and Andrea had formed a friendship, via the telephone and email over the past couple of weeks.

Standing down here he couldn't make out exactly what they were saying but got the gist of the warmth and camaraderie the three felt together on the porch. Linking arms Trish propelled them both into the cool of the house. Opening the back of the SUV he was surprised by the number of suitcases and other boxes they had brought. Out of a box on top of all the others he saw the origami softly laid so as not to get crushed or tangled. One by one John carried all and sunder into the house, then back out to the car to put on his new jacket before joining - the ladies as he now thought of the trio he had seen together on the porch. He could hear their voices and laughter in the back of the house, and went that way.

Pushing the door to a bedroom all the way open he stepped in, just as Trish turned to the sound of his footsteps. The effect of seeing John in the fringed leather jacket made both Trish's hands fly to her mouth. She burst into tears and then laughed and cried at the same time. John had no clue what he had just walked in on and was about to leave, when Trish leaned her head against him soaking his shoulder. Tears mixed with anguish and also a softness John translated as love he held her and wordlessly waited while it all came out.

Finally Trish pulled away smiling into John's eyes, she put a hand on either side of his face and in a quivering voice said, "That's Seth's jacket. When his dad left us he forgot his jacket. It was the only thing left behind and as soon as Seth could, he wore that jacket. All! The! Time! I didn't know it was still here....Seeing you come in just then, well you shocked me. I was expecting you and then all I saw was the jacket and I thought it was Seth walking through the door."

Turning to include everyone, Trish apologized for the outburst saying it's not unusual for her to just break down, "Especially now with Shelley gone too and no chance to ever see her again." With that said Trish got quiet while she tried to subdue her feelings.

Andrea placed an arm around Trish's shoulder and Heather took her hand. "I know how you feel Trish," said Heather, "when my dad died my mum was so sad and she still is." John, who had rarely given thought to Andrea's life before he came into it, was taken aback by this news. The story he overheard was that Heather's dad left right after Heather was born and two weeks later, before Heather was even a month old, he killed himself. But now, he guessed, how a person had died never changed the outcome, for both the living and the dead. The dead were gone from sight and those still living were left with their memories and with their grief.

JJ took the path and felt like a suitor coming to call. He remembered dreaming about calling on Trish; but then deciding to do the right thing and wait till she was old enough. And then along came Seth's dad, and he didn't have a chance. The funny thing was though; Trish thought he would be the ticket to get as far away from here as she could. But the guy liked it here, or so he said and they weren't going anywhere. Well not together at least! His loss... thought JJ at the time. And now he knew it was his gain.

Even though JJ and Trish had agreed to keep things private and under wraps, between the two of them, Trish couldn't resist giving JJ a lingering hug when she saw him on the porch.

Taking the flowers he offered and briefly holding his hand in a squeeze, she guided him into the house. JJ could tell Trish had been crying. She seemed happy now, but he did wonder what it had been about.

John stepped into the room in the fringed jacket, and he knew. It was the jacket. JJ was well aware of the significance of that jacket and remembered Seth, sporting it around in all kinds of weather. The long forgotten memory of a night surfaced, of himself drunk and behind the wheel of his beloved car.

He was on his way home from a house party. JJ knew he shouldn't be driving as drunk as he was, so was taking it very slow. Up ahead, on the shoulder of the road, he saw a figure walking fast with his back to the car. He knew it was Seth, because he saw the silhouette of the jackets fringe, swaying in the night. When JJ pulled over to offer a lift, it was as if Seth thought JJ was out looking for him. JJ said, "Hell no. I saw the fringe of that stupid jacket you have on, and knew it was you. Can't you just be grateful for the ride, why is it you're always so suspicious of everything I do?"

JJ was drunk and Seth knew it as soon as JJ started to talk. This night was the last night JJ saw Seth or talked to Seth. It was the night Seth told JJ off and left his jacket in the car. Seth leaned in car the window to say, "You're the one who's suspicious JJ." Tearing off his jacket in a fury, he threw it into the back seat of the car. "Give Shelley the jacket, it can remind her of a potential she would never be allowed to know." When JJ tried to make Seth take it, Seth turned his back and walked away but not before JJ heard him shout, "Give it to Shelley, you stupid old man."

JJ didn't remember giving it to Shelley, at all. But supposed he must have done and now here was John with the same fringe hanging from his arms. The look on his face held a mixture of self consciousness and pride standing there in the jacket among people he loved, and who loved him. And Trish, she looked as if she had seen a ghost.

Andrea broke the spell when she said she had brought a favourite main dish from the coast. "It is vegan mac and cheese John. Trish tells us you've been making salads from the garden?" Here Heather piped up and said, "You should tell her who you learned how to peel carrots from John... it was me. Wasn't it John? He stood next to me on a stool, when he was just a little, little boy and we peeled carrots together." Not Heather, and certainly not John or Andrea mentioned boiling water, peeling vegetables and setting the table was where Heather drew the line when it came to culinary skills. She frequently could be heard saying things like - I'm just not into cooking... or it's not my bag. Today she asked if she could set the table for them all including a place for Todd, if he decided to come.

Todd however never made it in time for dinner, catching up with them for smore's though at the camp fire. Todd brought his guitar too. Noticing the guitar Trish felt a familiar swelling of emotion, on a sea of memories. Seth and his friends, male and sometimes female too, all sitting around the camp fire singing, or in her kitchen, playing cards or crib at the table, usually surrounded by lots of food. Todd always had his guitar close at hand and would sit on the edge of the easy chair in the living room, one knee bent and close to his body where he rested his instrument with ease. And one long leg stretched out, his head hanging low to be mesmerized by the movement of his fingers, as he strummed.

The boys, she had been pretty sure at the time, drank the occasional beer never getting drunk, so she didn't mind too much. It was better they stayed here, she thought, than go out somewhere else to have fun. It was during this period in Seth's life of growing independence, when Trish had gotten the first small chesterfield to go in her bedroom. She wanted Seth to have space and freedom to do and say whatever he wanted without worry of her sensor. They got on well, she and Seth. She had a lifetime of memories and during the past two weeks many more had begun to resurface.

Bringing the guitar up onto his lap, Todd struck the old pose of years ago and began to softly play. Cozy, who had been snuggled in a heap across Heather's knee, became ultra alert. Sitting up to listen to the tune, she surprised Trish and JJ when she threw her head back and howled three long baleful howls before circling round again to find comfort in the warmth of Heather's lap. John reached out a hand to place on Cozy's back and he heard Heather say to the dog, just what he had been thinking. "The guitar reminds you of your mummy, doesn't it, Cozy? I know you really miss her…"

The next morning they all reconvened for breakfast over at JJ's house. JJ made pancakes for everyone and as a nod to the vegetarians he gave up his usual bacon. When the cat came slinking into the house, JJ was pretty sure, Bennett would miss the bacon too. And who knows, Cozy might have wanted some bacon as well. While thoughts of bacon swirled around in JJ's head, Todd turned up and the first words out of his mouth were, "What? No bacon. I thought we were having breakfast man."

Andrea had just come into the house from the porch to overhear their conversation and said, "JJ, Heather and I aren't vegetarian, if that's what you were thinking. John and his mum were… well maybe not John so much. Margaret… I mean Shelley was the real vegetarian. Even before she got cancer she gave up meat saying, she had grown up eating way too much meat and didn't intend to make it a lifelong habit. But me? I eat meat, especially bacon. Want me to make it?"

And so the morning went, everyone getting to know each other and getting used to each other. Andrea had arrived full of judgment for any family who could just so easily let someone so precious to them, as they made out, just slip away. She never understood why there was no contact and it wasn't something that was talked about except for the one time, when John was a baby.

But now that she and Heather were here, she appreciated the opportunity to get to know them. Listening to JJ explain things in an encyclopedic way from time to time, reminded her of John's mum. Now she knew where she got it from. There had been so much of JJ in Shelley they were so similar in such strange ways; even how JJ flipped the pancakes, right out of the pan, with a brief toss in the air – totally her all over.

Andrea's thoughts were interrupted when Heather asked JJ, what time they were going for their ride and should he make a lunch too. Andrea could see JJ's momentary discomfort but really admired him when he said, "Hey if you want to spend the day with an old man, I'll make sure you see all Shelley's favourite places. But I gotta warn you, I've got to get back here to help out with the Month's Mind preparations, and you do too. I've got a job all lined up for you in the barn, when we get back. Heather looked shocked as she was rarely put to work even though she was certainly capable of work. "What job? Or should I ask." Heather looked pleadingly at her mother, who just smiled and shrugged her shoulder. Trish had been in the utility room getting some fresh napkins. Handing them to Heather, to put on the table she went to the stove, standing next to JJ.

Placing her hand along his spine, she leaned her head ever so briefly onto his shoulder asking, "How long will it be?" Turning and leaning his head back so he could see her, JJ smiled and said, "Two minutes. Get everyone to the table." Heather was the only one who noticed the exchange and said, "Hey you love birds, knock it off, so we can eat." Trish went red but seemed to recover herself and no one else seemed to take any notice of what Heather had said. JJ, still with his back to the kitchen full of hungry people smiled inwardly as his chest expanded with sheer joy.

After breakfast Heather was quick to get ready for their ride, asking if JJ had a helmet she could use or if John should fetch one she saw hanging at Trish's place. "Yup Heather, I do have some helmets in the barn, and probably one that will fit. Do you want to try them out first? John, can you show Heather where the helmets are, and could you do me a favour, bring the horses over to the barn and start to get them saddled." Casting a glance at Trish, who was rising from her seat at the table and had her mouth opening, about to interrupt, he added, "Not in the barn though, just outside the doors…the barns too clean for horses today. Oh and could one of you fine ladies whip us up a bit of sustenance while I get my boots?

"Just water and some fruit ought to do it. We'll be home in time for lunch." From the porch seat where he sat to pull his boots on, JJ watched John walking with Heather to the barn. Heather apparently unused to the uneven surfaces held onto John's outstretched arm. They had done this kind of thing before. John had grown up learning to offer his arm to someone less firm. JJ sat still watching and saw the symbiosis in their relationship as Heather with ease snapped the lead onto John's horse and then onto Frida. Taking Frida's lead in her right hand she took John's right arm with her left and they carried on to the barn, each with a horse in tow.

Heather was, just as John had said - a real horse woman. So confident in her actions and John was too, as he handed Heather his lead and went into the barn. JJ stood up ready to shout out to Heather, that he would be right there to help. Lowering himself to sit again, he stopped himself. Watching as she tethered first one horse then the other to the corral railing, and went in search of John. He was still sitting watching the barn doors for activity, when he felt Trish sit down to share his seat.

"Andrea and Todd have started to clean up. Here's your snack." She placed a pack on his lap, and laid her hand on his thigh. JJ tucked his arm in behind and under hers circling back and over to rest his hand on top of her hand. The bench they shared had a lever on the side that turned it into a rocker. With his free hand JJ reached down and with a bit of effort released the lever, and they began to rock. To Trish he said, "There's been lots of times, I've wondered what it would feel like to have a special someone to rock back and forth with, when I got old." Trish threw her head back snorting out a laugh then punched him in the shoulder, "You're not old." Before he could reply, she hopped up and was gone into the house to help Andrea and Todd clean up their breakfast things so the rest of the Month's Mind, preparation in the barn could get going.

JJ got to the barn in time to turn a careful eye to how Heather managed her horse woman duties. He could see Heather's look of hurried panic as he approached so he held his arms wide and said, "I'm just here to watch." Pretty soon though Heather heaved a frustrated sigh and said to anyone who cared, "I can do a lot of things. But I can't lift the saddle myself." JJ and John both stepped in at the same time to help and Heather motioned John away saying, "Three's a crowd John. Do your own horse."

JJ wasn't sure if Heather knew it or not, but nobody except him rode Frida. By the time they got the horses saddled and ready, Heather was well aware she wouldn't be riding Frida. When she asked John for a box to stand on so she could get up, JJ laced his fingers together and told her he would give her a boost. "No thanks, JJ. I need a box."

Unlacing his hands and standing tall JJ said, "But Heather, we can't take a box with us so let me show you this way. If you get off your horse out there, you won't have a box. Come on, just step that pretty little foot of yours into my hands and I'll boost you up." Heather ended up wanting to do it twice for practice, before they headed off.

This was JJ's first experience with someone with a disability. Oh sure, he ran into people who had all kinds of disabilities all the time and interacted with them in various limited ways. But had never been alone with and responsible for anyone this fragile before. JJ glanced up at the house and could see the outline of someone in the kitchen window, watching the proceedings. Suspecting it was Andrea, JJ wondered why she or how she could trust him like this. A little voice popped into his head suddenly. It was Shelley's voice saying to him more than once while she was in her teens - You can't protect me from everything, JJ. Let me take a risk let me have a chance to fail. Haven't you ever heard of the dignity of risk JJ?

Taking a second look at the window he knew that is what Andrea was doing, maybe something she had learned how to do from Heather, through necessity. She was giving them both, JJ and Heather, the dignity of risk. So what if they failed. If life was lived for fear of failure, who would really live? With that thought JJ turned to Heather and asked, "Ready?' And off they went, slowly at first and then at a faster trot, so the horses could blow off a bit of steam.

They got lucky, about ten minutes out, when over a rise JJ saw the head of a moose up ahead. Thinking it might be the same mother and calf he and John saw on their way to the swimming hole, he stopped Heather and pointed. Sure enough, mother and calf came through the long grass. JJ held a finger to his lips, for silence as they watched. To his surprise, Heather slowly drew a small phone out of her shirt pocket and with great skill, zoomed in for a better shot of the two subjects. Carefully pressing the button a few times. Grinning and in awe, she turned to JJ and whispered, "My first wild life." After that all they saw were birds and a swarm of crickets exploding out of the grass just ahead of their horses footsteps. Heather and JJ went as far as the lake, just to have a look at the sign made out of rocks. When Heather read it out loud, she began to sing in a quivery, high pitched voice that held such a sweetness to it JJ had never known. He was touched.

Next, they rode to the stand of trees with all the various initials and expressions of love carved into the trunks. At her request, JJ helped her down from the saddle. They tied their horses in the shade, and Heather asked if her initials could be carved in a tree too. Pulling out his pocket knife, JJ asked, "What do you want carved." Heather surprised him again when she said, "Heather and Todd, BFF." Pausing while he got ready to carve, JJ looked at Heather and said, "OK. But why BFF, what does that mean anyway?" Heather's eyes twinkled behind her glasses as she had a laugh, at his naivety. "Oh JJ; It means, best friends forever. BFF, do you get it now?" JJ realized, not for the first time how out of the loop he was. Boy, did he have a lot to learn. He had actually heard the acronym many times, but never knew what it meant and truthfully, never cared enough to ask, until now.

In the shade of the trees, JJ and Heather sat on a couple of old stumps, talked and had a piece of fruit and a drink. Heather told him all about John when he was a baby and about Shelley helping her learn how to be independent. Oh, and how to be prettier. "John's mum told me, how to make the most of my looks and how to talk to people. She talked my mum into letting me learn to catch the bus on my own and tried to get mum to let me learn to cook too. But you know what JJ? Cooking isn't for me. I don't want to be a slave to the stove." This last bit made JJ laugh and he said, "I hear you Heather, I don't either. But when you're a bachelor you have to cook for yourself every day."

It was when JJ laced his fingers together to give Heather another boost up into the saddle, that she told him he wouldn't be a bachelor for long. Said with such a knowing smile, JJ was sure she had seen something significant between him and Trish. He didn't encourage her line of thinking though, instead he told her, "Once a bachelor always a bachelor." On the way back, JJ took Heather to a place John hadn't been yet. It was the patch of land where John's grandmother would have built her house. It had the best view around and was just a short way from his place. For a fleeting moment he imagined John building a house of his own here someday.

When they got back from their ride everyone was busy in the barn. JJ sent Heather inside to have a look see, promising to look after her horse. Once he got the saddles off them he gave them each a hose down, washing off the sweat and dust of the day. Cozy came out to look with interest up at the giant horses. He led them back to the pasture to turn them loose and watched as they trotted side by side over to the water trough. Cozy scooted under the fence to make chase or run alongside, JJ couldn't decide which. Once they stopped at the trough the little dog jumped up on the edge and teetered there for a second before falling right in. Surprised Frida, threw her head back and began to neigh and pad the ground with her foot. Cozy had no trouble getting back out of the trough, in one jump.

All wet though, she immediately rolled in the dust to get dry. "Oh man...you'll need a bath before you go in the house again. Cozy come." JJ patted his leg and called. With perfect timing just as the little dog shot out from under the railing, JJ was ready and scooped her up. Holding her squiring body away from his own, he took her over to the hose and gave her a rinse. Carrying her into the barn where he shut the big doors; there'd be no escaping, back out to roll in the dust.

With the doors shut, the barn was in darkness with shafts of slivered light piercing through here and there between gaps in the weathered wood. Dust motes swirled in a lazy dance above their heads. Trish hit a switch and the white party lights came on and the disco ball began a slow rotation. The white, silver and gold streamers were hung in the stalls and over the food table giving the whole scene more of a celebratory wedding look, than a funeral. This was just how Shelley would want things, there was no doubt.

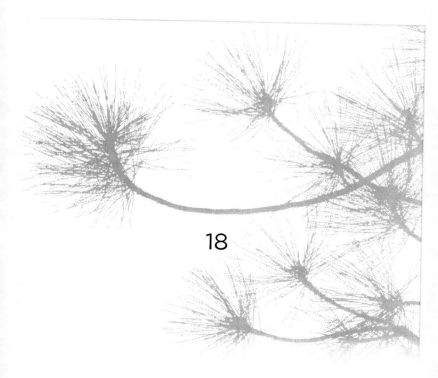

18

From behind the soft movement of origami hanging in the office doorway, John watched this tableau unfold. Trish in another of her flowing hemlines seemed to move with great fluidity in the dancing light. John caught the way JJ looked at her. While she sashayed around he felt sure that his mothers hope of them finding solace in each other, was coming to fruition. Watching as the five adults moved about placing chairs and tables, with a curious dog getting under foot, John moved out from his watching spot to join them.

Having Andrea and Heather around again, left John feeling a bit awkward at first. When he left them three weeks ago, he left as a boy wearing the hat of adolescent angst. He was filled with grief at the loss of his mother, and discomfort and apprehension regarding meeting his mother's estranged family. And

237

fear of what may lay ahead for him. So much had changed in three weeks. He had changed, in three weeks. John knew he was a different person. Daily, he was conscious of a shift taking place; he felt himself becoming comfortable with his new responsibility, with his decisions. He felt older, more mature. Both Andrea and Heather commented on it. Heather kept saying he was bigger and he had grown.

Putting into words, that gave a sense of what she might mean, Heather said, "You look taller John. I know you're, bigger... but you are standing in a different way, now. Did JJ tell you not to slouch? Maybe you're standing up straight now. You look like a man, and you sound like a man and you act just like a man. Mum says everyone, has to grown up."

This, he knew was in part, due to how JJ and Trish responded to him. They had no expectations of how he would behave, good or bad. - JJ and Trish treated him like he knew what he was doing. They looked to him, for decisions regarding the Month's Mind. His mother had left him in charge, because she trusted in him and his ability to take care of her party... Part of this new maturity allowed him to feel safe and comfortable with who he was becoming and with everyone around him. But perhaps most important, he didn't feel as self centered. He was more aware of others and their feelings. If he thought about it, he'd know how proud his mum would be.

On the day of the Month's Mind everything was ready. Trish, Heather and Andrea geared up for the possibility of some disco dancing later in the day as they watched the disco ball spin. As for the food, in the end Trish had taken the easy way out cancelling the potluck and calling upon the expertise of a caterer, asking John what kind of food his mum liked best. All vegetarian - was his answer so vegetarian it was. Andrea was relieved too, because no cooking meant a holiday for her as well. She had offered to help Trish out with the food. Andrea was always happy in the kitchen but right now she was having a different kind of pleasure.

The pleasure of being away from routine, the pleasure of seeing John look so well adjusted and actually happy and the pleasure of getting to know his mum's family. Trish had hung the bathroom walls with some extra photos of Shelley with John at various ages and stages and a couple of Shelley with Cozy, left over from photos Todd had brought over at the last minute.

The photos Todd brought were great; they spanned years; before John was born, they were candid shots, posed shots and blurry shots taken in summers, around Christmas, at an art show. Even one Trish had never seen featuring Shelley sitting on Seth's lap. Shelley was looking at the camera and Seth was looking at Shelley. When she saw the picture, Trish got a shock as the first thought that went through her mind was they were both looking so happy, relaxed and meant for each other. A wave of new guilt washed over Trish and she had to take a moment to get it together again.

When Trish expressed amazement by the volume of photos Todd had taken he confided to Trish that if Shelley hadn't had such a crush on Seth he would have made a move on her before it was too late. He also told her he had given Shelley, her dog Cozy about four summers ago when he was down there visiting. "Every boy should have a dog; right?" Todd just kept surprising her. She had a similar experience to JJ's with Todd.

For the past fifteen years or so whenever he saw her coming he'd head the other way. She thought he was uncomfortable talking about Seth because he and Seth had been such good friends. In fact she always felt she had lost Todd and some of the other boys too when they all stopped coming by completely. For years after Seth's death she longed to see Seth's friends and very few ever came around.

This week had been good for her to see Todd again; sitting down together to work on the music and to share a couple of meals felt so comforting after all this time. Having him sit at her table, felt natural. She could see he was happier and more light hearted too since he came clean about his special knowledge of where Shelley had been all these years and wondered at the damage a kept secret can cause.

By four o'clock the guests started to arrive. Parking in a field out behind the barn they came in carrying more food, beverages, photos or bringing with them stories to place in the leather journal. The stories spanned Shelley's whole life and after everyone was gone Trish thought she would put them in chronological order for John to read at some later date. John made his speech, just as he said he would, he took time to remind everyone this was a happy time, a time to remember his mum and be glad they ever knew her. Not a celebration of her life, because his mum told him she had already had a celebration of her life; on his birthday a couple of months ago. This party was a tribute to her and who she had been to each person there.

"She always called my birthday," and here John paused for a long time looking out into the faces while taking in the deep breaths he knew would stall the tears that were so close. The tears his mother had asked over and over no one shed. Finally settling his eyes on the comfort of Trish's face he said, "The day I was born, she called her own birthing day. Each year my birthday was celebrated, she celebrated what she called her birthing day, too. On my last birthday she made a speech, some of you were there to hear it… She made a speech saying the day I was born, she was reborn and it was the day her life really began in earnest. I had heard it all before and can't say I understand the love a mother has for her son. But it was also the day my life began… I silently said while my mum was making her speech that day.

"My mum gave me the best kind of life. It was full of diversity in the people we met, the things that occupied our time," holding up a finger John emphasized, "and she home schooled me which I highly recommend. This all done while she was going to school herself and working part time, as a self supporting artist from home. The last, an impressive feat in itself, she would say." Taking another long pause, his gaze looked across the sea of heads to the table beyond.

"On the table next to the food table you will see what is called, a diorama. I'd forgotten all about it until two days ago when Andrea unpacked the many things she brought with her from the coast for this day. I made the diorama with mums help when I was about ten. Mine is made in a round hat box. A box, mum found when she was dumpster diving…that's a story for another day." He paused as laughter died down.

"A diorama is, by definition, a three-dimensional miniature or even a life-size scene in which figures, stuffed wildlife, or other objects are arranged in a naturalistic setting against a painted background. Mum made me memorized that definition." John paused as more laughter from the audience erupted; when things had settled into a dull roar, holding up his hands for silence he took a deep breath and carried on with his speech.

"As I said I've set it up, the diorama that is, for you to see. It's next to the food table... I had mum's help with it and she actually picked the theme and did most of the work. After it was finished she asked me, would I like to live in a place like that? One time she told me, when she had finally grown up, she would go live in a place exactly like that. The theme of my diorama, though I didn't know it at the time; is this place. JJ's house, the barn, the pathway between our house and Trish's house, even a stand of trees in the centre marking the halfway point between the two houses.

"Out of paper-mache, we fashioned the landscape and re-painted farm animals to represent animals she could relate to she said... And you'll see five or six little people if you count the one in a big Cadillac driving away. There's a girl, a woman and a man in one yard and a woman and a boy in the other yard. You'll see a wee little fort in the trees and that was mums. And off behind some other trees are a coyote and a cougar too. Looking back over these last three years, when she was really sick, she had the round hat box close at hand. When she took the lid off and gazed inside she must have been thinking of being home. Home on the range." John briefly glanced at JJ and Trish before continuing.

"My mum was the person who taught me to look for the good, always live by the golden rule and always find humour in my daily life. She had so many quotes and expressions for positivity. One of her favourite quotes by an unknown author is written lightly on her studio wall at home in Vancouver, and I found it again written with many other quotes on a sheet of paper under a blotter on her desk in what was her office right here in this barn," looking up at JJ again, he said, "and now it's my office. It goes like this, the quote I mean."

Clearing his throat John began to recite, "It's impossible, said pride. It's risky, said experience. It's pointless, said reason. Give it a try, whispered the heart." My mum tried her hand at many things and was almost like a dog with a bone and wouldn't give up on an idea until she had success. She had another expression. It's from Finland and loosely translated means - never give up. The word is Sisu. Never give up! She said this a lot when she was sick and she said, as long as she was still alive she had hope. But now I know she did give up.

"She gave up on the life she could have had here – on the people back here, her friends and her family. It made her sad enough, and regretful enough, to want to send me here. My mother instilled in me a belief that it is never too late to do the right thing. By her sending me here in the special way she has - well, she did the right thing."

After another short pause meant to let the words sink in, John drew in a large breath then went on to tell the crowd his mum had actually handpicked most of the people in attendance in one way or another, and they had all been picked because they were special to her in some way. Either they had shown her a kindness of some sort, a look, a touch, or a softly spoken compliment, told a good joke, showed creativity. "My mum was a pretty special person. So much of today is her doing.

"Through many letters she wrote when she was ill, she guided me to this day helping me organize things just the way she would like them and had visualized them. My mum brought me life, and now she's brought me here for a second chance at life.

"A mother, granddaughter, niece, and like a daughter to more than one; she was an artist, a good friend, a comedian....

or so she thought. She was generous to those in need, and kind to those not expecting kindness. All her hard work for today is paying off. Soon we will have good vegetarian food and the music she liked. Songs she would have chosen if she were here, and there will be dancing too if you wish. But no tears - that was my mum's request when she first became ill… and if she were right here right now, she would say just take a few deep breaths and you'll not cry, just breathe." Pausing again John led the gathered group in an imitation of his mother. He closed his eyes and taking several long breaths in and then out he became visibly calm.

Opening his eyes and taking one last deep breathe he said, "You all have been given a glass with mum's drink of choice, sparkling water, please raise it now and make a toast to Shelley or Margaret or mum, whoever, whenever, however whatever and wherever you are mum, may all your days be filled with happy adventure." John raised his glass then and took a drink. From the front row Todd lightened the mood when he called out, "To Shelley."

Knowing there was no way for him to honour Shelley's wish of no tears today, JJ at the last minute couldn't speak because he was just too choked up and emotional after John's tribute but Trish spoke and so did Andrea. Heather surprised everyone except Andrea and John when she sang - The Wind Beneath my Wings, an old Bette Midler song, in her beautifully silky quivering voice, and she dedicated it to Shelley.

When Trish got up to speak all the sun burnished colour had left her face, the usually, steady hands shook as she clutched a sheet of paper and her eyes held the mist of unshed tears. John and JJ thought she looked solemn, and beautiful.

"A few minutes ago I opened a letter I'd been specifically asked not to open, until it was my turn to speak to you. I had a tribute all ready to go. In it I spoke of a child who could make the sun come out on an overcast day, just by smiling at you or finding the best hiding spot. I spoke of an adolescent who turned to temper, with her family at least, when things didn't go her way and I spoke of regret in not finding her and bringing her home sooner. In it I spoke of the many letters she wrote to me over the years keeping me in tune with her growing son…

"My tribute is now on hold until the reception when I will talk freely to any and all of you about someone who is so special to me. All these years of imagining she had just forgotten us, and now she has sent her son home. John's arrival and getting to know him, has been a gift for these past three weeks. Her parting gift to us I suppose.

"In these three weeks we've seen and appreciated all she did in her adult life. If she was an artist, John is her greatest creation. Shelley wants me to read a poem to you. A poem, she says helped to transform her life when she was ill and without hope. She says this poem helped her find the way to happiness. Because, and here is another one of her favourite quotes that guided her in life - There is no way to happiness, happiness is the way." Opening the sheet of paper she held, Trish began to read.

"The Thing Is, by Ellen Bass

to love life, to love it even
when you have no stomach for it
and everything you've held dear
crumbles like burnt paper in your hands,
your throat filled with the silt of it.
When grief sits with you, its tropical heat
thickening the air, heavy as water
more fit for gills than lungs;
when grief weights you like your own flesh
only more of it, an obesity of grief,
you think, How can a body withstand this?
Then you hold life like a face
between your palms, a plain face,
no charming smile, no violet eyes,
and you say, yes, I will take you
I will love you, again."

Trish stood still for a moment. Everyone could see and had heard in her shaky voice, the poem had been difficult to read. But she continued. "Shelley wants us all to embrace the last five lines of the poem. She did, during her worst times. Just love life. Again! And again, and again, love the heck out of life; no matter what, don't waste a minute. She wants me to remind you too that we all die sometime and of something. How we die though, that doesn't matter at all. What matters most is how we live our lives. All we know for sure is we only have one chance at life. We don't know how long we'll have that chance. All we know for certain is we won't be here forever.

"Shelley's last desire, her last wish before she died was for all the people she cared about to venture out of their comfort zone to have a life. Embrace the world, laugh, sing and turn to and turn on creativity, live in the moment. Not in the past or the future, just this moment right now. One last message from our dear girl is to turn on some music and have some fun, eat a little and dance a lot. Chat with each other, get to know each other and be happy, on this day."

Stepping away from the microphone Trish caught a glimpse of John smiling down into his lap. Heather was at his side with her head on his shoulder and holding tight to his hand. And JJ, he looked anything but happy he looked like he had been shot through with an arrow. Leaning back into the microphone, Trish made an open invitation to come up to say a few words or to share a story about Shelley any time.

John's speech had left JJ in tears of regret, and pride and gratitude to Shelley for not completely forgetting them. Pride in Shelley for bringing John up to be a strong, self assured, intelligent individual. And the pride an uncle could feel in his only living relation, his nephew when he stood so tall and spoke so eloquently of his mother. And regret he had missed it all. He felt regret about the past and apprehension about the future too. He worried that there may not have been enough time in these three weeks for John to want to remain in JJ's life. Tomorrow or the next day, Andrea and Heather would be returning to the coast and John was expected to return with them.

As afternoon turned into the night, between songs, people got up to speak spontaneously. They talked about how they met John's mum and what particular attribute they loved the most about her. After they stepped off the podium they would come along to introduce themselves or to just say hello if they hadn't seen John or JJ or Trish in a while. Whether John had met them or not they all came to say hello and give him a hug. All John's mother's friends, who knew her as Margaret, told John what he already knew, she was kind, generous, humorous, an exceptional artist and that he was the centre of her world. And everyone who grew up with her and knew her as a kid and a teenager said many of the same things; kind, funny, creative, quiet ... and always seeming so calm. Soon John got to know a little bit about everyone that was there and felt he knew his mum just a little bit better too as memories were shared.

The mother of Tiger Lily who Todd had been asked to invite came up and introduced herself, saying what a wonderfully evocative speech he had given for his mum's party and even though she had met his mum only one time she felt a kindred spirit in her. Regretfully she told John she had to get home to a sick mother of her own.

The daughter he had played with when he was two...she would have been four, he was told, had come to pick her up. "Would you like to come say hello to her, I'm sure she'd like to meet you again. She's outside, just come out to the car to meet her for a second and then I've got to go." Gladly John stepped out into the fresh air of the night, walking over to the car with its motor running and head lights on.

When he got there and he could see behind the wheel, he laughed; it was the same girl from the restaurant and from the phone store. She turned off the car and leaned out saying into the sudden quiet and darkness, "Third time's the charm. I knew I'd run into you again." Startled her mum said, "Oh I see you've already met Tiger Lily." Before the girl could reply beyond an exaggerated eye roll directed at her mother, John reached out his hand to shake hers, saying, "We haven't been properly introduced. Good to meet you Tiger Lily. My mother told me about you, she especially liked your name." Tiger Lily's mum smiled proudly at that, and hurried around the car to get in the passenger seat. Before driving off, Tiger Lily said, "Now that I know who you really are, I guess I'll see you again..." With all three waving goodbye, off Tiger Lily and her mum went into the night.

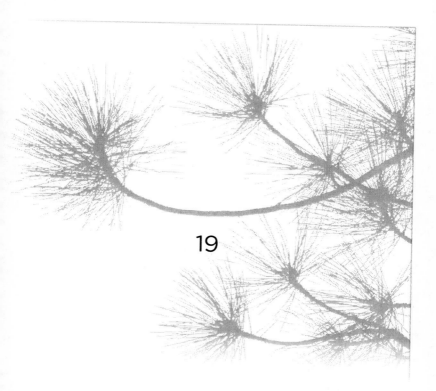

19

Right at that moment the first crack of lightning was heard, followed by thunder. Gentle drops of rain began to fall and soon several people made their way out of the barn and into their cars, saying their goodbyes along the way. All the remaining people made a run for the house, some with platters of food, others carrying bottles of drink. And running alongside of Trish and JJ was a still very excited Cozy. When everyone was settled into the inglenook, kitchen, lounge, porch and remaining areas of the house and making sure they were all having a good time, very quietly John left the party that had moved indoors.

By then some of the people who had come up to the house to say their goodbyes, had gone home and the rest were still as lively and happy, as Shelley would want them to be. Laughter and conversation and some dancing too, had ensued in the barn and some of that had come up to the house and was in full swing. As he headed up the stairs to his mother's old room he heard music, and laughter accompanied by the happy bark of his mother's dog. Just as he turned for one last look, the barking dog was seen jumping up and down in the hope of getting a bit of attention, as JJ and Trish tried to have a slow dance together.

In the beginning John didn't know how good this idea of his mum's would be. But she did the right thing sending him here; the whole three weeks had been totally cathartic. He couldn't imagine how he would have managed this period after his mum's death at home with Andrea and Heather. He'd have been just milling around in a daze of grief, with Cozy and Andrea and Heather also in deep grief. His mum did know him best. And she knew too that even though time, lots of time, had separated her from her home, all the things about the place and all the people she still loved and valued, were here; for him to love too.

This place, this experience, the treasure hunt she planned was just as Trish had said, a parting gift to him. Opening the last letter, John paused. He wasn't sure any longer if he wanted this adventure to end or if he just wanted to stay awhile longer, or if he would stay forever. His decision, he knew was his alone to make.

Andrea had cornered him in the barn to let him know she and Heather would return to Vancouver in the next day or two. She told him, she had the suite repainted and new tenants had moved in; a young mother and her four year old daughter, also a student. Andrea said that she never imagined the possibility he wouldn't come back to live with them, but seeing him here with JJ and Trish she could see how he might be torn. "Your mother wrote me letters too, I told you that before you left. She prepared me for every scenario saying in the end she felt you are old enough now to decide what you want in life. I didn't agree. To me you were as young as Heather, just a kid.

"Oh John, Heather and I love you so much. We want you home with us any time. And I hear JJ and Trish want you to make a home here too. You know that. What you might not know though John is that this truly is your own decision. You're the one to decide. And that, my boy, comes straight from your mum. All of us are here for you."

As much as he felt safely grounded by all the memories he had in Vancouver, he couldn't get away from a desire to make this place his home too. New memories of his mum were here. All around him in her room, with all the boxes unpacked he felt her near. He knew though wherever he went, he would carry her with him long after these first weeks of grief, long after he adapted to life without his mother. But right now he was feeling a different kind of grief.

He was feeling her grief, at leaving this place never to return. The place she grew up, her childhood home, where he had been sent with his mother's assurance; where he had come with excitement and trepidation. He had carried her ashes here and still had not found box number 9 but imagined he may not and that was OK.

Because now that he was here, he knew she just wanted her ashes back at the place she thought of as home all along. Putting the letter back in his shirt pocket, he wanted to delay the moment; he'd save the last letter to be read later. Turning his attention instead, to the wall and the big hand appliqued and quilted tapestry JJ's mum, Jean, had made for her own daughter.

The tapestry covered a large portion of one whole wall, it touched the floor and almost the ceiling too. In the letter numbered seven his mum had written, she had asked him to carefully roll up the big tapestry. It was to be packed up and taken home for Heather to enjoy in her room. A gift for Heather, she had instructed. The tapestry was very beautiful and inspired by a tapestry called - Interlude - Old World - JJ had told him. The original tapestry, where Jean drew her inspiration featured an idyllic scene of women taking an afternoon rest, in the gardens of a villa. There were trailing, vines surrounding and uniting them; weaving them together. The young women were all dressed in the same blue flowing gowns giving the idea of ladies in waiting or ladies of leisure. And as his mother recalled, the woman on the left looked out into the room, following movement with her eyes. Her dress was a slightly different style and shade of blue setting her apart from the rest. The tapestry was apparently heavily lined on the back and had a tunnel sewn across the top edge of the back side for easy hanging. There was a rod that passed through the tunnel and finials on each end. John could see these were held up by brackets on the wall.

He thought he'd need help for this job because the tapestry looked so heavy; JJ had offered to give him a hand the next day. Right now though, John decided to go for it on his own. Getting a chair he climbed up, lifting the rod off one end of the bracket. Losing his balance as the weight of the fabric shifted; his hands shook while he lowered the other end. Avoiding dropping it before it hit the floor, was heavy work.

John mentally began a plan for stretching the tapestry out on the floor, to get all the wrinkles out before rolling it up. Glancing back at the wall where the tapestry had hung, he saw something had been hidden behind the heavy cloth; a large set, of wooden double doors. Turning his back to the wall once more and taking a deep breath of air in, he moved the chair, the night tables and shifted the bed a couple of feet so he could stretch and straighten the tapestry making it ready to be neatly rolled for transport.

Stepping back to take another look, his breath held tight inside clamped shut lungs, his eyes locked on the set of double pocket doors. The same kind Andrea had in her old house in Vancouver, between the dining room and living room. He knew all he had to do was place a hand in the inset handles of the door panels and give a mighty push. The two doors would glide apart and some new treasure would be revealed. His mind wasn't letting his hands do it though.

With heart beating down the walls of his chest, he felt a certainty that behind the doors waited a secret that had been there for a long stretch of time. When he finally tried the doors, like all the doors to his mother's other private rooms, these too were locked. The only key at his disposal yet untried was an old skeleton key found in the seventh box now unpacked. Tucked tightly in his front jeans pocket, he pulled the key out. For several seconds the key lay in the dampness of the palm of his hand. Nervously stepping forward, jiggling the key into the lock, it turned. Hearing a click and feeling it too; the lock was open. With a deep breath in, he pulled out the key, replaced it in his pocket then inserted both hands pushing the doors apart.

With the same vacuum effect he had experienced in the barn's office room, a swish of air blew out and on its breath the sound of a soft moan. What John saw was like nothing in his wildest imaginings. A hidden room; a room his mum had talked about as a wish. A wish for a secret space, she romanticized the idea of hidden rooms, until one day her dream, became John's dream too.

John reached across a spacious work desk to push a button that he knew would make the roller shutters blocking his view come to life. Squealing as it rose; a window from which he could see for miles by the light of a moon just coming out from behind storm clouds. Rolling hills, a few stars peeking out from a clearing sky, the night sky, full of distant lightning strikes.

Sitting down on the hard backed chair, John placed his hands on the dusty surface of the desk and looked out. He knew what he saw, he saw what she had seen, and he sat, where she sat. Running his hands across the top of her desk, he could almost feel her hands beneath his own. The lamp hanging over top of the desk, had a long string attached just begging John to grab it and pull; so he did.

Reaching his hand up to give the string a gentle tug, silently saying as he did, "Let there be light." There was a slight delay and then a golden light came on, casting a life of its own to everything it touched. A golden glow, washed over previously unseen objects in the room. JJ had said there had been a window in his mother's bedroom. Did JJ really forget all about this hidden room, or did he want John to find it on his own?

This room with its shuttered window, an expansive desk and beside the desk now exposed by the golden light of the overhead lamp was a box. A wooden box with a large metal hook in its lid; a sheet metal hook made to look like the number 9.

Tears of disbelief and sheer joy wet John's eyes as he stood and very carefully lifted the lid of the box straight up to hang the loop in the nine on an overhead hook. A sound like rustling leaves fills the room. With the lift of the lid, out floats, dances and shimmers in the shadowy light, hundreds of origami creatures attached to the underside of the lid by silvery threads. The rustling, swooshing, whisper the origami creatures make, fill his head, fill his chest and fill his heart with deep emotion. The sound the creatures make, take him back to the first moments of life alone without her, and to the first letter and what his mother had said. Find 9 and you will find me.

His gaze touching on the delicacy of dancing colourful creatures, he imagines his life as a circle, a continuation of connected events intertwining to create something just as beautiful as the tapestry rolled up at his feet. His mind's eye takes him back to the other origami his mum had made; the ones that hung as a curtain in her studio and now graced the barns office doorway. Visualizing those other lively creatures he could see that day unfold, as she hid behind the origami when they played hide and seek. He could not see her. But she could see him. It was with this memory, he heard the very clear whisper of his mother's soft voice say - You have found me, I am here.

Finding the box with a nine attached wasn't the end of his journey. Deep in his heart he knew that by his mothers design this was the beginning. By leading him on this treasure hunt, she had set in motion the growth of relationship with his family. She had offered him a sense of belonging that he felt deep within his soul. And had planted firmly in his mind, the answer to what it was all about. John saw with clarity the path he was meant to take; he knew what he would do and how, and he was pretty sure it was all part of his mothers bigger plan for him.

Spreading out the last letter, he sat down at her desk to read the final words of wisdom she would have for him. Knowing she would predict he would be sitting in her chair, at her desk, and reading by the light of her lamp, gave him a kind of comfort in the knowledge she would always be with him. In the quiet of the room he heard the distant sound of laughter, music and people having fun.

Calmly he read, then re-read her final letter and without hesitation folded it up neatly, opened the desk drawer, and with great care, tucked it inside. Reaching up to grasp the string hanging overhead; he pulled the room into darkness. Watching the changing night sky for just a moment more, he heard the gentle rustle of origami sway and imagined what his mother's voice would sound like, as she urged him to go to join the others and a world without her; giving permission to love life again.

THE END

CPSIA information can be obtained at www.ICGtesting.com
Printed in the USA
LVOW08s0915270916

506362LV00001B/11/P